SEVEN LASSES

and a

LAIRD

LAIRDS OF THE NORTH - BOOK TWO

KARA GRIFFIN

SEVEN LASSES *and a* LAIRD

LAIRDS OF THE NORTH - BOOK TWO

All Rights Reserved.
Copyright © 2021 Kara Griffin

Cover Photo © 2021 All rights reserved – to be used with permission.
Cover design by Sheri L. McGathy

This book may not be reproduced, transmitted, or stored in whole or in part by any means, including graphic, electronic, or mechanical without the express written consent of the publisher except in the case of brief quotations embodied in critical articles and reviews.

This is a work of fiction. Names, characters, businesses, places, events, and incidents are either the products of the author's imagination or used in a fictitious manner. Any resemblance to actual persons, living or dead, or actual events is purely coincidental or used in historical view or context.

This book contains adult material, reader discretion is advised.

ISBN-13: 9798702831466

DEDICATION

For true love believers.

And to AAW & BEK welcome to the world, little ones.

The best thing to hold onto in life is each other.
~Audrey Hepburn

SEVEN LASSES *and a* LAIRD

Lairds of the North - Book Two

Keith Sutherland, the son of a powerful clan, is called home to take over the role of chieftain. The elders impose one stipulation—that he takes a wife. He is given the choice to marry one of six lasses from the most prominent clans in the north. As he courts the lasses, he realizes the one woman who ignites his passion is forbidden to him.

Marren Macleod gave her heart to Keith long ago. When he returns home, her desire for him deepens, especially when his kisses spark her unbridled passion. As Marren tries to win Keith's affection, secrets come to light as to why she was sent to his clan for fostering. She is furious to learn she's nothing but a pawn, going from one laird to another in their game of alliances and enemies. To prevent marriage to her guardian's choice, Marren must force her betrothed to break the agreement set by his father.

At first, Keith wholeheartedly courts the lasses, but then mysterious happenings occur. Some lasses fall ill and some flee his castle in fear they have been hexed. He refuses to name the lass he intends to marry and delays his nuptials, much to the chagrin of his clan. With seven lasses at his disposal, one laird should be able to find a woman likable enough to marry. If only he might win the heart of the woman he most desires and put behind him the family discord that could be his undoing.

Character List

Sutherland Clan
Keith Sutherland
Hendrie – Father
Vera – Mother (d.)
Ophelia (Philly) – Aunt
Aulay – Commander-In-Arms
Marc – Gate Watchman
Emmett – Stable Master
Vinn – Soldier
Dain -- Squire
Samuel – Elder clansman

Lasses
Trulee Macleod – Waif
Caroline Gunn – Cook
Eedy Fraser – Prim & Proper
Iona Grant – Bird lover
Lindsey Gordon – Plain Jane
Robina Robertson – Warrior

Heroine
Marren Macleod
Ronal – Father (d.)
Jennet – Mother (d.)
Cassie – Friend
Duncan Macleod – Uncle
Loreen Macleod – Aunt

Other Notables
Wynda – Village Hawker
Grady Mackay – Best comrade
Chester Mackay – Grady's uncle
Jumpin' Joe – Tavern/Inn owner
Father John – Joe's brother and Priest
Callum Sinclair – Comrade
Violet Sinclair – Callum's wife
Peter -- Sinclair gate watchman
Eric -- Sinclair smith
Kieran Mackenzie – Clan Rival

CHAPTER ONE

Wick Village, Caithness
Northern Scotland
March 1390

Winter's wrath banged the shutters on the old inn's windows. Keith Sutherland groaned at the incisive noise. He'd wanted a wee bit of shut-eye and hadn't slept for more than a few hours in days. There was no better place to get rest than at Jumpin' Joe's Tavern and Inn. His good comrade kept rooms in the back strictly for his use. Yet he wouldn't get a wink of sleep with the shutter banging repeatedly. He shot a disgruntled glance at the window casement and pulled the cover higher over his head. The noise jarred him awake, but he wouldn't leave the warm bed to correct the issue. It was too darned cold to traipse to the window. And besides, the bed was too comfortable and the woman next to him too alluring to leave.

Another bang came. Keith shouted an expletive and disturbed the lass he'd spent the night with. She shifted the covers over herself and grumbled but didn't fully awaken. If he ignored the bang, he might fall asleep again. At least, that was his hope. By the sound of the wind, it was unlikely the shutter would close on its own. The annoying clash would persist to drive him mad, unless he did something about it. He pulled the cover higher and groused because there was nothing to do but secure the damned shutter. The wooden closure flew open and a gust of frigid air flowed into the room. Snow speckled the window ledge and floor.

Another bang came. He left the bed and marched with heavy, ireful steps on the frigid floor to the window, secured the latch, and muttered under his breath. "Bollocks."

The chamber door burst open and Grady Mackay, his longtime comrade, entered. He stood by the door threshold and grinned. "Didn't you hear me knocking?"

Keith returned to the bed and peered crossly across the small chamber. "I thought it was the shutter. You should've come a minute sooner then you could've secured the damned window."

Grady raised his dark brows and chuckled. "Aye? You need to roust yourself. There's a visitor in the tavern. Where are your garments? No wonder you're freezing your arse off." He snatched his garments from a nearby chair and tossed them to him.

Keith shot a loathsome glance at his friend. "I never sleep with garments on and I'm not about to start now. Leave me be. I need to sleep." He hastily lay upon the bedding and burrowed beneath the heavy covers and closed his eyes. "Be a good chap and bank the fire and shut the door on your way out. It's getting bloody cold in here."

Grady bellowed a laugh. "Did you not hear me? You have a visitor and you need to roust now. He awaits you in the hall. You might want to meet him before he takes to drinking and is too sotted to speak to you."

Keith muttered another curse. "I'm not leaving my bed. Who dares to bother me in the middle of the night?"

"It's not the middle of the night, my friend, but only nears the supper hour. Why it's only just getting dark." His comrade gripped the cover and yanked it from over him. "You should leave your ladylove and rejoin the living." Grady chortled in laughter.

"Keep your voice low or else you'll wake her. She's had a long night." Keith peered at her but she didn't move, awaken, or show signs of being bothered by their low-voiced discussion.

Grady chuckled humorously. "I would wager she has. Come on, move your arse."

Keith wanted to thrash him, but instead, he threw his legs over the side of the bed and rubbed the sleep from his eyes. There was nothing to do but dress and find out what the visitor wanted. Mayhap he could then return to his bed and get needed rest before he woke his amorous partner.

"Bloody hell, I'm up. Cease nagging me."

"Uncle Chester came an hour ago. He says he has a message for you."

"Chester? Why would your uncle bring me a message?" Keith pulled a tunic over his head, belted his tartan at his waist, and tugged on his boots.

"Well now, I suppose it's from your aunt, but Chester didn't say."

"Couldn't you take the missive and bring it to me? If it was dire, wouldn't he tell you? It must not be important. Tell him to leave it and I'll read it in the morning." He was about to turn around and head back to bed.

Grady scoffed, held onto the door, and opened it wide. "He said he needed to put it directly in your hand. You know how persistent your Aunt Ophelia is. And Chester wants to see you, so you'd best hurry."

He tried to make sense of it, but why bother when he'd see the man in a few minutes. Keith opened the door and snatched his heavy tartan to set around his upper body. The room he stayed in was located at the back of the inn, and there wasn't an opening that led into the main tavern area where Chester awaited. They had to trek around the building in the blustery cold to the front and enter through the main entry.

Jumpin' Joe, a childhood comrade, purchased the inn when he came into an inheritance. His comrade got his nickname by chance when as lads they had camped near the Sinclair holding. They'd challenged Joe to run through the fire embers of their camp. Joe couldn't run through it because the embers were still bright with heat and he jumped over the pile and shouted curses. Ever since that night, he and his comrades called him Jumpin' Joe. The name stuck. He was a good sort and often gave them a roof over their heads.

Joe's brother though, John, the local priest, was a vexing man who berated anyone he chanced upon about their sinful ways. John preached about damnation and the saving of their souls. But none at Jumpin' Joe's tavern wanted to receive his religious preaching, not when their cups were the only solace they sought. Keith grinned to himself as he thought about the titles he and his comrades gave the brothers—the Saint and Sinner of Wick.

The brothers were opposites too. Joe had light hair, his brother dark. Joe had green eyes and his brother had brown. If they stood next to each other, one wouldn't distinguish whether they were related, let alone brothers. If he had a wee bit of luck on his side, he'd avoid the Saint this day.

Snow fell lightly, and he suspected soon, the ground would be white with its flakes. By the time Keith reached the inn, the cold penetrated his garments and he shivered.

"Let's get inside before we freeze to death. It's too cold out this night. Oh, bollocks, there's Father John. Let us hasten inside, Grady, before he reaches us."

He opened the door to Jumpin' Joe's and once the door closed behind him, he breathed a sigh of relief at avoiding the Saint. The Father derided people for sins even if they hadn't committed an offense. John was aware of the many sins he'd committed, and he didn't want to answer for his misdeeds, not this day. He'd probably commit a few more sins before the day was through.

A fire blazed in the hearth at the end of the great hall. The warmth from within instantly eased him. Rows of tables flanked with benches set the confines, and though it was early evening, partakers drank and filled the hall to capacity.

"Jumpin' Joe, I mean to settle my debt soon," he said as he approached his comrade and clasped his arm in greeting. He hadn't paid for his room or for the large tab he'd surmounted in the tavern. All his coins were safely tucked away at his father's keep, and he'd have to retrieve some to keep him housed. His comrade was patient though, but Keith detested being indebted to anyone.

Joe guffawed. "Aye? You keep telling me that, but you'll sort it. I know you're good for it." He yelled at a patron who fell back off the bench on which he sat. "You blighter, get out. These sots never know when to leave. Go on, get yourself home."

Keith clasped his hand and nodded. "My thanks, Joe, and if I can't come, I'll send the coin for the amount I owe you."

Joe nodded and set off to throw the patron from the inn. Keith spotted Chester at the farthest table, the one as far from the fire as could be. A shiver wove its way through him as he scrunched his eyes in objection at having to leave his bed for nonsense.

Chester Mackay was well-groomed, his slightly graying beard trimmed neatly, and his garments in an impeccable state. He took care of himself, and Keith suspected he did so because he was interested in the ladies. There were rumors he spent a good bit of time with them, probably as much as he and Grady did with the fair lasses.

He grumbled again at the inconvenience of being pulled from his bed. "This better be important."

Keith slid upon the bench across from Chester, and Grady took the spot next to him. Grady didn't resemble his uncle in looks at all, and he'd taken after his mother with his almost black hair and eyes and darker skin tone. Chester often boasted with pride that he had the Norse blood of his ancestors and was much fairer than his nephew.

"Chester, what brings you here? Grady says you have a message for me."

Chester raised his blood-shot eyes and grinned. "Och, lads, finally, I thought ye'd keep me awaiting all night. Here," he said and handed him a sealed missive. "I visited your clan, Keith, and saw Lady Ophelia, the sweet woman asked me to deliver this and to put it directly in your hand."

Keith set the missive on the table and instead of reading it, he reached for the pitcher of ale. It was still warm and newly batched. Jumpin' Joe made the finest ale in the north, which rivaled what the monks made. He poured a tankard and filled it to the rim. Before he attended to his aunt's news, he drank his fill and swiped his hand over his sparsely whiskered chin. Grady shoved him and reached for the pitcher.

"Damn it, Keith, you hardly saved me any."

Chester laughed and motioned to a servant for service. "There be more where that came from, Grady, cease your complaint." He raised his hand and twitched a finger to the serving lass, who finally noticed him. Within minutes, another pitcher was placed on the table.

Keith waited for his comrade to finish taking his share and snatched the pitcher again. He and Grady were alike in that neither could out drink the other. They'd been close since at the age of eight when they were sent to foster with the Sinclairs for training-in-arms. Throughout their childhood, Grady had confided in him about the discord between him and his father. He was probably the only person who understood Grady's sentiment on the matter.

Keith shot a glance at the missive but was hesitant to find out the news. "Is this bad news? If it is, I'd rather not read it now. I'm in too good a mood."

"Phee… ah, Lady Ophelia seemed in fine spirits when she gave me the missive. She's as bonny as ever. Mayhap it bears good news. If you open the missive, ye might find out."

Chester turned to Grady. "Och lad, how are you? You haven't been home in a while. Your da mentioned he might call for ye soon."

"Aye? Tell him to kiss my arse. I'm not returning to Mackay land, ever. I have nothing to say to him. Tell him that when next you see him."

Chester took a chunk of bread from a platter the serving mistress placed in the center of the table. "This rift between you and your father must end soon, especially if ye'll take over the chiefdom when your da passes. Now is the time to make amends, before it's too late."

Grady's dark eyes stared at his uncle until he bellowed a laugh. "I'd rather be run through with my sword than deal with him. I'll go to my grave before I make amends with that fiend."

"Ye always were a stubborn lad," Chester said.

"Keith," Grady called, "Open the damned missive so we can send Chester on his way. I won't listen to his prattling about my father, and I want to know what your news is."

After Keith finished his second tankard of ale, he set it down with a bang. He took the missive and cracked the seal. His eyes scanned the short lines his Aunt Ophelia had scrolled. Philly, as he liked to call her, had gone into little detail. "She writes that I should come home. My father has news and my days of carousing are ended."

"That's all?" Grady laughed. "When does she expect you?"

They glanced at Chester for an answer, but he wasn't forthcoming until their glares forced him to appease them. "She said nothing to me about how soon ye need to come or why your father calls you. The woman never tells me what's on her mind. Och, methinks you might want to get home soon, especially before the storm reaches us. We may get heavy snows with this one."

Keith detested traveling in snow. "Then we'll leave this night."

Grady smirked. "To hell with that. I'm not going with you. You can travel with Chester since he's headed that way. Mayhap I'll stop by in a fortnight to see you, or perhaps when the weather warms… Spring will be soon enough. And besides, a lass is warming my bed."

He glared at him with envy. Grady would have a woman awaiting him, and he wished he didn't have to hail off. He would've entertained the woman warming his bed this night too, but instead, he'd be freezing his arse off on the journey home. Keith expected he'd have to one day return home and take on duties for his father. Now was as good a time as any. As laird, his father ruled a large clan with a vast area of land. Guilt plagued him somewhat that he hadn't helped his father much in recent months, years even in the caring of their clan.

He wondered if the Mackenzies were giving his clan troubles. Their rival was always pestering one clan or another. Perhaps his father needed his aid. It was the first time he'd asked, and Keith cared for his da and all those within his clan. He wouldn't say nay, and besides, he'd had enough carousing to last him a lifetime. He was ready to settle himself and return to clan life. Duty awaited him.

Since he'd turned fourteen winters, he'd just about been on his own. With no mother to gainsay him, and his father busy handling laird duties, he left home and lent his sword to the Sinclairs. That was how he met Callum Sinclair, his good comrade whom he often stayed with. Years of training prepared him to lead his father's army and to defend their clan against their enemies.

For fourteen years, he traipsed the northern region of Scotland and took on jobs and duties at whatever keep he and his comrades visited. He and his comrades had even journeyed across the channel and offered their service as guards for clergy and political figures for a few years. They'd had an adventure and gained enough coin to weigh down their horses. It was high time to end his adventurous life and return home.

Keith missed Philly too. Though he saw his aunt occasionally in the village, and infrequently stopped to see her at his father's fief, he hoped she was well. The woman aged, yet still beheld beauty and a sharp wit. Her teasing endeared her to him, and he missed their banter. That got him to thinking; he needed to stop in the village before he headed home. After a few hours of listening to Chester try to convince Grady to return to his clan, Keith had enough.

He threw his hand out to Grady, who shook it. "I'll see you soon then at my keep. Don't dally, though. Who knows what I'm walking into? You might want to come at the soonest to find out." Keith grinned and motioned to Chester. They left the warm confines of the inn and walked the village lane.

"I'll meet you at the stables and will get the horses readied," Chester said and marched off.

Keith reached the cottage he sought. A small bell alerted the hawker of his arrival. He ducked beneath the doorway and entered. Inside, a small fire lit the hearth. The abode darkened and few candles offered light. Scents drifted about and he recognized the herbs and floral odors. Situated around the chamber were tables laden with goods the mistress made. She was reputed to be a wise-woman or a white witch and made concoctions and remedies for those needing it.

Wynda also made jewelry of all sorts and sold the items to enrich her purse. She had remarkable talent and her craftsmanship above any, at least, of those in nearby towns. He perused the tables for the perfect object as a gift for his aunt. As he walked along, he passed by the small bottles of potions, pouches of scented items, and various medicinals.

When they were children, he'd often protected Wynda from the village lads who were bent on making mischief. They teased Wynda and often made her cry. Keith and his comrades took an oath as part of their warrior training to uphold chivalry and vowed never to harm a woman, though she wasn't yet a woman at the time. Still, it gave him a sense of pride to aid her.

Wynda approached and pulled the length of her long brown plait over her shoulder. Her face was somewhat bonny and her light brown eyes softened as she peered at him.

She smiled widely. "Good eve, Keith. You haven't come here in a while. What brings you by?"

"Fair lass, it's been a long time, hasn't it? I seek a gift for my aunt. Have you something she might like?" He scanned the broaches and didn't give her another glance.

"Oh, I saw Lady Ophelia last week. She stopped in and admired the blue-stoned broach there," she said and pointed to the one that drew his interest. She picked it up and handed it to him.

It was finely made and golden, with one large blue jewel in the center. Around the edges, a delicate scroll etched its luster. He nodded. "I'll take it. How much is it?"

"Two pence… I mean four pence. So you're going home? She mentioned she hoped to see you soon. I got the sense she had news, but she didn't speak of any."

"I wasn't aware my aunt was in the village. How did she appear? Did she come to you for a medicinal?" Keith grew concerned because if Philly visited Wynda, she must've had a good reason. His aunt rarely left Sutherland land and only visited the village perhaps once a month. He only hoped she didn't have an ailment.

"She sought herbs for the Sutherland cook on her monthly visit. Do you want me to wrap that in a cloth?" Wynda gazed at him with bright eyes and a winsome smile on her lush lips.

"Nay, I'll take it as is. It was good to see you, Wynda. You're as bonny as ever. Good day." Keith dropped four pence on the table and secured the broach inside his tunic.

"I haven't seen you in a while. Will you return to the village soon?"

"Nay, I'm headed home and won't likely return for a time." He gave a quick wave and left hastily when she appeared to want to keep him there with idle conversation.

Wynda was a peculiar woman. The way she watched him and spoke to him made him uneasy, but likely he made more of her looks than what she intended. Perhaps she was attracted to him, but Keith didn't find the woman to his liking. She'd never drawn his regard in a romantic sense. If rumors were to be believed, for a price the lass made hexes and potions for people to use against others. He was uncertain if such a thing was possible, but he wasn't about to ask or find out firsthand, if there was truth to the rumors.

Keith met Chester by the hostelry and took his horse's reins from him. Winddodger was eager to get on the trail and snorted for him to hurry. Once he mounted, he rode from the village in a swift gallop. "Philly better have a damned good reason for calling me home in this weather."

Chester grunted, but otherwise, he remained silent during the ride.

Night prevented Keith from taking in the enchanting view he knew to be there along the route. As they rode, the snow fell heavier, and by the time he reached his clan's lands in the early hours of the morn, there were a few inches on the ground. His upper tartan was covered with a dusting of white. He was pleased he'd made good time and wasn't hampered much by the weather.

Chester left him when they reached the cross path where the Mackay land bordered the Sutherland's. The man's eyes appeared tired, and he suspected Chester would seek his bed as soon as he reached home. That's what he planned to do as well.

Keith continued onward to his clan's holding and another hour later, he stopped at the gates. Marc, the gate watchman, let him inside. The muscular man wore a tartan at his hips, but nothing on his chest. How the man wasn't affected by the frigid air, Keith was unsure. It was beyond him, but Marc always was a strange fellow and rarely wore a tunic or tartan on his upper body, regardless of the season or weather.

Marc tugged at his dark beard and grunted a greeting. "Och, it's the wee Sutherland, home at last? Good to see you, Keith. Welcome home." He threw a hand out in greeting and Keith took it.

"Good to see you, Marc. I'll come by later and we'll catch up," he called over his shoulder, nodded to him, and continued on to the stable.

There, Emmett, the stable master, took his horse's reins. He bowed his head to Emmet. The man's long light-brown hair hung over his face when he returned the gesture. He'd grown to a spry young man and had a neatly trimmed beard, but he reeked of horses. As Keith strolled away, he heard Emmett grumble at his horse who nipped at him. Winddodger didn't like many people, and he hoped Emmett didn't have a hard time with his steed.

Four tall towers set the corners of the main keep's building. Many windows were situated between the towers on the three floors that seemed to reach the sky. Flattened stone flanked the ground in the courtyard that led to the steps. The heavy, ten-foot door was closed, but he quickly entered. Inside, the main entry was darkened, and it didn't appear anyone was up and about yet.

Keith reached the great hall and hastened to the fire. There, he held out his hands and warmed himself. Someone had banked the fire, and the heavy flames sent welcomed warmth throughout the chamber. Memories of his childhood flooded him. He'd spent many an hour beneath the large trestle table in the center of the room playing with his wooden soldiers.

With no other siblings, his childhood was a wee bit lonely. It might have been enjoyable if he'd had a brother or even a sister to share those times. Yet his parents only had him, and his mother died when he was but four in years. She'd perished from an illness, an outbreak of the Black Death which fortunately quickly subsided in their region. His father was brokenhearted. Vera was the love of his father's life, and he refused to marry again.

In view of the table, remembrance of a lass who had stayed at his father's keep came. He recollected days of relentless torment on her part. Marren, a lass who was placed with his aunt for fostering, followed him everywhere he'd gone. From what he recalled of her, she was a sweet lass, and perhaps a wee bit bonny. He wondered if she'd left the holding, but his thoughts were interrupted when a sound came from the hallway that led to the great hall.

Keith didn't hear anyone approach, but he turned hastily when his name was called.

Aunt Philly ambled forward. His aunt always looked the same. Her short grayish-brown hair stuck out in places beneath the head wrap she wore. Her dark-blue eyes beheld affection in their gaze. She was a slight woman who wore austere garments. Rarely did she drape a tartan around her shoulders. Though she possessed beauty, she'd never married. He thought she was meant for the church, but Philly never left their holding or owned to want to be a nun. Keith had never asked why.

"Ah, lad, let me look at you," she said and held his face in her hands. "You're as handsome as ever. You haven't changed. You still have your mother's coloring with your fair hair, and her beautiful blue eyes, and your father's height and build. Oh, but your hair is a wee bit long. You might need a cut soon."

"Philly, I've missed you." Keith snatched her in his arms and swung her around. Her squeal sounded and she shouted for him to put her down. "I have a gift for you." He reached inside his tunic and handed her the broach.

"You always do. Oh, it's the broach I eyed at Wynda's. It's lovely, my thanks. I shall wear it with pride." She held the item as if it was worth a fortune, and her eyes shone as she peered at it.

"Why have you called me home? I came as soon as Chester gave me your missive."

His aunt's cheeks brightened. "All is well and there's nothing to cause worry. Sit with me and I shall speak with you before you seek Hendrie." Philly moseyed to the table and sat in her usual chair, the one nearest the fire.

Keith took the bench on the side and appreciated the heat that overwhelmed the hall. He sat back and watched her curiously. "You asked me to come and here I am. Say what you will. Is my father ill? Has this to do with him?"

His aunt firmed her lips, and she didn't have the typical shine to her eyes. "Your father is of good health. Nay, it's his wanderlust. He aims to take to travel and wants to leave the clan."

"This is the first I've heard of his desire to travel. He cannot leave the clan, he is the laird."

She shook her head. "No longer, my lad, your father has relinquished his role. He is laird no more."

"What are you saying?" He drew a frown at the news. Why would his father give up the lairdship? Did that mean he was no longer the heir and wouldn't one day rule his clan? A hundred questions plagued him at once, but he had to be patient. Philly would tell him all.

"I'm saying, lad, it is time you took the position as the laird. You have had plenty of time to gallivant with your warrior comrades. Surely you've learned all you need to know about life by now."

"Is this what Da wants?"

Philly clutched his hand. "Aye, for he has said so. My brother is tired. Hendrie has given his years in service to the clan and only wants his last years to be a comfort. He will speak with you about it further."

Four serving lasses entered the hall and placed the morning fare on the table. He leaned forward to snatch a piece of warm bread, but Philly smacked his hand. "You need to meet with your father at the soonest."

"I'm ravenous. Can I at least eat something before I go to see him?"

"Clan matters before pleasure, my lad. I'll set aside a trencher for you."

The lasses giggled as they hurried away.

Keith scowled when his stomach grumbled. "You don't intimidate me, Philly. I will have a piece of bread before I set off to meet him." Keith disregarded her frown and took a sizeable chunk of bread. He smeared it with a fruit mixture and shoved it in his mouth.

"Come and find me after you visit with your father. There is more we shall discuss and there is someone here you'll want to see."

Her eyes took on the shine she was renowned for and he raised a brow. He quickly swallowed the bread. "Why don't we discuss whatever you want to say now? Who is here?"

"Nay, you won't get it out of me, but I shall tell you later. Be gone with you. See to your matters and we will speak later and I'll reveal the rest of the news." Philly pulled a trencher forward and dismissed him with a wave of her hand.

Keith smacked her face with a quick kiss and left her. He removed the weighty, damp tartan he'd worn on his travel, and set it on a bench by the stairs. With heavy steps, he took the stairs two at a time and reached his father's solar. He knocked and heard his father's voice. On his approach, he looked for signs of his da's ailment. Surely that was the reason he had called him home, but Keith saw none.

His father appeared healthy with good color in his face. The dark strands of his hair grayed a good bit and his face wrinkled in places by his eyes and mouth. Yet the brows that often scowled at him as a lad when he'd reprimanded him, remained dark and full. His father hadn't fattened around the middle and he was lean, but perhaps his muscles were not as rigid as they once were.

"My son, you have returned," his father said as soon as he spotted him. "Come and join me. I'm taking in the view of the grounds. It is always bonny after it snows."

Keith joined him at the windowpanes and peered at the sweeping landscape of his home. It dawned on him how much he'd missed the land and his family. "The view is as enchanting as ever. How are you, Da? What is this I hear about your wish to travel?"

His da enfolded his arms around him in an embrace and slapped his shoulder. "I'm well. You're looking in good health…and fit. God, how you resemble your mother. She was so bonny. I vow I fell in love with her at first sight. 'Tis good you came quickly for I mean to leave soon."

"Philly told me that you want to travel. This is the first I've heard of your desire to go off on an adventure." His da motioned for him to sit. Keith settled on the thickly padded chair, stretched his legs out, and folded his hands over his stomach. He waited for his father to speak his peace. "Da, what's this about?"

His father sighed. "I have given my life to this clan… but now that I'm beyond in years, I long to travel, to fish, and to visit with my comrade Calvin MacDonald. He lives on the isle… on Skye and has invited me to stay for a spell. It's time ye took your place here, son. I'm afraid time has battered me and without your ma here to comfort me, I long to be away."

Keith's chest tightened at his father's words. "Da, I shouldn't have stayed away. I should have come home sooner. I am sorry you were lonely, without close family, save for Aunt Philly."

"Ah, the desires of youth had you ensnared. I understood and didn't want to rush ye. But there comes a time when a man must take on his responsibilities, and for you that time is now."

"I won't disappoint you, Da. You never mentioned Calvin. Who is he?"

"Och, he's a comrade who I fought with years ago, when I was but a lad when we supported the Bruce's son in keeping our independence. You'll make me proud, won't ye?"

Keith took his da's hand. "Of course I will. If this is what you want, then I'll support your decision. You really want me to be the laird?"

His father leaned forward, turned his hand, and placed in it his ring. Keith scowled at the silvery object because it was a ring handed down from laird to laird, from father to son, since the inception of their clan. Its significance brought a lump to his throat. The ring held a large ruby, and he'd remembered it well from his childhood.

With a nod from his father, he pulled back his hand. "You will wear this with Sutherland pride, lad, and be a good and just laird. I have never doubted that."

"Are all in agreement with me taking over? I won't have any opposition?"

Hendrie shook his head. "None will oppose ye. I have spoken at length with the elders of our clan. All are in favor of you taking control. The younger men are thrilled at the news since you've made a name for yourself. It's a fact that you've fought alongside the Sinclairs and Mackays. Peace has reigned for some time here in the north. Our only adversary, the Mackenzies, have been quiet of late. We've had no squabbles with them, but it's always best to be prepared."

"I've heard the Mackenzie's war with the Roses. There's an issue with the land borders. But you're right, we should be prepared, should they come to seek war. When do you plan to leave? It's not a good time to travel with winter at its harshest, and I wish to spend time with you before you go."

"Calvin expects me soon. I will hold up at his keep until the spring melt and then he and I shall embark on a trip farther north. We'll visit our comrades in Norway for a spell. I leave the clan in your capable hands. There's just one wee thing that must be done before the matter is settled…"

"What matter?"

His da rose and peered through the windowpane with his back to him and his hands clasped behind his back. After a minute of silence, he spoke, "Our clansmen worry that you're irresponsible because ye stayed away and hadn't returned to take to duties. You're quite young and our clansmen stand firm that something must be done to ensure you remain here. They insist you prove your loyalty. There were a few worthy suggestions, but all agreed to one stipulation… To become laird, the only covenant the clansmen insist upon is that ye… You must take a wife."

Chapter Two

The overwhelming scent of herbs permeated the solarium. Marren Macleod stood at the table where she concocted scents which she consigned to the local village hawker to sell. She'd gained a good amount of coins from her diversion. The long strands of her brown hair kept restricting her vision as she bent over the table. She pulled her hair back and secured it with a ribbon she obtained from her overdress.

The solarium was the quietest and most relaxing place within the castle. Marren gazed about the solarium, the only place she felt solaced. Though it was unroofed and open to the elements, the cold didn't seem to penetrate her warm, heavy cloak. Stone walls on two sides butted the castle walls and kept the gusty wind from breaching the area. Sections had been left open to afford sun and rain to nourish the many plants that were situated about in wooden boxes and various planters.

A brisk chill set the air and whipped at the evergreens at the solarium's entry. Even the cold day did little to dissuade her from attending to her tasks. With three layers of garments, she was warm enough. The exit of the solarium led into a massive garden that overflowed with flora and fauna when the weather warmed. Hues of bright greens and various other colors faded to browns and black on the leaves and stalks. Lanes made for a walkway past the ornate bushes and fancy shrubs that were tended to by two men Lady Ophelia employed when in season.

Her favorite part of the garden boasted several types of roses in almost every possible shade of color. Now and then, Marren snatched a few rosebuds to add to her collection and hoped Lady Ophelia hadn't noticed. She'd never hear the end of it, had the lady realized her thievery, because she wasn't one to share her blooms.

The domain was strictly for Lady Ophelia's pleasure, but she allowed her entrance. The lady's father, the previous Laird Sutherland, had the solarium erected for her use. Lady Ophelia adored gardening and tended to the greenery throughout the year, regardless of the season. Ophelia tutored her and gave her one table for the practice of her passion. Marren was fortunate the lady gave her a table at all. All called the place a solarium, but the lady called it her secret garden.

Marren had a talent for mixing the more alluring scents women often used to keep odors at bay. But the batch she'd mixed this morn was dreadful. She couldn't get the ingredients right and was about to dump the mixture when Cassie, her dearest friend, strolled into the garden.

"There you are. I tried to find you. I should've known you'd be here."

"Good morn. Where else would I be? What are you about this day?" She barely glanced at Cassie as she took another whiff of the scent she created and blanched at the awful mixture.

"I'm hiding from Lady Ophelia. She's in rare form this morn and you would do well to hide from her as well. I went to tidy her chamber, but it was already done."

Marren frowned at that. As Lady Ophelia's chambermaid, Cassie was responsible for all things within the lady's bedchamber. That included cleaning it, emptying the chamber pot, making the bedding, and keeping the lady's garments laundered and ready for her use. Cassie also helped their lady to dress each morning. That the lady hadn't awaited Cassie signified something was amiss.

"I wonder what has our lady up and about this early in the day. She never rises before the morning fare is set upon the hall's table."

Cassie snorted a derisive laugh and hoisted herself up on the table. She swung her legs over the edge and picked up a sprig of chamomile and took a whiff of it. "She's been awaking earlier these days. It appears her nephew has returned. I heard the hall maids talking about it, shrieking more like. Lady Ophelia is having a feast this eve to welcome him home."

Marren dropped the container of the scent she held and it spilled down the front of her cloak. "Oh, drat, now look at what I've done." The mention of the laird's son caused her clumsiness. Keith returned? How she longed to see him again. She'd always been infatuated with Keith. For years, she hoped he would come home, and he had on occasion, but he never stayed long enough to visit with her. She'd missed seeing his handsome face and him jesting with her.

Marren continued to clean up, but wistfully, she set the cloth she held to her chest. In the years since she'd been at the Sutherland's keep, she'd seen Keith a handful of times. The first time, she was wee and only about eight years in age. Then he'd teased her as children often did. Even then she found him endearing. Each time he came for a visit, she found herself longing for his attention. Why did her heart have to betray her and fall for the only man she couldn't have?

"I've never met him, but the hall maids are all a-gush over him. They wouldn't cease talking about him and their giggles were more akin to shrieks. They're a bevy of hens if ye ask me."

She chuckled at her friend's jest. "Aye, perhaps they are? Well, he is handsome and I suppose he'd cause a stir amongst them."

Cassie set the chamomile twig down and laughed. "You never confessed that to me, that he's handsome. I have never seen him. What's he like?" She pulled her knees up to her chest and closed her arms around them to keep her legs secure.

"I have known him since we were young. He's kind enough, I suppose. When we were younger, he'd often tease me as lads are wont. When he got older, he went off and I hardly saw him. He's only returned a few times for short visits." Marren smiled to herself as she recalled the first time she met him. She was newly arrived at the Sutherland keep. He had pulled her hair, tripped her, and he was annoying as lads often were at such a young age. But otherwise, he was a quiet sort and barely spoke to anyone besides his aunt. His demeanor then had been somewhat sullen or perhaps he'd been a shy lad. "Lady Ophelia adores him. I imagine she's excited he has come for a visit."

"Oh nay, he's not here for a visit, but here to stay. Milady has all the maids giving the entire keep a thorough cleaning for his welcome home feast."

"So that's why you're hiding in here." Marren laughed at her friend's impish grin. Cassie detested cleaning with the maids.

"I would rather empty a hundred chamber pots than spend a moment with those silly maids. Milady comes, oh I must hide." Cassie jumped from the table and hastily hid beneath the cloth over her expansive worktable.

Marren would have joined her, but she wanted to find out what was going on. Often, she'd hid beneath the table in her hope to escape Lady Ophelia when she was in a state of displeasure too. Yet, the news of Keith's return was too tempting to hide from the lady. She wanted to know what was going on and why he'd returned. Her lady breezed into the solarium with her usual enthusiasm. She typically wore a serious mien, but this day she smiled and there was an unmistakable shine in her eyes.

"Good morn, Marren." Lady Ophelia approached but stopped short. "I see you've been at your concoctions. What is that awful odor?"

Marren glanced at the lady briefly but continued about her task of cleaning up the table. She peered down at the stain of the liquid on her cloak. Her lady had a good nose. "It's a scent I was trying to perfect but I couldn't get it right. I spilled most of it on myself, but it matters not because I was going to dump it anyway."

"Aye? It is not as pleasant smelling as what you usually concoct." Lady Ophelia pulled a stool from the wall and placed it a safe distance downwind from the odor of her cloak. "I've come to seek your aid. This eve I shall have a welcome home feast for my nephew, and I would like you to meet with the cook to ensure the meal is planned and served on time. There's much to do and I haven't time to see to it."

"Of course, Milady, I would be pleased to handle that for you. Is there anything particular you would like served?"

"I'm certain you can come up with a delicious meal menu."

Marren nodded. In the years she'd fostered under Lady Ophelia, she'd learned everything about keeping a home, being a laird's wife, and all the duties required of such. Day after day, she toiled under the lady's tutelage, and the woman was relentless in her pursuit to teach her all she needed to know. Most of which was easy, like changing the rushes, doing launder, directing the servant lasses, and such. It was the keeping of the castle's stores of goods, ensuring all within had enough food, and handling important festivals and feasts that were tiresome.

"I shall be gladdened to help. So he's finally returned, has he?" Marren smiled to herself. She took a cloth and brushed the scattered remains of the chamomile leaves to the ground. She'd sweep them up later, but now she wanted to hear about the lady's nephew. "I imagine you're thrilled, but he's returned before and left again. What makes you think he shall stay this time?"

"Oh, he must stay. He will be named the laird by the day's end. We shall have a grand feast this eve to celebrate. Be sure to arrive for supper early so you don't miss it. Oh, and garb yourself suitably. Ye might want to launder your cloak or wear another if you must." Ophelia winked at her. "Make certain you clean up well before you're through here. There's no time to dally. Now, I must be off. There's plenty to do and I must make certain all is ready." Without another word, the lady left as hastily as she'd come.

Marren liked order and cleanliness and didn't need to be reminded by her lady to clean up the mess she'd made. She never left disorder in the solarium. Ophelia had often remarked that she was efficient, dependable, and a stickler for order. It was just her nature to be so and not due to the lady's encouragement or command. She found if her surroundings were orderly then so too would her life be, except her life was in somewhat of a shamble.

"You can come out now. She's gone."

Cassie crawled from beneath the table and stood. "She sounded rather chipper, didn't she?"

Marren smiled. "Aye and she has a good reason to be, I suppose."

"When you're finished with the cook, come to your chamber and I shall help you get ready for the feast. You'll need to be garbed in a fine gown."

"I could use your advice on what to wear." She wasn't one to be frivolous in her attire or to have a care how her hair was done, or even to take notice if she'd worn matching stockings. Such things hadn't mattered to her, and she focused more on her scents and the order of her herbs and flora. Her workstation was never out of sorts, but her attire left more to be desired.

On the outside, she was plain, at least to her she was. She wasn't one to flirt or be brazen with men, so her desire to attract Keith's attention was nil. It wasn't that she wasn't a passionate woman. She wanted love, wanted to love, and hoped to one day have a kiss worthy of causing her heart to flutter. She hoped to one day have a husband and children where love abounded. Perhaps a romantic stirred beneath her lackadaisical manner.

"With your bonny dark hair, I'd say a light-colored gown would be best. Perhaps we'll choose a cream-colored or white gown. You shall look like a grand lady. Here, let me," Cassie said and took the broom from her. She laughed as she swept the remaining flower petals on the floor. "Lady Ophelia has put you in a state of nerves, hasn't she? Usually, she leaves you alone when you're in here. She didn't give you any other direction besides attending the cook? I vow she makes you attend to the duties to keep you busy and to do those she doesn't have a care for."

Marren sat on the stool, certain her face showed her confusion. "Nay, she doesn't like to deal with the cook on a normal day, let alone this one. But she didn't give me the task of the day… It's strange, because with the feast this night, you would think she would have a list as long as her arm…"

Cassie pulled her light blonde hair over her shoulder and continued to sweep.

"I suppose our lady is beyond excited to have Keith home. Did you hear what she said? That he'll be named as the laird by the eve? I never thought he'd return for good, but I'm pleased he has. I just hope Laird Hendrie is well and that an ailment hasn't caused him to step down."

Cassie snickered as she went about sweeping. "The laird's son had to come home eventually. Oh, I hadn't thought of that. Hopefully, our laird doesn't ail, but let me guess… You're thrilled Keith has returned as well and not because he'll be the laird? I always thought you were smitten with him and saw the way you looked when he was mentioned. He's all you ever talked about when it concerns men." She shoved her shoulder and laughed.

"I cannot help it. He's too handsome and I… You know how I feel about him. Yet I cannot do anything about it because I'm going to marry a Mackay."

Her friend scrunched her brown eyes and smiled. "Don't

despair. It might not be as ill-fated as you make it sound. Who knows maybe your betrothed will be as handsome as Keith."

"None are as striking as he is." Marren laughed. "Listen to me sounding like a doltish lass who has no sense at all. I have only ever shared this with you. You mustn't say a word because I don't want him to find out about how I feel..."

Cassie set the broom aside. "Of course I won't tell a soul and I shan't betray your confidence. Would it be terribly awful if he found out how you feel about him? It's unlikely the Mackay laird will ever send your betrothed to fetch you. Maybe he has forgotten you. Will you not finally tell me why you were sent here? I have often wondered why a lady of your standing would be put in such a predicament."

"There's not much to tell. When I was wee, about six in years, my parents perished at sea. They'd gone to travel to France to meet with a good comrade of my father's. Their ship supposedly sank in the channel and my uncle took guardianship of me. He told me I would be sent to his ally and would wed one of his ally's followers."

"How wretched, to be torn from your family at such a tender age." Cassie was enrapt at her tale and leaned against the large table in wait for more of the story.

"My memories of those days unsettle me because I was young and didn't understand the importance of the situation. But when I arrived wherever my uncle sent me, I recall seeing a man who was so fearsome, even more so than Laird Mackay. He frightened me and I might have cried."

Cassie clasped her hand and squeezed it. "I've heard Laird Mackay is a cross man and his face always beholds a ferocious stare. You must've been frightened to death by the other laird."

"I was scared and remember being alone. I often wondered who that man was, but I had never asked and no one ever told me. After a fortnight, I was sent to the Mackay keep and the Mackay laird was as terrifying as the other man was. It wasn't as daunting though as being at the other holding. At least Laird Mackay left me alone except for his rebukes. He often shouted at me and called me horrible names. I spent nearly a year there until Laird Mackay sent me to foster with Lady Ophelia." Marren took the broom from Cassie and continued to clean the floor.

Cassie paced the length of the table. "You were most fortunate he allowed your leave. So you were sent here to train at being a wife? If you ask me, that's horrendous to send a wee lass to strangers. Besides, being a wife comes with experience."

"Laird Mackay told Milady that he wanted me trained to be a laird's wife. I always thought he meant to marry me himself. The thought of it sickens me." Saying the words put a sour taste in her mouth. Who wanted to be married to a man as aged as Saint Andrew?

"Oh, blighter it, I wouldn't want to marry him either. You're most fortunate that Laird Mackay hasn't called for you yet. Let us hope he never does."

She set the broom against the wall and pulled Cassie to stand with her. Marren smoothed her hand over the fabric cloth that covered the entirety of the wooden table to the floor. Now that the table was cleaned, she could go about mixing a new scent when Cassie left.

"Are you afeared he will call for you soon? You say he's forgotten you, but what if he has not? Who could ever forget someone as pretty as you?"

Marren took a deep breath at the contention of their conversation. "You're a dear sweet friend for saying so, and so are you, pretty that is." She peered at the table as memories of that dark time came back to her. "He must have forgotten me. At the time, when he sent me here, I was relieved to be in the care of a woman. I hadn't been around another woman since my mother... There were few women at the Mackay holding and none ever spoke to me." She took a cloth full of herbs and dumped them on the table. They needed to be sorted.

Cassie stood next to her and helped her to divide the

herbs. "You're beyond marriageable age. Most women your age have children by now. If he wanted to wed you or betroth you to one of his followers, and it's alleged to be a laird, perhaps he changed his mind?"

"I despair that I'll ever marry and I deem he hasn't chosen a groom. If Laird Mackay had, wouldn't he have shown himself by now? As much as I wish to marry, I don't want to return to the Mackay holding. There was something evil about the place. Of course, that could've been my youthful fear playing tricks on me. I vow I heard strange noises of a man yelling and a lad crying. I've never forgotten those dreadful months there and how my heart wrenched at hearing the sorrow of the lad's sobs."

"Oh, that sounds terrible. And here I am complaining about being cast out of my ma's home. I was always loved as a child and now I must help support my brothers and sisters. Still, our parents care for us as best they can."

Her friend's words disheartened her. She was forgotten by her family, by Laird Mackay, and her betrothed. Even though she was displeased at the situation, she was grateful she hadn't had to leave the Sutherland holding yet. Marren didn't want to leave Cassie or even Lady Ophelia. The lady was a force to be reckoned with and often lectured her on the do's and don'ts and the rights and wrongs of being a wife, she never tired of her. Occasionally, the lady made her laugh with her sternness and strict rules about wifely duties. She had hope that her husband, whoever he might be, wouldn't care about such trivialities as what Lady Ophelia put her through.

As much as Lady Ophelia could be harsh or difficult to please, she had a caring heart and sometimes teased her. Marren cherished the times the lady had spoken of her nephew. Ophelia's voice softened when she had spoken news about Keith and her eyes shone with happiness. She adored her nephew. If the woman cared that much about her nephew then she wasn't such a bad sort.

Most of the serving lasses feared Lady Ophelia, and she did as well, but most often, the lady had their best interest at heart. Although, she could do with softening her approach to such matters and perhaps command in a kinder tone. Still, she was thankful the woman took her under her wing. Perhaps one day, she would put to use the skills she'd obtained or at least some of it.

"I only wish I understood why my family sent me away. When my parents died, my uncle took control of my father's fief and his family came to stay at our home. I was pleased to have my aunt and cousins come to stay with me, but then within days he sent me to the frightful man's holding." She never understood and wished to know why her family had no care for her.

Cassie hugged her. "It matters not now because you're here and we care for you. All will be well. I should get back to my chores and let you get back to your scents."

She waved to her friend and turned back to the table. Displeased with the scent she created, she dumped the rest of the liquid out into the garden and decided to start over. She took the dried petals from the chamomile stalk and ground them with a pestle until they were smashed and almost powdery. It took a long time to get the petals to the stage where she'd add water and the other herbs to heighten the scent.

Marren had promised to supply at least ten jars of fragrance to Wynda, the hawker, by month's end and she was pushing her time limit. She was a planner by nature and that she was behind schedule tensed her shoulders. Until she got the fragrance perfected, it would take time. But once she had the exact recipe, the concocting would be easy.

She went about her tasks and her thoughts muddled about her guardian's lack of care. Marren considered writing to Laird Mackay, but she thought better of it. He wouldn't take well to being called to task for his inattention of her. He had rarely spoken to her, even when she'd arrived at his keep when she was but seven years old, although she recalled his ridicule and harsh words. As far as she was concerned, he was a knave, pure and simple, and she'd rather avoid him if she could.

Marren tried to put her troublesome situation from her mind since there was naught to do about it. As to the situation with Keith, he'd be named the laird. Life was about to drastically change at the Sutherland holding. And yet, in her elation, she couldn't wait to see him. She was certain he was as handsome as ever with his alluring eyes and winsome body. With his return, she might be able to persuade him to help her. But even if she only got to glimpse him for a short time, it would have to be enough.

CHAPTER THREE

Banging came at the bedchamber door. Keith groaned and rolled onto his stomach and ignored whoever it was. It was much too early to rise and he hadn't gotten enough sleep. Throughout the night his mind turned over his father's edict. *To become laird, the only covenant the clansmen insist upon is that ye... You must take a wife.* He'd spent hours rationalizing what he needed to do. He had to take a wife immediately.

His father's words echoed in his head like the sounds in Fingal's Cave when the waves crashed through its rocky walls. The terms of him being proclaimed the laird prevented him from getting a single wink of sleep. It wasn't that he was opposed to marriage, but he hadn't given it much consideration or had met a lass who he'd given his heart to.

Most men wanted a comely wife and he was no different. But there was more to a woman than her beauty. He wanted to marry a woman who had wit, a wee bit of intelligence, and someone merry to be around. He certainly wouldn't marry a shrew or a woman who abhorred sex. That reminded him of his good comrade Callum who had married a harridan that cuckolded him. Fortunately for his friend, his wife died. Callum was recently remarried to a woman whom he loved and his life had taken a turn for the better, one toward happiness. He was elated at his friend's good fortune.

He certainly wouldn't allow himself to marry a woman like Callum's previous wife. Keith had seen what it had done to his friend and how downtrodden he'd become. With her death, his friend turned his life around and he'd married a woman he adored. If only he met someone akin to Lady Violet, his problems wouldn't be as daunting. He'd always hoped to have children and wanted a handful of sweet bairns. He wanted what his friend had: an endearing wife, sweet bairns, and a clan that revered him. It would take all he had to obtain each of those fetes.

The bang came again at his door and he muttered an expletive. Whoever it was, wasn't about to go away until he answered them. He shouted, "Be gone," in hopes to sway them to leave.

The door burst open and his aunt flounced in. He grabbed at the bedcover and quickly covered himself. "Really, Philly, can a man not get rest? And I'm not garbed…"

She smirked and chortled with laughter. "Aye, I see that. But my lad, it's not as though I haven't seen a man's naked arse afore. You must roust yourself. We need to discuss what's to happen."

"You couldn't wait until I rose? What's the hurry?"

"The sun rose hours ago, but you'd know that if you woke at a decent hour. All are about their day, but you. We have much to discuss before the eve arrives, my lad."

"You know what my father decided and…about the clan's edict? They are forcing me to take a wife. Bloody hell, this is a quandary."

She tossed his tunic at him with vigor. "One that I'm certain you shall handle. I am privy to all. Hendrie told me that the clansmen have decreed you should take a wife and I'm in agreement. It's about time ye married. You're of marriageable age, well past, and a woman might settle ye. It would do well to fill the castle with bairns. Oh, how I long to hold your children. You must get around to it before I'm too old to enjoy it."

"You're a selfish old lady," he said in jest and she scoffed at him.

"Perhaps I am, but you cannot fault me for wanting to see your bairns before I meet my maker. It's been years since the castle had children playing in the hall. How delightful to know one day soon we shall hear the merry laughter of their sweet voices."

He nodded and pulled his tunic over his head. "You have this all figured out, aye? There's no use in me putting in my view."

Philly grinned and leaned against the bedpost. "I have a sound plan, my lad, to help you choose your bride. Listen well, for I have sent word to some of the most prominent clans here in the north. They shall send their daughters to us and you shall court them. You should be able to find a woman amongst them to be your wife."

Keith scowled at her speech. "What say you? You expect me to court all of them?"

"I sent a missive to the Macleods, Gunns, Frasers, Grants, Gordons, and the Robertson clans. All of whom have daughters of marriageable age. They shall send their daughters here within a sennight and ye shall begin the courting. When you have decided which lass is to be your wife, I shall have Father John fetched from Wick to come and perform the sacrament. It shall be done quick and painless."

He raised a brow at the word *painless*. His heart tensed at her words and a smidgen of discomfort seemed to settle in his chest. Keith drew a deep breath to settle himself. "I can find my own wife, Philly, and don't need your aid. You didn't have to do this."

She tossed his tartan at him. "Nay? Well, if you had met a lass you wanted as a wife by now, ye would've married her. I see no wife. Besides, I heard about the women you take to Joe's inn. Do you deem I don't know what goes on there? Those women… They are unacceptable and unworthy to be the laird's wife, especially the wife of a Sutherland. Now, these lassies are from good families and it would do well for you to marry one of them. Not that we need an alliance with them, mind ye, but it couldn't hurt to have their support if ever we might need it."

Keith lay back upon his pillow, pressed his face with his hands to abate his sleepiness and the angst of their conversation, and moaned. "I cannot believe I'm being forced to take a wife. It's barbaric. Does the clan believe I would leave off if I were made the laird? I wouldn't do so. Can you not tell them this is absurd?"

"Your father tried, but they wouldn't hear of it. They insisted the covenant be set or else they would take a vote and choose another as laird. Hendrie almost had heart pains over that. But he talked them into accepting you and ye would do well to follow their dictate. You must marry. Will you disappoint me, your da, or your clan?"

He shook his head. "Nay, of course not, but I should speak to Da this morning about it. Maybe there is a way to convince them to forgo the stipulation, at least for a time. Such consideration shouldn't be made in haste. There are more important matters to see to like the soldiers' readiness and upkeep of the land. I should be more concerned about those issues…clan matters, not a bunch of wearisome-husband-seeking lasses."

"He's gone, your da, so you will just have to accept the covenant to your rule."

"Gone?" Keith threw his legs over the side of the bed and made ready to seek his father. "He wouldn't have left without talking to me. Are you certain?"

"Aye, he set out early this morn before the sun rose. He left a missive for you and before ye read it, I want your promise to take this matter seriously, my lad. You must choose a lass from those who will come. This matter is grave and should be handled with discretion and importance."

"I am displeased da left without saying farewell. But aye, Philly, I will promise to pick from your lassies and I shall consider the matter most carefully. Besides, I haven't ever met a lass I didn't like. I'm certain one of the lasses would do well enough as a wife." He flashed a grin and his aunt scoffed.

"Clean yourself up, my lad. This night we will have a welcome home feast and Samuel will announce to the rest of the clan your lairdship. I expect you to attend in your finest garments and present an upstanding image. Most of the clan will be invited. You should find fresh garments on the table there. I had a maid bring them this morn. I suppose she got an eyeful of your bare arse, did she not? Ye might want to put something on for sleeping in the future so you don't cause my maidservant's blushes." She handed him the missive and reached the door. His aunt turned and smiled. "I'm pleased you are home and have missed you."

"I've missed you as well, Philly. Best tell your maids not to enter my bedchamber until I've left it. I won't wear garments to bed and if they are abashed by it then so be it."

"I suppose I must do so since you insist on causing havoc amongst my maids. Best hasten and be about the day. There's much to do and we cannot dally. Your da left his squire, Dain, to see to your comforts and needs. You might want to direct him in his tasks, yet he's eager to assist ye. He's rather young and inexperienced, but you'll have to make do."

His father hadn't mentioned a squire. Hell, he'd looked after himself most of his life and didn't need a snot-nosed lad to see to his comforts. Somehow, he'd have to find something else for the lad to do, tasks that didn't interfere in his daily routine. Keith peered at the missive and was eager to read his father's message.

"After you've dressed and eaten, come and find me. I'll probably be in my secret garden."

"Aye, very well, I'll see you soon." He waited until she closed the door to tear open the missive from his father and glanced over the words:

My dearest son, I could not bring myself to say farewell, but worry not for I shall see ye again soon. You will be busy in your role as laird and I beseech ye to take guidance from Aulay. He is privy to what's happening within the clan. My sweet sister has a plan to help you choose a wife. Listen to her as she's always given me sound advice. Perhaps by the time I return, I shall have a grandchild or two to bounce on my knee. At least, that is my hope. God guide ye in your role as chieftain. Be well, son. Da.

Keith laughed with a scoff at his father's words. Hendrie Sutherland had his life planned down to his bairns. He wasn't opposed to the clan's decree, but he'd always thought he would choose his wife when he was ready and that he would decide when to have children. Had they chosen the number of bairns he would have as well? The question lingered with a slight affront, but he supposed as laird he had to secure his family's succession. Their forcefulness bothered him but there was little he could do to refute them if he wanted to lead their clan.

Hopefully the women his aunt selected for his bride were acceptable. But that didn't much concern him either. What worried him more was whether the lassies would find him acceptable? Keith needed to be confident and not only with the lasses, but with his clan. He'd never had issues with the woman he'd wooed, but courting a woman for marriage was an entirely different sort of wooing. Not one to admit such a cowardly view, he shook his head and wouldn't consider it.

Before he'd meet with Philly, he wanted to see Aulay, his father's steward and the most trusted amongst the Sutherlands. Keith secured a heavy tartan over his tunic, certain the weather was as cold as it had been the day before. The tartan at his hips was thick and reached his knees and would keep him somewhat warm. When he left the chamber, he bumped into a lad who stood before his door as if he guarded it. Dare he tell him the sentry was unneeded?

"M'laird, I'm Dain, your lairdship's squire. I await my duties." The lad bowed and when he straightened, he was only as high as his chest.

Keith scowled at the dark-haired lad who peered at him with fearful brown eyes. Dain was a scrawny boy with no muscle to show for his age. Though Keith studied him for a moment, he couldn't guess his age. "How old are you?"

"I just turned ten this past autumn, M'laird."

"Ten? You don't look that old. Have you fostered for training yet?"

Dain shook his head.

"I do not need a squire. Find something to do." Before Keith sauntered off, he noticed the lad's crestfallen gaze and the way his chin nearly touched his chest. But he had no time to care for the lad's tender heart. It might do well to toughen him a wee bit if he might squire for a knight or train at arms. Most lads his age had sufficient training and were well on their way to squiring.

He strolled down the stairs and heard his aunt giving directions to the servants in the hall. Keith hastened past the doorway in hopes to avoid her. He wasn't ready to hear the sordid details of his aunt's devious plan to shackle him to an ally's daughter.

Near the barracks that housed the unmarried soldiers, he turned his gaze in search of Aulay. Though he'd known the man most of his life, they hadn't ever been close. He was uncertain if Aulay respected him. That might well be the cause of difficulty between them and a power struggle might ensue. Keith spent most of his time with his comrades rather than his father's soldiers. He was practically an outsider for all the years he'd spent on Sutherland land.

Aulay, the commander-in-arms, and most seasoned soldier in the Sutherland clan stood near the stables. The man's staid expression told him Aulay's mood bordered on annoyance. Whether he was annoyed with him or his brother, Keith was uncertain. Aulay spoke to Emmett, his younger brother, and they hastily ceased their discussion when he approached.

"Aulay, Emmett, I don't mean to interrupt but I need to speak with Aulay," he said with his hand on his hip in wait for their accord.

Emmett grinned with a nod. "You didn't intrude. We

finished our talk for now. I'll see about getting your horse ready, Aulay."

Aulay struck his leathered hand with the harness he held and appeared more than annoyed. "So the laird's absent son returns, aye? Your da visited me early this morn and told me that he gave you his ring. He awoke me from a dream and gave his orders."

Keith arched a brow at the commander's admission. "Aye, he did." He raised his hand and flashed the bauble to prove it. "I suppose your dream was one of pleasure then, given your glare."

Aulay smoothed a hand over the dark strands of his tied-back hair and his eyes narrowed. "I have nothing but pleasant dreams. We need to talk."

Keith nodded and was surprised his da spoke to Aulay, but the man was his most trusted soldier and he too was the keep's steward. His da depended on the man and he needed to find out if he could rely on Aulay too.

Emmett tethered his brother's horse to a pole, waved, and sauntered off.

Aulay motioned him to follow and they walked along the short trail toward the fields. The commander kept his gaze ahead when he spoke, "Your da has faith in you, should I?"

He took a breath and realized he needed to reassure Aulay that he meant to be a strict, forceful, laird, and one who wouldn't take shit from his soldiers. There was no time for nonsense when their rivals and others waited in anticipation of overtaking a clan that didn't protect themselves or their borders. He needed to proceed with caution and surety if he was to safeguard his clan from peril.

Keith turned to face him and blocked him from continuing onward. "You definitely should have faith in me. Maybe you think I'm not worthy to be the laird and wish you were chosen instead?" There, the question was posed. The commander's leadership put him in esteem and likely in a positive position in the elders' eyes.

Aulay shoved him hard on his chest. "Bloody hell, I

don't want to be the laird. If you can defeat me, perhaps I might deem you worthy. I won't give my respect until it's deserved or gained." He shoved him again and his fist came at Keith's face.

He ducked in time to avert Aulay's strike. Keith retaliated and landed his fist on the side of Aulay's jaw, and before he fell backward, Keith gripped his tunic to keep Aulay steady and on his feet. He wasn't about to back down and wouldn't allow the commander to confront him when it was unnecessary.

There was no reasonable cause for Aulay's discord and Keith wanted to assure himself that he had the man's respect. What better way to gain his respect than to thrash him to the ground in a brawl. Otherwise, he might have to oust him and name a new commander-in-arms. That wouldn't do at all. From all accounts, Aulay was a good man and a fine leader of their soldiers. There was no time to try to find a replacement or one as trustworthy.

Aulay grunted and scowled. "Well now, you might be a wee bit worthy. When you're ready, come and see me. We'll discuss the soldiers and what's to be done."

"We should discuss the clan issues now. There is no time to dawdle on the matters and with the Mackenzies threatening war on most of the clans hereabouts; we should be prepared to face any threats." Keith blocked his exit.

Aulay grinned and rubbed his jaw. "Now is not the time. You haven't been named as our laird yet, even though you wear your father's ring. When ye are named, we'll talk. As to the Mackenzies, they're too distracted by the Roses. I doubt they'll want to war with us." With that, he shoved him out of his way and marched toward the fields.

Keith didn't know what to make of his standoffish attitude. Did it bode ill for him and his leadership of his clansmen? Would the soldiers dislike him being their chieftain? Not only did he need to prove to Aulay his ability to lead them, but he also had to ensure his clansmen followed his orders. He wasn't about to stand for dissension amongst the ranks. Keith wanted to follow him and demand they continue the discussion, but he was too far away and immersed in conversation with the soldiers.

Dain ran toward him and stood in his shadow. "M'laird, I took care of your chamber and Milady told me to have all your items taken to the laird's chamber."

Having a squire might not be so bad after all. "My thanks, Dain." Keith was ready to make off again when the young lad sauntered after him.

"Is there aught else I can do?"

"Nay." Keith didn't like the look of defeat on the lad's face. "Aye, go and have your morning fare. Fill your gullet, lad. I'll think of something for you to do and will find you later."

Fortunately, Dain ran off to do what he'd asked. Keith ambled along deep in thought of how to win over his soldiers and how to keep Dain busy. His steps led him to his aunt's solarium, her secret garden. Memories of his aunt toiling away at her plants came. He'd spent a good number of hours in the solarium as a wee lad, but then he was still wet behind the ears and attached to her apron strings.

The stone walls opened wide and he entered the large area overrun with various plants and trees. Most greenery browned with the cold season, but some plants kept their foliage. As he traipsed through the lanes, he spotted a woman standing at a table. She muttered to herself and let out an unladylike expletive. His smile widened at her blasphemy.

"Bollocks, I will never get this right." She tossed aside a small bowl and picked up a sprig of a leaf and took a whiff of it.

He cleared his throat to alert her of his presence and startled her.

She nearly jumped a foot. "You frightened me. Didn't anyone tell you it is impolite to sneak up on someone? I didn't know anyone was there. It's you."

"Aye, it's me." He gazed at her and instantly remembered her from his childhood. *Marren.* "I apologize and didn't mean to frighten you." She wasn't the same wee lass who had teased him when he was a lad. How she had changed. Her blondish locks of hair had darkened and matched the dainty brows over her lovely blue eyes. He couldn't tell whether she was slight or not since she wore a heavy cloak about her body. "What is that awful smell?"

"It's nothing… Ah, my first error of the day. It's good to see you, Keith. You're looking well. I heard you had returned."

"Aye, and you, Marren, are a sight to behold. You're still here? I would have thought you'd be long gone off to marry some unfortunate man." He chuckled at his jest.

"Still here," she muttered and continued to labor and crumbled a leafy stem into a nearby bowl.

He neared and stood beside her. "What are you doing?"

"I am trying to make a scent but it's not going too well. I'm distracted this day and cannot get it right. This is my third batch." She fastened her bonny eyes on his and smiled.

Keith remembered her smile and he couldn't for the life of him take his eyes from hers. He wasn't the sort to be demure around a woman, but she rendered him so. It was an uncomfortable feeling and one that tensed his shoulders. Was it her loveliness or that she blatantly stared at him with alluring eyes that caused him to be staid?

"Your aunt was here earlier. She's in a rare mood this day and has everyone within the keep in a dither about your homecoming. The maids hide from her."

He drew his brows at that. "Philly? She's never so. You must be mistaken because she always smiles and is of a pleasant nature."

Marren snorted. "Maybe around you she is, but the maids fear her. Oh, I think she's coming. Come on." She grabbed his hand, lifted the cloth over her table, and pulled him beneath it.

Keith crawled next to her and sat close. He would have laughed at the situation he found himself in, but remembered she'd often hid beneath the table as a young lass to escape household tasks or Philly. His aunt never suspected they'd hidden there as children and they'd often gotten away with forgoing their chores or punishments.

They listened to his aunt talking to a woman as she passed the table. It was light enough under the table to see Marren and she peered ahead at the cloth as though her secret hiding place was in jeopardy of being discovered. The white fabric was thin enough to afford light to filter through, but thick enough to shield them. They were well hidden and safe from being found.

After a few minutes, silence came to the solarium. He stretched his legs out and leaned against the stone wall the table butted against. Keith was in no rush to leave the quiet, intimate place, or the woman who sat beside him.

Marren shifted back and folded her legs beneath her. She turned her face to him and her nose almost touched his as close as she sat. Keith should've shifted away, should've called upon his knightly code of honor, or he should've left the hiding place as soon as Philly vacated the solarium. But something held him there, next to her, and he was unwilling to admit what.

"Do you recall the last time we hid under this table?"

He grinned at the pleasantness of her voice. "Aye, I kissed you."

"You did and it was my very first kiss. We were so young then and innocent." She smiled and set her hand on his thigh.

Keith peered at her hand and almost groaned at the desirous sense that overtook him. "Neither of us was any good at kissing then." She didn't move away and with her face near his, he swallowed hard at the thought of kissing her again, only this time it wouldn't be the innocent kiss of youth.

"We were young and foolish, weren't we? I suppose you've had many kisses since then and are probably much better at it now."

Keith set his hand on her shoulder and slid his fingers to the soft skin of her neck. "Let us find out, shall we?" He pressed his lips on hers but was certain she'd push him away.

But she didn't and when her arms embraced him, Keith took the kiss to a more lustful place. His throat rumbled a bit from a pleasurable moan. He couldn't resist and added his tongue to the mix. She matched his passion in a duel that sent them both gasping for breath.

When their kiss turned more brazen and he was persistent with his onslaught, she pulled away. Keith was disappointed and suspected he'd frightened her again, but he was proven wrong when she leaned close to him and smiled. He kept his eyes fastened on hers and lost himself in the sensual aura of her gaze.

Marren continued to hold him and her lovely blue eyes stared back. "I would say you most definitely improved."

Chapter Four

For a feast, the great hall was oddly quiet. Marren approached and stood in the entryway and hesitated to enter. It wasn't because she didn't want to celebrate Keith being named as the Sutherland laird. It was because she was completely chagrined by her actions in the solarium earlier. To think she'd let him kiss her and she wholeheartedly returned his passion.

Why had she allowed him to kiss her? And more importantly why had she teased him about the many kisses he had since their first kiss in the solarium? She knew well why. Keith was too darned attractive to resist. Wasn't it her heart's fondest wish to kiss him? She'd done so, but now she wished she hadn't. It would only lead to her brokenhearted dismay.

Still, she needed to remember she was betrothed to an unknown man and she should save her kisses for him. If only she had a name and face to put with the ideal of her future husband. Until she met the man or he was named, there was naught to do but wait. Wait forever it seemed and she was impatient to begin her life as a wife and one day, mother.

Now that Keith returned, she wanted to leave, especially

since it was Lady Ophelia's duty to see that he chose a wife. Marren didn't want to witness him being tied to another woman who would perhaps win his affection, get to touch him whenever she wished, and spend a lifetime with him. A sorrowful, envious mien overtook her spirit.

She peered about the hall until her eyes fell on Keith. He looked rather irked with the company he stood with. But she was acquainted with Aulay, the leader of the soldiers. He'd often tried to court her until she asked Lady Ophelia to set him straight—that she was unfortunately unavailable to any of the Sutherland men.

That included Marc, the gate watchman, a man whom all the ladies loved to watch. It wasn't because he was handsome, which he was, but it was due to the fact that the man forwent wearing a tunic or tartan about his muscular upper body. At least he had a pleasing figure to gaze at.

Emmett, the stable master, was as handsome as his brother, Aulay, but he always appeared disheveled and reeked of horses. He'd professed to one and all that he'd rather spend the day with the clan's horses than the people. She doubted any woman would let him get close enough to her, let alone woo her.

Keith didn't appear to appreciate his company and she edged closer to listen to their conversation. She got as close as the hearth and pretended to warm herself. But being in the same room with Keith was enough to send warmth through her and her cheeks heated. She certainly didn't need the hearth's fire to ignite her insides.

"Your bloody horse got loose twice this day. He's after the mares." Emmett laughed coarsely. "I suppose he takes after his master and wants to rule the roost. He's a handful, aye just like ye."

"Winddodger is not used to the stables and doesn't like to be closed in." Keith glared at Emmett with affront. "He'll settle down. It's your job to make certain he does, unless you want me to put a more experienced stableman in your position."

"Hah, aye, you wouldn't dare? There's no other with more experience than me. I do my job but your horse is a difficult, ornery beast. He's a wild one and broke through the stall's wood within minutes. That horse sure likes to run. It took me over an hour to catch up to him. I don't know what to do to settle him."

Keith frowned. "It's not my place to tell you how to take care of the horses, Emmett. Why don't you let him choose a mare and perhaps he'll settle down? He's not used to being around so many females either."

Aulay bellowed. "Sounds akin to the situation you're in. You might be able to handle one lass, but six? You're a damned fortunate blighter, but you'll have your work cut out for you and your pick of the lassies if what Lady Ophelia says is true. Hmm…who will he choose? Mayhap a broodmare who'll pop out some bairns posthaste?"

"Cease your jests. This is a serious situation. The clan wants me to marry and I have no choice in the matter and must heed their dictate. It's either marriage or naught. Unless you want someone else to be named the laird, I'd suggest you accept me and cease your banter." Keith turned his back to her and muttered something to the men.

Marren couldn't hear the rest of their discussion. The men laughed and Keith joined in. She wished she'd heard what they found so humorous. Likely they continued to bait Keith about his upcoming nuptials and the women who were to soon arrive.

Cassie joined her by the fire. "I knew you'd look fetching in that gown and I told you if we pulled back your hair behind your neck it would accentuate the bodice. The color suits you."

Her gown was a plain cream-colored one with a squared bodice that showed a little too much skin for her liking. It was somewhat demure in its fashion, which was perfect for the occasion. And she adored the way Cassie had done her hair. There wasn't a single wave until it reached the tie behind her head. Waves cascaded down her back and curled at the ends. She felt a little exposed and her neck open to the chill in the room.

"My thanks for helping me get ready. You look beautiful this night too. Are you trying to draw Marc's eye again?" She laughed when Cassie gasped and nodded vigorously.

"Definitely, but he never notices me. I shall gain his eye one day. Oh, you will never believe what Lady Ophelia told me." Her friend spoke low and moved closer. Cassie purposely diverted the conversation away from Marc as she typically did when Marren teased her about her infatuation with the bare-chested Marc.

"If you wish to gossip, I don't want to hear it—"

She spoke low and used her hand to shield her mouth, "I tell you, you'll want to hear this. Lady Ophelia said by week's end six lassies will arrive. They come so her nephew might choose a bride from amongst them. He will court them all and shall decide who will be his wife. Are they not the most fortunate women?"

Marren nodded but her heart sank. She already had heard Lady Ophelia's plan from the woman herself and was despaired by it. How privileged were those lassies. She followed Keith with her eyes and returned her gaze to Cassie. "I cannot fathom why Lady Ophelia wouldn't just pick a wife for him. She's outrageous enough to do so."

Cassie snickered. "She probably would if he'd allow her to, but he doesn't seem to be the sort to let someone pick his wife. Look at him. I could sigh at his handsomeness, but I won't resort to being silly like the hall maids."

Marren had to agree, but only nodded and didn't voice her dejection at the situation. Keith made the rounds about the hall and twice she'd caught his gaze. He didn't smile, nod, or make any indication of whether he was pleased to see her. Their kiss meant nothing to him and she tensed at the thought that he would, within the week, be kissing others. He looked even more handsome than he had in the solarium, under the table, in her secret hiding spot, where he'd all but melted her heart.

"Your face is flushed. We should move away from the fire." Cassie linked her arm with hers and pulled her forward.

They walked at a slow pace around the massive table in the center of the room. Her cheeks heated but it wasn't from the hearth or the closeness of those in the hall. She kept her gaze on Keith as her friend continued to ramble on about the happenings and lord knew what else she'd spoken of. She barely listened.

Keith had cut his hair and now instead of flowing past his shoulders, it reached just below to his nape. He wore a dark blue tunic and a Sutherland tartan about his lean hips. She tried not to notice how strong his arms appeared where the tunic rolled to just under his biceps. He even wore new boots and a gleam of a large stone ring glinted on his finger. She recalled Keith's father wearing the same ring, the laird's legacy. Keith was taller than most of the men in the hall except for Aulay, Emmett, and Marc. All were fit men, but none rivaled Keith in their attractiveness.

Lady Ophelia entered the hall and spoke with one of the servants before she marched forward with vigorous steps. The woman eyed them and set a course in their direction.

"Oh, she comes. I must go. I'm sorry, Marren, I don't mean to abandon you, but she's wrath with me for disappearing this morn. I must go before she lays into me again about how I shirked my duties. I vow she gave me an earful."

Before Marren could stop her, Cassie ran off and left her standing alone.

Lady Ophelia approached and stood next to her. "The feast is grand, is it not?"

"Good eve, Milady. It certainly is festive." Marren curtseyed and smiled.

"Cook says you selected a good menu for our supper. You have my thanks for handling that tiresome task. As you know that is my least favorite duty, selecting the meals. You make me proud, lass. Now, come and sit next to me while we dine. I should like to hear how your scents are going."

Marren had no choice but to follow her to the end of the table when she took her arm. She'd rather sit elsewhere and didn't want to hear the sordid details of her lady's plan to get her nephew hitched. Once the lady took her seat, the rest of the clan ambled to theirs. The meal was served as soon as the lady took her seat and with her signal to begin.

Keith sat on the other side of Lady Ophelia and smiled at her. Why did he have to have a heart-melting grin? She closed her eyes and a glimpse of their fervent kiss flashed in her mind. Marren quickly opened her eyes and tried not to think about the way his lips felt on hers, but it would probably haunt her for a good long time.

Lady Ophelia motioned to a man across from her. Samuel, the clan's most elder man, rose and banged his wooden cane on the floorboard and drew everyone's attention. He had dressed for the occasion and wore his finest tunic and tartan. Samuel had even combed the few wisps of white hair on his head. He winked and Marren was uncertain if he winked at her or Lady Ophelia.

"My good clansmen and women, I call your attention. Our fair and just laird has left us to go on a grand adventure. We pray he has a safe, joyous journey and one that solaces him. Hendrie leaves us in good hands and in the care of his son. Raise your cups and we shall toast to our new laird, his gracious and deserving son Keith. To Laird Keith Sutherland, may ye prosper and bring good fortune to our clan. We go forth Sans Peur, aye, without fear."

All cheered and raised their cups at hearing the Sutherland's adage and drank.

Marren leaned forward and clinked her cup to Keith's and then to Lady Ophelia's. "I'm happy for you, Keith. You'll make a fine laird for the clan."

He grinned and took a sip of his drink. As he did so, she narrowed her eyes at the movement of his lips which brought forth another glimpse of them pressed against hers. Marren chugged her drink. Fortunately, Lady Ophelia had poured her wine and had filled her cup to the rim. She needed something stronger than ale to get her through the night.

Supper was served and for the rest of the night, she tried not to ogle Keith, but paid attention to Lady Ophelia's conversation with him. Unfortunately, the lady spoke of nothing but the lasses who would arrive and be wooed by Keith. After three cups of wine, Marren's mind started to muddle and she couldn't catch a single word of what they spoke. It was torturous to be close to him, and yet, unable to do as she wanted—to touch him, to feel his hands on her, or to kiss him again.

The feast began to wind down as most of the clans' people had left. Marren finished the last of the wine in her fifth cup of the night. She giggled to herself and was unsure of what she found humorous, but the drink had gone to her head. The hall wavered when she stood. After she bid her lady a good night, she glanced to where Keith had sat; only he wasn't there.

She hastily left the hall and ambled outside. The cold fresh air felt good and helped to clear her head a little. Marren walked toward the stable and wanted to see Keith's horse. From what Emmett said he was a rowdy beast.

"Where do you think you're going, lass?"

Marren whirled around and bumped into Keith. She almost fell flat on her face, but he stood close enough to touch her, and he steadied her with his hands on her hips. "It's you. You frightened me again. Do you make it a habit to scare people?" She stumbled away and reached a good sturdy tree to lean against.

"It's not my habit, nay. I didn't mean to frighten you…again. You shouldn't be out here alone, without an escort. Come, I'll help you back to the keep, you look like you need it." His smile was infectious.

Marren laughed lightly but she sobered when he reached out to her. "Nay, don't touch me."

Keith sidled next to her and set his arm around her back. "I cannot leave you out here alone and will see you safely inside. Why don't you want me to touch you?"

His touch seared her with wantonness and her head spun with the urge to kiss him again. She gazed at his face which was free of whiskers, and yet, masculine with a shadow of the day's length. He waved a little before her eyes and she shook her head to abate the strange sensation. "Because when you touch me, I cannot help but want more. It's too dangerous."

"Dangerous? For who, you or me?" He chuckled. "Come, lass, you've had too much to drink and don't know what you're saying. How many cups of wine did you drink?"

She shifted on her feet and her head began to spin ever faster. "I lost count. Too many, I suppose, and it's entirely your fault. You make me want to…" Marren closed her mouth and would say no more. She'd already put her foot in it so to speak. Her face burned with heat. The embarrassment was too much to bear.

"I'll get you safely to bed."

She clutched his arm because he gave her no choice. "That's what worries me. You won't join me, will you?"

He chuckled in his manly, affecting tone. "Nay, I promise to keep my hands to myself."

Marren leaned against his hard body and sighed. She wanted to wrap her arms around him and feel his hard muscular body. If she was brazen enough, she might even lean up and kiss him on the lips. "What a shame… I was afraid you would say that."

Chapter Five

The day the lassies were set to arrive finally came. Keith had spent most of the week with Aulay and was given the rundown of the tactics the soldiers had undergone. The men seemed pleased he was named the laird and cheered at the gathering of the announcement. Four hundred men had stood on the field, all attentive to Aulay's command. They'd trained hard and he was impressed with their vigor and devotion. Rival clans would have a force to defeat if they chose to instigate them. That eased Keith's mind on that matter and he didn't worry that his soldiers were inept. They were more than ready to take to arms should they need to defend their lands.

He met with Emmett, and still, Winddodger hadn't settled down. Emmett had yet to find a suitable mare in the stables for his randy, cantankerous warhorse. Keith had faith that the stable master would eventually get his horse to relax and take to his surroundings. Although, the man grumbled about it each time he saw him.

Then there was Dain. Keith hadn't come up with a list of daily tasks for the lad. Dain followed him everywhere and was practically his shadow. Keith couldn't get a moment alone, not with the lad constantly chattering away about how ardent he was about his duties. Try as he might, Keith couldn't find a suitable position for the lad. Dain wasn't yet old enough to train with the soldiers, and he was too old to be kept with the women. Something would come to him, but Keith hoped he'd figure it out sooner rather than later.

Throughout the week, Keith had gone to the solarium in hopes to see Marren again. It was obvious she avoided him because she couldn't be found. He didn't want her to hide from him especially if she was only embarrassed about drinking too much wine at the feast. Keith feared that Marren would avoid him after their last encounter. When he'd taken her to her bedchamber, he was riddled with contention. He tried to be gallant but couldn't shake the vision of the kiss they'd shared in the solarium. There was definitely an attraction between them and he was uncertain what he should do about it, if anything.

Thankfully her friend came a moment after they arrived at her bedchamber and he was saved from having to get Marren undressed and settled in bed. He imagined how bonny her body was, unclothed, and lying about the bedding waiting for his touch. Temptation taunted him, but somehow he resisted.

Keith groaned at the thought of touching her as he'd envisioned that night. Marren hadn't spoken more about him joining her in bed. If she had, he probably would have appeased her and himself. Hell, he would've enjoyed it. He desired her and after he'd questioned his aunt about her situation, Philly told him that she was unavailable and unfortunately betrothed. His aunt refused to discuss her and wouldn't name the man Marren was betrothed to.

He could have remedied his marital situation easily if Marren was available. She was bonny and everything he'd hoped for in a wife. Marren was intelligent, his aunt liked her, and she made him laugh. Never mind her beauty which had drawn his innermost thoughts and taunted his desire for the last week. But it wasn't to be, much to his dejection. She'd be wife to another.

A knock came at his door and interrupted his pondering of her. He was happy to have something to divert his thoughts from Marren's avoidance. He reached for the handle to open it.

Aunt Philly barged in and pushed him back a few steps. "What are you doing wasting the morn away? You mustn't dally this day. The lasses will soon be here and we must get you ready to greet them. Let me look ye over…"

"You mean inspect, do you not?" He stood at attention as he had many times when he'd been a lad awaiting his aunt's approval of his appearance when they were to attend an important function. "This is my best tunic and my tartan was laundered yesterday." Keith gave her a quick smile to assure her he'd done his best to look presentable.

She pressed a hand over the fabric of the Sutherland tartan he'd draped over the left side of his body. "You do appear handsome. I'm certain the lasses will find you so as well and more than acceptable. Let us get outside and await them. I hear a carriage coming up the lane."

Keith laughed because the lane was a good distance off and there was no way she could discern a carriage's arrival. He followed her and they reached the outside steps. Next to Philly, he stood with his shoulders back and his stance relaxed. Philly was more excited than he was to greet the women. She wouldn't stand still. Even so, he found himself eager to meet the lassies though. Perhaps he'd meet his intended wife this day? He hoped one of them would be suitable.

His gaze moved about the servants who stood at the base of the steps until his eyes fell on Marren. She stood next to the blonde maid, the woman who helped Marren on the night he'd put her to bed. Marren wore no smile, but she didn't frown either. He couldn't take his eyes from her, but she appeared disinterested in the event. Although, he couldn't blame her for trying to remain impartial. With the arrival of six lasses, his aunt's attention would be in high demand. Where would that leave Marren? But he had no time to consider Marren's position when the first carriage appeared at the end of the lane.

Keith shifted his stance and reminded himself to be confident and amiable. The carriage came to a stop and the outrider opened the door. A woman with the longest black hair he'd ever seen stepped out and neared them. She had a bonny face with dark eyes and a sharp nose. Her limbs were long and her body thin which was covered with a white tunic and a grayish overdress of skirts.

"Good day," she said and curtseyed before him. "I'm Robina of Clan Robertson."

"It's a pleasure to meet you, Robina." He inclined his head and noticed she held a handful of arrows and a small bow. "Do you practice arms?"

She raised her hand and showed him her weapon. "I do and I would be honored if you showed me your skill. That is if you have time."

He smiled at the tone of her winsome voice. "I would be delighted. Perhaps I'll arrange a target for us."

Aunt Philly stepped forward and intercepted the woman. "Entertainments will be arranged." She appeared affronted by the suggestion of target practice. But Philly was a stickler for convention and she likely had many droll afternoons planned. Philly waved the woman onward. "There is refreshment in the great hall. Go and take a rest from the journey, lass. We shall be along shortly."

Robina curtseyed again and strolled into the castle.

Keith's eyes followed her inside and he barely took a breath when the next carriage came. A young woman departed the carriage and hastily stepped forward. She wouldn't look him in the eyes and her gaze peered at her feet. From what he could tell, she was rather plain looking with mousy brown hair, but her green eyes were attractive, he supposed.

"Milady, welcome to Castle Dunrobin."

"Good day, Laird Sutherland. I'm Lindsey Gordon and my da sent me to—"

Philly cut her off and waved her onward. "We know why you're here. Come inside, lass, and we'll be along shortly."

Keith whistled low when she hurried past him. She was bonny enough, he supposed, but he'd have to find out more about her. She was a coy lass and wooing her wouldn't be easy. Yet, a sweet demure wife was exactly what he needed. He turned and his gaze found Marren watching him. She smiled and that simple gesture allayed him somewhat. He relaxed and stepped forward to greet the next lass with more confidence. The woman stepped from the carriage and held out her hand. She was garbed in a flowing green overdress that covered every inch of her. She wore a wimple on her head and from what he could see she had light brownish locks of hair.

"It's good to meet you, Laird Sutherland."

He bowed and smiled. "And you, Milady." She tried to move past him, but he stopped her. "Who are you?"

"Oh drat, I forgot to give you my name… I'm Iona Grant. Do you have a falconer here? I should like to go hawking every day and I have a fondness for all birds."

He wasn't sure if there was someone who tended to the hawks on his land. Keith should know that shouldn't he, but he was uncertain. To appease her he said, "Of course we do. I'm sure our lands are laden with many kinds of birds." Who the hell knew if that was true, but he wanted to please her and by her smile he had. She bowed and marched hastily inside.

Another carriage rolled up and another lass departed. The woman was beyond beautiful and wore her hair rolled on the sides. There was a reddish glint to the golden strands. She had brown eyes and fair skin, and a dainty look about her. She stood straight and had the bearing of a queen.

"Milady," he said and bowed.

She curtseyed and looked at his aunt. When Philly didn't speak, the woman stepped toward her. "I don't speak to men I have not yet met. Will you make the introduction?"

Aunt Philly hurried forward to do as she bade. "Oh, certainly, lass, I shall. This is my nephew, Laird Keith Sutherland. Keith, this is Lady Eedy Fraser."

"It's a pleasure to meet you, Eedy." He was about to take her hand but she stepped back with a look of affront on her bonny face.

"It's Lady Fraser, Laird Sutherland. Do you mean to be forward? Only my husband has the right to touch me and to call me by my given name. You haven't proposed yet and I haven't accepted you."

He wanted to laugh given her stern putdown. The woman was prim and proper and a wee bit resolute. That didn't bother him, because he could use a bit of decorum in his life. Courting her might be vexing though. He'd be fortunate if the woman allowed him to bed her on their wedding night. Keith didn't answer or remark on her tersely worded affront. She bowed and thankfully, Philly hastily guided her inside.

Next, came a lass who meekly ambled forward. She wore her hair completely wrapped which bulged atop her head with her hair's length secured. There wasn't a single loose strand to give him a clue as to what color her hair was. But her face was bonny enough and she was slight. She wore a white tunic covered with a blueish overdress.

"Laird Sutherland," she said and held out her hand, "I'm Caroline Gunn."

"Good day, Milady," he said and clasped her hand in greeting. Her hand was cold and limp with uncertainty. "Welcome to Dunrobin Castle, Lady Gunn."

"I look forward to speaking with you. And I do like to cook. Perhaps I shall make a meal for you whilst I am here. I'm told I made delicious meals."

"I would like that and I look forward to sharing a meal with you." Keith released her hand and found her pleasing enough even though she was a mite meek. If she could cook, being married to her wouldn't be so bad. If she was a good cook, he'd likely be fattened around the middle by the time they had their first bairn.

"Come, lass," Philly said and led her to the door of the castle.

Only five lasses down with one to go before the hairy ordeal was finished. Keith searched for Marren again in the crowd that had gathered, but she was no longer there. His shoulders slumped a little and he wondered where she'd gotten to. His aunt stood next to him and nudged him with her shoulder.

He turned and faced her.

"This lass is quite a favorite of mine. Be noble, my lad, and don't frighten her."

He spun around to face the walkway when the lass vacated the last carriage. Keith stepped forward to greet her. She was beyond lovely with shiny brown hair which was perhaps a shade lighter than Marren's. She had kind blue eyes and a winsome smile. The lass reminded him of Marren and had some of the same facial features. They had the same button nose, lush lips, and heart-shaped face. This lass was of medium height and was about the same size as Marren with the same slender build. Her skin was honey-colored and not too fair or sickly looking.

"Good day, Laird Sinclair, I'm Trulee Macleod. My da sent me to present myself. I'm pleased to be here and am gracious for your invitation."

He quickly stepped forward to lessen the space between them. "It's a pleasure to meet you, Trulee." Keith took her dainty hand in his and smiled. She was a Macleod and he wondered if she was related to Marren. Given their similar looks, he supposed they might be related. But he wasn't given time to consider it, or to ask her if she was, when his aunt had taken her away.

Keith stood there unsure, awkward, and wondered if he should join the lasses in the great hall. He waited for his aunt to give him further instruction. When she returned to his side, he sighed. The women were unexpected and he was quite impressed with the lot of them. Courting them would be pleasurable."

"My lad, what do you think? Is there a lass amongst them that might suit ye?"

He flashed a wide grin. "Perhaps there is. They're all beautiful and seem kind enough. I would like to get to know them though before I choose. If you'll allow me to, or do you want me to pick one now?" He laughed when Philly swatted his arm.

"Oh, you knave, of course not. I only wanted your initial thoughts. They are lovely and any one of them would make a good wife. Let us give them a few moments to rest and recover from their journey. We shall have a feast this night, but only a few shall attend. The ladies will, of course, and you."

"And Marren?"

"Marren? I suppose she should attend. Maybe she could offer advice to the lasses. Marren is the most reticent lass and has never acted immodestly. She might be able to offer you guidance as well in how to deal with the lasses."

He kept his expression blank because his depraved mind envisioned the kiss they'd shared in the solarium. Immodest? Keith would have laughed. If only his aunt knew of their encounter, but she didn't know Marren as well as she thought. "I would appreciate her counsel."

"Supper will be served earlier than usual so don't be tardy." Philly sauntered into the castle and left him alone on the steps.

"Are you impressed?"

He turned on his heel to find Marren standing behind him. "There you are. I wondered where you'd gotten to."

"I left the fire on beneath one of my pots in the solarium and had to turn it off before it set everything ablaze." Her eyes shone with mirth. "Why do I get the sense you're as frightened as a buck being hunted?"

He raised a brow. "If I could flee like a buck, I probably would."

"Come now, it won't be so bad, having all those lasses'

attention. Walk with me?" She took his arm and pulled him forward.

Keith peered at her arm linked with his and wished he could snatch her in his arms and kiss her. As they walked along, she kept her gaze ahead and their silence brought forth an awkward mien. She unsettled him in a way no woman had ever affected him. Why couldn't he find words to evoke a lighthearted conversation? It baffled him.

"I have complete faith that you'll make the right choice."

"What if I don't? I cannot be saddled with a woman who doesn't care for me."

She patted his arm in a comforting manner. "Then you shall make certain she does care for you before you ask her to marry you."

He sighed wearily at how to do so. "I'd rather be here talking with you than courting any of them." His confession came before he was able to stop it from passing his lips.

Marren laughed and the merry sound lightened him. She smiled and continued to walk on. "You shouldn't say such things, but I'm pleased you enjoy my company. I'm always available whenever you need to talk. I suppose you need someone to confide in."

He stopped her from walking ahead and kept her arm linked with his. "Why did you hide from me then this past week, lass?"

"I am sure I don't know what you're talking about."

He chuckled at her softly spoken words. "You speak a falsehood. Admit it, you hid from me. I want to know why."

She dislodged her arm and kept her gaze lowered. Marren leaned against the fence of the horse corral and watched the two horses that moseyed nearby. Keith whistled to Winddodger and he galloped toward him. He held out his hand and petted his warhorse's chest. His horse seemed pleased by his visit and wasn't as rowdy as Emmett had let on. He needed to exercise the beast though before he caused more havoc in the stables.

"Are you going to answer me?"

She stretched out her arm to pat the horse's head. "I couldn't face you after that…night, the night of the feast when I made a complete fool of myself—"

"There's nothing to be embarrassed about. You did nothing untoward. Aye, you giggled a lot and were sweet."

Her face flushed a little. "Still, I thought I said some inappropriate things to you."

"Oh, like how you wanted me to kiss you? And that you thought I was handsome. I am, am I not, handsome?" Keith laughed when she punched his arm.

"Aye you are, but none should tell you so and swell that big head you're carrying around. Still, I shouldn't have confessed that I thought you were handsome."

"If it makes you feel better, I think you're bonny. Your beauty is probably the cause of many a man's mishaps when you walk by them. If I didn't have to court six lassies, you can be sure I'd tell you so and often."

"You're a knave, Keith Sutherland."

He lifted her chin and stared into her beautiful blue eyes. "Bollocks. Life is not fair, is it? How can I find myself attracted to them when all I want to do is take you in my arms and kiss the breath from you?"

"Keith, please… You shouldn't tell me that or speak inappropriately. I wish you could kiss me again, but we shouldn't—"

He leaned forward and was about to touch his lips to hers when he heard someone clear their throat. Keith closed his eyes and drew a sharp intake of breath to settle himself. The intrusion couldn't have come at a worse time.

Emmett leaned on the fence with a smirk on his face. "Well now, is this not a grand show? Go on and kiss her if you are wont, but remember she's not part of the deal, Laird." He winked at Marren and chortled.

Keith cursed under his breath and released her. He scowled at the stable master and regrettably stepped back from Marren. "He's right, lass, and I have no right to court you. But I do need your advice about the women. You'll help me, won't you? Please say aye."

Emmett chortled louder. "Since when do ye need advice about women, Laird? What advice could Milady Marren offer?"

She frowned but replaced her expression with a splendid smile. "I would be happy to give you advice, Laird Sutherland. And Emmett, you are a black-hearted fiend." Marren marched away with angry steps.

"What'd I do to her? Why did she call me a black-heart?" Emmett shrugged his shoulders in the pretense of being offended.

Keith grinned because Marren had grit. He liked her more and more. "Maybe because you're an arse, Emmett, and deserved her insult. Hasn't anyone ever told you that you're a dimwitted oaf?"

Emmett guffawed and hunched his shoulders again. "Aye, perhaps a lass or two. Are ye calling me senseless, Laird?"

He wanted to pummel Emmett for interrupting them. If he hadn't, at that moment he would be kissing Marren again. With a shove to his stable master's chest, he said, "You bet your senseless arse I am."

Chapter Six

Marren waved off Cassie as she passed her at the castle entrance. She wanted to be alone and sulk. Why had Keith told her he wanted to kiss her? Now that's all she could think about. If she didn't know how forbidden it was, she might be excited at the prospect of holding him and being with him again. They couldn't act on their attraction regardless of how affected they were.

She took the steps to her bedchamber and hoped to escape for a short time. On her traipse up the stairs, Marren thought of Emmett. She owed him an apology for her insult, even though he was a crass man and deserved such a slight. He had saved them from making a drastic mistake and she shouldn't have cursed him.

The closer she got to her chamber; she discerned the sounds of laughter and voices coming from within. Marren entered and found three lassies inside. They had unpacked their satchels and made themselves at home. In the years she'd stayed at the Sutherland keep, she hadn't had to share her bedchamber. It was large enough to house at least four people, but the idea of having to be in their company completely dismayed her.

"What are you doing in here?"

A woman greeted her with a wave. "Good day. Lady Ophelia told us this was our chamber whilst we visited. I'm Caroline Gunn and that's Eedy Fraser and Iona Grant."

Iona giggled and drew Caroline away. "You cannot tell me he's not handsome."

Caroline scoffed. "I didn't say he wasn't."

Marren ignored their conversation and glances. She wouldn't join in the drivel of their discussion which centered on Keith's attractiveness. Yet if she was a young lass who had come to be courted by the laird, she might have been excited as well. She couldn't stay in the chamber when their voices rose in a debate as to who Keith would choose for his bride. Their argument boasted their skills from cooking, to being a gracious lady of the keep, and to the unaccountable ability to care for birds. The lasses' talents were as passionate as what she beheld of perfumery.

She pressed her forehead with the back of her hand and was certain it would ache for the rest of the day. Marren grabbed a pillow from her bed and hastily left the chamber. She sought the serenity of the solarium where it was good and quiet and positively free of the lasses' pitched voices.

When she reached the secret garden, she expected to find Lady Ophelia there tending to her plants, but she wasn't in the solarium. Usually, the woman cared for her plants from midmorning until late afternoon, but she must be too busy to see to the chore what with the many guests in the keep. Marren scoffed at that. She tossed her pillow beneath her table and settled upon it. With woe in her heart, she couldn't blame Keith for the situation he was in. He needed to marry someone to retain his title and position. How she wished she was one of the lasses he got to choose from. But alas since she was already betrothed, she wouldn't entertain the idea.

Someone entered the solarium and she heard footsteps which stopped near the table.

"I know you are under there. May I join you?" Cassie

lifted the tablecloth and crawled to lie next to her. "What are you doing here, hiding? Lady Ophelia is looking everywhere for you."

"I needed a few moments of peace."

Cassie took her hand and entwined her fingers with hers. "I met your bedchamber guests. What silly lasses they are, except for Eedy. That lass is so somber, she must have a broom handle up her arse."

For the first time that day, Marren laughed. "She is quite prim and proper, is she not? I cannot see Keith marrying a lady as drab as her. She'd bore him to an early grave."

"Nay, but who knows what kind of woman he wants. Perhaps she suits him."

Marren wished not to discuss Keith's marriage because she wanted to be the kind of woman he desired. "Are you hiding from Lady Ophelia again?"

Cassie giggled. "Nay, not her, I hide from the lasses. She asked me to stay in the bedchamber with some of them. I'm glad to leave the servant's quarters because there's never any room. I met the lasses a few minutes ago and they seemed to be offended that I'll stay with them. Me, a nobody...but a mere servant. There's a lass who has a satchel full of weapons and it's all she talks of. I vow Robina is a frightening woman, but the other two are harmless enough. One is a dowdy thing, but she's sweet though. I think her name is Lindsey. The other lass has her head in the clouds and wears nothing but black garments. Not a smidge of skin shows on her arms or upper body. She's Trulee."

"Truly what?"

"That's her name...Trulee. She's sweet though and her face is pretty, I suppose. I hope Robina doesn't scare the poor waif to death."

Marren thought she'd heard the name Trulee before but couldn't think of where. She shrugged her shoulders in defeat of remembrance. "I should be about my scents. There are only a few days left before I must take the containers to Wynda. I fear I shall fail in the effort because I can't seem to get the fragrance right."

"It's not like you to mess up your concoctions. Something troubles you." Cassie lifted her arm and settled their joined hands over her stomach. "What's wrong with you? Are you upset about the laird's return?"

"Nay, I'm not upset or troubled, except that I cannot seem to get the scent right, is all. I'm just...frustrated." Marren couldn't tell her the truth—that she was devastated that he'd marry one of the lasses. It was best to keep her view of the situation to herself.

Cassie squeezed her hand. "You speak falsely to me because I know it's not your scents that bother you. When you're ready to talk to me, I shall be here for you. I should leave you to the chore then and will see you at supper."

Once she left, Marren crawled from beneath her hiding spot and removed her cloak. She pushed up the sleeves of her overdress and reached for a bowl. With her efforts of mixing the chamomile, she put it aside and grabbed several dried buds of blue water lily and combined them with the petals of roses she'd stolen from Lady Ophelia. To the mixture, she added myrrh, saffron, cardamom, and cinnamon, all gotten on her last journey to Edinburgh with Laird Hendrie. The herbs were said to have an aphrodisiac quality. The scent was truly fit for a queen. It had a pleasant floral scent about it and the liquid was a little stouter than what she usually mixed.

As she proceeded to mix the ingredients, she took a whiff. The scent smelled of lilacs, mixed with a slight hint of roses, and was light and fragrant. *Perfection*. She finally got it right. Marren continued to mix the recipe until she made enough for ten containers. Come the morrow, she would take them to the village and meet her goal.

"Ah, lass, there you are. I've searched for you. I need a favor."

She set the last container down and turned to greet Lady Ophelia. "Good day, Milady, I'm happy to help. What do you need of me?" Now that she had perfected her scent, Marren could use a diversion—anything to take her mind off of Keith and his courtship.

"As you know, Keith is tasked with finding a wife. He must court the lasses that arrived this morning. I need you to chaperone their outings and such."

Marren's breath ceased because that was the last thing she wanted to do. She stared at the lady as if she'd gone mad or had no God-given sense. When she was forced to resume her breath, she turned away. "I shouldn't be the one to chaperone them. Why can you not do it?" She almost gasped as the words left her lips. It wasn't her place to question her lady or refute her request.

"I don't understand why it bothers you," Lady Ophelia said and placed a hand on her arm. "But I shall be busy seeing to the keep and the entertainments for the others whilst he meets them individually. I need to make certain nothing inappropriate takes place. I've promised the lasses' families they would be safe, protected, and in my presence the entirety of their stay."

Marren swallowed hard. "But—"

"There is no one else I trust more than you. You'll need to be discreet because I don't want him to know you are chaperoning him. Keith wouldn't take it well that I trust him not around the lassies. Yet I must ensure the lasses' safeguard."

Marren's mouth hung open in shock at what Lady Ophelia asked of her. What's more, how could she do what she asked without Keith knowing? She found herself nodding and agreed to her lady's request. "I shall do my best, Milady."

She patted her shoulder and continued, "I knew I could count on you, lass. You must befriend the lasses and gain their trust. If you do, it shall be easier to join them on the outings and festivity. I have it all planned, down to the last minute."

Poor Keith. His aunt was positively set on getting him married. Marren nodded but wasn't pleased to have to mingle with the lasses or to witness their courtship. She'd spent five minutes in their presence and they'd given her an ache in her head, which was why she'd sought refuge in the solarium. What about her perfumery? She'd have little time to herself if she agreed to accompany Keith and the lasses on their outings. There would be no time to perfect the scents she planned to make.

"I am pleased you'll do me this favor, Marren. The lasses' reputations must be protected."

Marren nodded and watched as Lady Ophelia left the garden. She stood by the table and was disheartened that she'd have a first-hand view of Keith's engagements. She hoped he found one of the lasses to his liking quickly and his courtship would be as painless as possible—for them both.

Chapter Seven

Keith awoke refreshed and ready for the day. His bedchamber was as messy as he'd left it and none of the maids had ventured inside. That was a relief since he wasn't about to sleep with garments on and he hadn't caused his aunt's maids blushes. Dain was forbidden to enter too. The lad was under his feet all the time and was becoming a nuisance. Keith hurriedly dressed and opened the door to find the squire, Dain, standing in the hallway in wait for him.

"M'laird."

His sigh raised his shoulders in his quest to avoid the young one. "Lad."

"What tasks do you have for me this day? I'm happy to do whatever you need of me. Shall I tidy your chamber? Milady Ophelia said that the maids were forbidden to enter."

Keith reached back and opened the door for him. "Aye, tidy the chamber. Then get yourself some food, lad, because you look as though you could use it." Dain was too thin and if he would make a worthy soldier one day, he'd need to fatten before he could gain muscle. The lad entered his chamber with a whistle. At least he was enthusiastic about his chores and would be busy for a time.

Keith rushed down the stairs. At the bottom, he heard the women's voices in the great hall. In his lightest steps, he bypassed the doorway and almost reached the exit of the keep and his freedom. But it wasn't to be.

"Where are you going?"

He stopped short at his aunt's voice. If he was of sound mind, he'd ignore her and go through the threshold and keep going. But it was Philly and he couldn't bring himself to be rude to her.

"Good morn, Philly. I need to meet with Aulay first thing this morn, and I mean to take to the training fields for an hour, and then I must go to the village. As laird, I have duties to see to."

"I understand, my lad, but you cannot leave the keep. I forbid it." She set her hands on her hips and gave him a look of disapproval. "The lasses await you. Did you forget your sacred duty? You won't disappoint them, will you?"

He resisted sighing in objection but gave her a stern look with a frown. His aunt dared to command him when he was the laird, and yet he wouldn't reproach her. Sacred duty, hell, how could he forget? She reminded him at every turn. "I have forgotten nothing, you minx, and you well know it. The lasses won't be disappointed. I must go to the village because I sent word to Grady and he hasn't replied. It's unlike him to not respond. Something troubles me about it." Keith hadn't spoken untruthfully. He had sent word to his comrade but he had yet to hear back. Grady wouldn't put him off and that concerned him.

"Your friend will need to wait. There are matters you must see to here, such as finding a wife. What shall the lasses do all day if you're not here? You're the very reason they have come."

His brows rose with her authoritative tone. Bollocks, his aunt was right. The lasses came and expected to be courted, yet he had no time to see to it this day. "You must explain that I'm detained elsewhere for now. I need to check on

Grady and find out why he hasn't replied to my missives. Give me one more day, Philly, and I promise I shall be all yours. A courting I shall go." He flashed a grin and thought how humorous it sounded but more akin to being tortured.

"It's not me that you will need to regale yourself of but the lasses. And I fear if I let you go to the village, you won't return. Are you running away?"

He grinned at the thought. "As much as I'd like to leave off, Philly, I vow I'll return before it gets dark. I'll meet with Aulay and will forgo my training this day. If I head out now, I'll be back before supper. Will that please you?"

"If you vow so then very well, go. But I shall hear no excuses for your delay in returning. On the morrow, you will begin the courtship. We cannot put it off another day. Marren is headed to the village this morn as well. Perhaps you might escort her. The lass often goes on her own and I have warned her against not taking a guard, but she won't listen to reason."

He gave her a nod. "I must go." Keith smacked her cheek with a farewell kiss and rushed to the stables. He was met along the way by Aulay who appeared cross. "I was going to come and find you. We have much to discuss but it might have to wait."

Aulay had a concerned gaze in his eyes. "There's no time now, Laird. One of the soldiers was hurt this morn during exercises and I'm off to the healer to find out how he fares."

"How badly was he hurt?"

"Vinn's leg was sliced deeply. We had trouble stopping the bleeding. Hopefully, the healer will save his leg. I'm off to see him now." Aulay's concern showed with his grimace.

"I'll find you this night when I return from the village. I'll stop by and visit with Vinn too." As Keith approached the stables, Marc exited with Emmett.

"Laird," Marc said with a nod and scratched the bare of his chest.

Emmett handed Marc the reins of a brown stallion and returned to the stables.

"Where are you off to?" Keith whistled to Winddodger

and his horse crossed the corral within seconds. He returned his gaze to the gate watchman and surmised the man was in an oddly pleasant mood. Marc took a moment to answer. With a glare, Keith gave the indication he wasn't pleased with his hesitation. "I asked you a question. Where are you going?"

"I'm going to the village to get medicinals for the healer. She needs them for Vinn's wound. Vinn got in the way of a sword this morn and is in a good deal of pain. And since I'm going, I thought to escort Milady Marren."

Keith turned when she exited the stable and for the life of him, he couldn't recall what he was about to say to Marc. Marren stood beyond with her horse and muttered a greeting. He narrowed his eyes and took her in. She looked lovely and dressed warmly for the trek.

The thought of the wily gate watchman being alone with Marren discomfited him. Keith turned back to Marc. "There's no need to escort Milady Marren, Marc. I'm going to the village and will bring the medicinals back."

"But Milady Marren—"

"Will be in safe hands with me as her escort. Return to the gate and do your duty unless you'd like to be reassigned?" Keith wouldn't be gainsaid and gave him a stern glare to get him to obey his command.

Marc shook his head, grumbled under his breath, led his horse to the corral, and tied him to a pole. He marched away with angry steps and twice glanced back at him as if he wanted to refute his order.

"Where is Marc going? He was supposed to ride with me to the village," Marren said and approached. She mounted her horse with ease and looked down at him prettily.

"He has duties to see to. I will escort you."

"You? Your escort is unnecessary. I usually go to the village alone and told your aunt I didn't need an escort. Surely you're too busy and with all those lasses awaiting you, have no time for a jaunt to the village." She patted her mare's head and stared at him.

For a moment he thought she was angry with him. He

smiled and took the saddle from Emmett who strolled from the stable. As he went about getting his horse ready, he said, "I have been given a day of reprieve. We'll have a fair ride. The weather has warmed a wee bit."

Emmett snorted a laugh. "I'd wager you'll have a fair ride alright, Milady, and if you have any sense, you won't let him—"

Marren cut him off. "Emmett, did I apologize to you for my rude behavior the other day?"

Emmett held the reins of her horse and his face brightened. "Nay, but you don't have to apologize. Worry not, Milady, you're not the first woman to curse me and you won't be the last."

"Get back to your duties before I also curse you." Keith mounted his horse and kept from laughing at the disgruntled gaze of his stable master. He led the way to the gate and they rode a mile in silence. Along the path that led to the village, he wondered what was going on in her clever mind. She seemed deep in thought but he wouldn't intrude on her musings.

"I cannot fathom that your aunt gave you a day of freedom when you're in such an all-fired rush to marry."

So that's what she'd been thinking of, his marriage. He almost grinned. "Aye, Aunt Philly took some convincing, but I need to go to the village. My comrade hasn't replied to my missives and it's unlike him. Remind me to fetch the medicinals from Wynda before we return."

"I shall and since I'm going to Wynda's, we won't forget."

"Why are you visiting her? Have you an ailment?" Keith hoped not, but most only visited Wynda to purchase medicinals. Not many had the means to buy the other items she sold.

"I often visit her but not for medicinals. I must stop by the millers to pick up fabric for Lady Ophelia as well."

They continued the ride and didn't stop to take a rest along the way. Keith felt eased in her presence as if words weren't needed between them. When they reached the village, he helped her down from her horse and removed her satchel, and handed it to her.

"Will you be well until I meet you at Wynda's or do you want me to escort you? I need to go to the tavern." He glanced around and didn't notice anyone who didn't belong or of anyone that he'd be wary of. She'd be safe enough.

"I will be well and usually come to the village on my own. Go on. Oh, there's Father John. I want to give him my confession while I am here."

Keith blanched at the sight of the man. If he was caught by Father John, he wouldn't cease his sermon and he had no time to listen to the priest's lecture. "Don't dally too long. If we want to make it back before supper—"

"My sins are not that great in number so it won't take long. I'll see you soon." She set off to meet with Father John.

Keith grinned to himself. Marren didn't look as though she'd ever sinned, let alone any number. He walked in the opposite direction and reached the tavern. As he entered, he spotted Jumpin' Joe who stood by a barrel. He dunked a cup and handed it to him with a nod.

"Ah, my good comrade, news has reached us of your good fortune. Compliments are in order, Laird Sutherland. We've heard you've been made laird of your clan."

"Aye, I have. My thanks," Keith said and took the offered tankard of ale. He pulled a small sack of coins from his tunic and handed them to Joe. "This should be more than enough to settle my debt. I'm sorry it took so long to get it to you."

"I'm sure this will cover what's owed, my friend. Is this what brings you here to the village? I hope ye didn't come all this way to bring the coin. I could've waited for it. Business is good these days. I'm sure you have more than enough to keep you busy at home in your new position." Jumpin' Joe took a cloth and wiped the nearest table and bade him to sit.

Keith set his cup down and looked about the hall. Though there were some patrons early in the day, none were his comrade. "Aye, and I wanted to find Grady. Has he been here?"

Joe shook his head. "Nay, he was, but he left a few days after you did. Said he'd be gone a while and I suspected he went to see his ladylove."

He frowned at Jumpin' Joe's speculation. "What ladylove?" This was the first he'd heard of Grady having a love interest besides those he cavorted with at the tavern.

"He didn't tell me her name and only said he was off to see his lady." Joe shrugged his shoulders and smirked. "Do you want me to give him a message when he returns?"

"Tell him I need to see him posthaste and that I sent him missives explaining…"

"I received the missives you sent and hold them for him. When Grady comes, I'll be sure to give him the missives and your message."

Grady's uncle sat across from him and smiled. "Good lad, is it true that your father left and gave you the chiefdom?"

"Aye, Chester, it is," Keith explained why his da left and the covenant of his taking the position as laird.

Chester chortled with mirth. "Your clansmen are wise to get you settled. Once ye do, you can ensure the clan will prosper and beget heirs for the future." He poured himself ale from the pitcher Joe left on the table.

Jumpin' Joe hailed off when a servant dropped four cups of ale on the floor. His scoff and lecture to the woman could be heard well across the village as angry as he was.

Keith peered at Chester and wasn't allayed by his agreement with his clansmen. He didn't need a wife to settle him and to ensure anything, let alone heirs. Why couldn't they understand that he meant to be a good laird and would stop at nothing to make certain they prospered?

"Och your da was lonely. I visited him a month ago and I deem he misses your ma. She was a good woman. There was no finer lady than Vera, except of course for Phee, ah, Lady Ophelia. How does your aunt fare? Well, I hope?

Mayhap I should stop and visit with her soon?"

Keith raised a brow in wonder that Chester might be beguiled by his aunt, since he mentioned her often enough. But he wouldn't dare ask. That was the last thing he wanted to envision, his aunt and Grady's uncle…together in any sense of affection. "Maybe you should visit her. She could use the diversion." Anything to dissuade her, even for a short time about his marriage. "What's this about Grady going off to see his lady? What do you know about this? He never mentioned anything to me about having a lady."

Chester snorted. "Nay, but ye know how tight-lipped that lad can be. I am not aware of a woman or at least Grady hasn't told me of anyone. If I see him, I'll be sure to ask about it."

"You do that. I need to go. Someone is awaiting me…"

Chester raised his cup with a nod. "Farewell, Laird Sutherland. I'll be sure to spread the news of your clan's prosperity. It would do well to make sure certain clans are aware of your land's protection." He winked at him.

Keith knew who he hinted at—the Mackenzies. As much as he preferred to keep his matters private, it might not be a bad thing that the Mackenzie clan was told about his new position.

He ambled along to Wynda's cottage and thought it strange that Grady left the area without telling him. Although he wasn't beholden to him, Grady never withheld his whereabouts or who he was with. Until he spoke to him, Keith had to put the matter aside. He'd get his answers when Grady returned.

He entered Wynda's shop and it was empty save for the hawker herself. Marren wasn't there and there were no other patrons inside. A pang of worry hit him. "Good day, Wynda. Has Marren been here? She was supposed to meet me."

She startled, turned quickly, and knocked over a jar of liquid. "Oh, Keith, I didn't hear you come in. You just missed her. She was here earlier but left soon after. How are you? I heard about your da and his leaving."

He wondered where Marren went but recalled her saying she had to go to the miller. He pretended to be interested in the bottles on the table. "I'm well. Da is off on his adventure. How much for these?" he asked and picked up a bottle and smelled the contents. The fragrance was delicate and reminded him of Marren.

"Those are not for sale and have only come in. There are other scents over there that you can purchase." She led him across the room. "These are ready and the seal is dried enough for sale."

He picked up a bottle and smelled a light fragrance of heather through the thin layer of wax. "I'll have all six of them."

Wynda flashed a smile. She collected the bottles and put them in a woven sack and handed them to him. As he paid for his purchase, Marren entered.

"There you are. I wondered where you'd got to and worried about you."

She smiled and raised the satchel she'd gotten from the miller. "I'm ready to return now. Are you? Don't forget the medicinals for Vinn." Marren waved to Wynda who frowned at her.

Wynda bent and retrieved the medicinals. "The soldier who came earlier told me what was needed. It's all there and should be a good help to Vinn. I hope his wound heals."

"My thanks, Wynda." Keith wasn't sure why Wynda's mood changed the moment Marren entered the shop, but he took the small satchel from her and followed Marren outside.

"It shouldn't take long to reach home. The air has warmed and I won't need my cloak." She removed it and set it over her arm.

Keith took the satchel she held and walked beside her.

"Did you find your comrade?"

Keith wanted to hold her hand or to put his arm around her as they ambled along the village lane. He didn't have the right to make a show of fondness toward her and that sunk his shoulders a wee bit. "Nay, he's left the village."

"That's too bad." She peered at her horse when they reached the hostelry.

They retrieved their horses and set out. Winddodger was in a difficult temper and bucked twice before he got him to settle down. His horse was smitten with Marren's mare and the randy beast wanted to be set free. Winddodger followed his commands though and he cantered along almost contrite at his earlier behavior.

He rode close to Marren and couldn't help but watch her. The thought of kissing Marren and how passionate they were in the solarium came to him, but he shook the visions away. He tensed at the way she'd felt in his arms. Before he could reason it, he sidled next to her and pulled her from her horse, and settled her on his lap.

"What are you doing?" She gasped and held tightly to his arms. "Honest to God, if you let me fall I shall—"

Keith answered her by pressing his lips on hers. He couldn't get enough of her. With his arms clasped around her waist, he kept her pressed against him and his mouth on hers. Their passion ignited an urgent sense of longing within him as if he could never get enough of her.

Winddodger maintained an easy pace. Keith dislodged from the kiss and peered behind him to make certain Marren's mare followed. The horse sidled next to his. When they reached the forest adjacent to the Sutherland land, he dismounted and helped Marren from his horse.

"Let us walk a bit. I'm not eager to return."

"Me either." She clasped his hand and kept her gaze ahead on the dirt path. "We shouldn't be kissing. You're to marry and I'm betrothed."

"Aye, you're right but I cannot help myself." He led her to a stream where the ground was soft with moss. No grass had grown even though the temperature rose. After he tethered their horses, he pulled a tartan from his chest and placed it on the ground for her.

Marren knelt next to the stream, cupped her hands, and drank.

The current of the water wasn't too fast, but it was deep and clear. He wished it was warm enough for a swim, but the weather hadn't yet reached the warmth needed to afford so.

"I won't kiss you again if that's what you want." He stood afar from her, certain that if he got any closer, he'd take her in his arms and wouldn't be able to keep such a promise.

She sat upon the tartan and focused on the flowing waters of the stream. "What I want I cannot have."

He refuted his thoughts because she all but suggested she wanted his kisses. Keith dejected at her woeful words and that he'd caused them. He sat next to her on the tartan and took her hand and sighed because he felt the same. "Aye, unfortunately, we are beholden to our pledges."

"Neither of us is married…yet."

Her words tensed his chest. Keith frowned as he tried to discern what her words meant. Did she imply she wanted to be with him? It wasn't a falsehood and they hadn't taken vows to anyone…yet. He left the tartan and stood by the water in deep thought of what to do. Never in his life had he wanted anything more than to be with Marren. The conundrum of it tensed his shoulders and the quandary of it reverberated in his mind. Would being with her bring more troubles than he hoped for? Would once be enough? Would twice be enough? Keith doubted it would be.

He kept his gaze from seeking her when he said, "We are not yet married, that is true, but—"

"Shhh. I care not about anything. Only you. Only what happens in this moment."

When Keith turned, he found her standing directly behind him. She threw herself in his arms and he held her tightly as if he'd lose her forever if he loosened his hold. Her breasts pressed against his chest and caused a desire to swarm within him. He set his mouth on hers and moaned when her hands played with the hair at his nape.

While he allowed himself the pleasure of touching her, he was caught in the desirous effect of her caresses. He shifted her overdress from her shoulders and pressed his hand over the softness of her bared skin. They rasped from the excitement of how their kiss sent desire pulsing from one to another. Keith set his lips on her neck and trailed them to the naked center of her chest and then to the swell of her bosom. He cupped the weighty flesh in his hand and used his tongue to heighten her lustful urges.

Marren leaned lethargically against him and he held her so she wouldn't fall. But his knees weakened as his passion took hold. Keith picked her up and settled her on the tartan. She peered at him with sensuality in the depths of her bonny blue eyes.

He was never so enrapt by a woman's gaze and it would be his undoing. Keith flanked her and perused his hands over the softness of her body as his lips slid over the naked flesh of her neck and throat. It only took a moment for him to be completely beguiled by her.

"Keith...this is incredible. What you're doing is...marvelous." Her breath came in short rasps and she moaned as he continued to pleasure her.

He grinned at her while he helped her remove her overdress. Her body was pleasing, so beautiful, and sent him to a state he was unable to recover from. Hardness effectuated him with an ache between his legs and his need spurred him onward. Keith yanked his tunic from his belt and he continued to assail her with passionate kisses until she broke free of the kiss.

"Nothing else matters but us together in this moment."

"Aye, lass, nothing. You were made to fit perfectly in my arms."

Marren withered beneath him and her moans of pleasure nearly did him in. He flung his tartan from his waist and leaned on his elbow. He wanted to be gentle and to give her as much pleasure as he could. But she made it difficult and urged him on by rubbing her leg against his. The slight movement wove lust throughout his body and he was in an unsteady state as it was. His restraint slipped and was nonexistent. There'd be no turning back if he didn't desist in kissing her or touching her body. He goaded himself to cease, but his hands wouldn't obey his thoughts.

Keith gritted his teeth and took a deep breath to settle himself. "Lass, we need to slow down."

She pressed a hand on his face and smiled. "Nay, I don't want to." Marren pressed him back and leaned over him. She caressed his body with the gentle strokes of her fingers. His body heated with an insatiable fervor. "I have wanted to do this for so long…to touch you…to kiss you…and to have you do the same to me."

Her raspy tone brought on his moan. "Are you certain you wish to—?"

She wouldn't let him finish and set her mouth on his. His question vanished and he wasn't sure what he wanted to ask. His censure was long forgotten and all he could do was enjoy her touches. Keith pressed her back and rolled to settle himself between her legs. He placed kisses on her navel and stroked the center of her. She moaned and huffed. He suspected she ached for more than his touch there, just as he ached to be joined to her.

He pressed onward until his erection was halted at the barrier of her womanhood. Keith groaned because he would hurt her and it was the last thing he wanted to do.

"Lass, sweetness, if we continue—"

"Don't stop. Please." She cajoled him onward and held onto his shoulders. "I want this…you."

Keith pressed forward and with a quick thrust, he planted himself. Warmth and softness surrounded his hardness. His arms shook and his body tightened and taunted him to move, but he swore by all that was holy he wouldn't budge an inch until she was ready.

"Tell me when you're ready, sweetness…," his words were barely a whisper on his breath as he grated them.

She opened her eyes and they shone with unshed tears. The beauty of her gaze caused his breath to cease. He hoped with all his heart that her desire forbade her to refuse him. But if she did, he wouldn't be dishonorable. The last thing he wanted to do was hurt her.

"Ready for what?" Marren continued to hold him in a death-grip and he shifted his body. She gasped and clung to him. He purposely moved slightly to give her a sense of what was to come. "Oh...aye, I am."

He withdrew slowly and the madness to thrust overtook him. Keith could no longer hold back and his movements mindlessly brought his desire to the brink. Marren got the hang of their pace and met his thrusts and their bodies clashed in a great war of pleasure and pain.

"Hold me, lass, hold me tight." Keith used every stratagem to arouse her passion.

She smiled but then she moaned and cried out. He thought her body was beautiful to behold but it didn't compare to the way she responded to her culmination. She nearly shrieked with pleasure and when the euphoria settled, Keith felt the tension of his ecstasy entwine in every part of him. It clashed in his heart and would surely end him.

"By my faith, that was..." She didn't continue but kissed him with passion.

The kiss heightened his desire until his body was no longer controllable. He kept thrusting until he was completely done in. All his muscles tightened and his blood rushed through him as though it was an unstoppable collapsed dam. Keith closed his eyes and focused on the brutality of his orgasm. When his breath calmed and he returned to some semblance of normalcy, he placed a gentle kiss on her lips.

Marren clasped her arms around him and she placed her head on his chest as he lay back. His heart drummed madly and he felt the thumping in every part of him. Neither spoke. He wasn't ready to face what they'd done or the culpability of it. Yet as much as it was wrong to be with her, it was perhaps one of the greatest moments of his life. It would take a lifetime for him to forget the intimacy they shared.

She's betrothed to another man. You cannot have her. You're to marry another.

The reminder of the pacts that forced them to accept

their inability to follow their hearts displeased him. His words echoed in his mind and he couldn't curtail the woebegone nature of them. Life's reality wouldn't abate and he was forced to admit that even if he was pleased with their encounter, he should have had more control.

"I'm sorry, lass. What we did, shouldn't have happened—"

She pressed a finger on his lips. "Don't you dare apologize, Keith, I will not listen. It's too late for either of us to be noble. This moment is too perfect. Don't ruin it with regrets. I'm not contrite in the least about being with you."

He smoothed a hand on her cheek and yanked her body next to his. "Well then kiss me hard, lass, because it'll likely be our last."

Chapter Eight

Marren was wracked with guilt even though she refused to regret what she and Keith did at the stream. It wasn't as if they had betrayed anyone since neither of them had yet committed to their betrothals. Still, a great penance was needed if she would be dissolved of the guilt that plagued her. Although she had yet to befriend any of the lasses, she felt as though she'd betrayed them. The culpability weighed heavily upon her. She was abashed though at having to admit her sin to Father John. He'd probably scold her or worse, give her a penance that would last an eternity.

After they reached home, Marren bid Keith a farewell with a passionate kiss, one that she would never forget. It was likely the last she'd ever get from him. She'd spent the night listening to the lasses discussing Keith and their hopes to win his favor. That put her in a foul mood which hadn't abated when she woke and began her day.

She detested that she'd all but thwarted their plans to win him as a husband. Since she couldn't marry Keith as she wanted to, perhaps she could ensure he ended with the right woman at the altar. Marren wanted him to be happy, even if that meant he loved someone else. With that in mind, she had to get to know the lasses, and when she discerned which woman was the best wife for Keith, she'd help her win his heart. Although, it would undoubtedly break her heart.

She quickly finished dressing and overheard the conversation between Eedy and Iona.

"No one wants to hear more about your silly birds. Can you not shut your mouth for one second?" Eedy said with nastiness in her uppity tone. "Honest to heavens, who gives a fig about birds? If you deem to win the laird with that nonsense, you'll be sorely let down."

Poor Iona appeared crestfallen at the woman's put-down. Marren liked Iona even though the lass was a little obsessed with birds and spoke of nothing but. Still, that didn't give Eedy cause to be mean-spirited. She had to go. As soon as she met with Lady Ophelia, she'd ask her to move Eedy to the other bedchamber or perhaps even send her home. Keith wouldn't want such a harridan for his wife and it wouldn't take getting to know the woman to reason it. The woman's surly nature wasn't what a man wanted; at least, Keith wouldn't want someone of her ilk.

Eedy approached and stopped her from passing. "Two of my gowns need to be laundered and I need my bed tidied each morn. Be sure to see to it." She flapped her hand as if she should attend to it immediately.

Marren would have laughed if she wasn't so affronted by her demands. Imagine her being Eedy's maid. It was quite laughable. She was about to correct her when Iona spoke up.

"She's not your servant, Eedy," Iona said. "She's a lady and Lady Ophelia's companion. Is that not right, Lady Marren?"

She nodded, but otherwise didn't elaborate on who she was or why she was at the Sutherland keep. It was none of their affair. Marren was surprised the lass stuck up for her, but she didn't need her aid in dealing with Eedy. "I'll be sure to tell the maids of your needs, Lady Eedy. But we really should get moving. The morning fare will soon be served and

Lady Ophelia doesn't like it when we're late to arrive." Marren motioned them from the room.

In the great hall, all the lassies assembled. This was the first day Keith would court them and there was a buzz of excitement in the air amongst the young women. They stood about in groups of two and their conversations were whispered but seemed fervent.

Lady Ophelia stood and addressed them after all had finished their morning fare. "Ladies, I have put your names in this chest and shall pick who will be the first to meet with Laird Sutherland." She thrust her hand in the wooden chest and withdrew a small piece of parchment. "Robina, you will join Keith after the noon hour. I will find out what he plans so you may garb yourself appropriately."

Robina appeared nonchalant and the other lassies looked dismayed and envious that she was chosen to be his for the day. Lady Ophelia left and Marren made the rounds with the lasses. She had to befriend them if she was to do what her lady had asked her. And if she would keep her vow to find Keith the perfect woman, she needed to find out more about them.

She sat next to Robina. "You must be thrilled to be the first to meet with Keith. I understand you use weapons? You should get along with him then because he likes weaponry and often joins the soldiers—"

Robina didn't let her finish her sentence and held up her hand. "Whoever you are, I need not your company or advice. Please, go away and leave me be. Refill my cup and then be gone."

Marren frowned and couldn't reason why the woman was so hostile. Keith entered a moment later and spoke low to a servant before he gazed about the chamber. His long stride took him closer to the women and he stopped before them. She was too far from him to hear what he said to the lasses, but they wore smiles. The man was gallant and his charm could win over the most demure of women. The thought that he'd woo them, narrowed her eyes. He took

Robina's arm and she wore a smug smile on her face. Keith led her from the hall and the other lasses were quiet and appeared saddened by his departure.

Marren's heart ached because he hadn't given her a single glance. Yet they promised after the journey to the village the day before that their liaison was a one-time event. That didn't mean her heart wasn't affected though.

Cassie tried to stop her, but Marren waved her off. She hadn't meant to be rude, but she needed to be alone, and she had to hurry and catch up to Keith and Robina. Lady Ophelia expected a report later and she wouldn't disappoint her. Yet the thought of fabricating a report appealed to her so she wouldn't have to spy on them.

When she reached the outside, Lady Ophelia stopped her in front of the keep. "You shall be my eyes, lass. He intends to take her to the fields where the men practice their archery. Later, he asked me to place a table and chairs in the solarium where they might dine alone. Come to me after so I may learn what transpires betwixt them. I deem she might be the right lass for Keith and the Robertsons are an agreeable clan. Her beauty should win him over." Her lady winked at her and continued to amble along.

Marren bowed and nodded. "I must hasten if I'm to catch them. Good day, Milady." She picked up her steps and reached the quintains which were set up as targets for the soldiers' arrows. She kept at a distance and stood beside a tree. The absurdity of spying on him brought forth an odd sense as though she watched something she wasn't supposed to.

Although she couldn't hear their discussion, her line of vision afforded her a good view. They spoke and Robina wore a pleasing enough smile. She supposed the lass was happy to practice arms given that she was obsessed with weaponry and she'd spoken of nothing but since she'd arrived.

Keith handed her an arrow and allowed her to set and release it. The arrow missed the mark and Robina stomped her foot with ire. Marren couldn't see him marrying the lass. He was the Sutherland laird and needed a woman to look after matters of home and hearth, not on the battlefield or the rampart. Additionally, Marren held no fondness for the woman mostly because she wasn't a pleasured natured lass, given her attitude after the morning meal and the way she spoke to others. She was a crass lass and had not a selfless bone in her body.

Robina certainly didn't bring joyfulness to those around her. Didn't all men want a woman who eased them and didn't bother them with unimportant matters or ill-mannered tempers? That was one of the lessons Lady Ophelia had instilled within her—to make certain her husband was comfortable, his home clean, his home matters seen to so he didn't have to lift a finger. A wife didn't trouble her husband with mundane matters of home when he had duties that beheld more importance. And regardless of how irked one was with her husband, she didn't show it.

Marren stood by the tree for what seemed forever. They took their sweet time and nearly two hours later, Robina collected the arrows by the quintain. By the grace of God, they had finished and she blew a relieved sigh. Marren thought she'd fall asleep out of sheer boredom of their task. It seemed a mindless task to her. Set the bow, release it, and repeat. Droll, quite droll.

When Keith reached the quintain, he dropped to the ground with a shout. He lay on his stomach and he'd pressed his arms over his head to cover it in protection. Robina had released one last arrow and it nearly killed poor Keith. She missed him by mere inches. If Marren wasn't so concerned for his safety, she might have laughed at the humor of the situation.

Keith bellowed though and his laughter reached her. He had a deep manly laugh. If only she stood where Robina was, she certainly wouldn't care about such practice. They walked forward and Marren slunk behind the tree so they wouldn't see her.

"You did well, lass, and hit the target a few times. There are soldiers within our ranks who have yet to hit the mark. I'm impressed."

"I will hit it next time with all my arrows," Robina said boastfully and set her hand on his arm. "Shall I change and meet you for supper?"

"Aye, lass. I have duties to see to and will meet you in an hour." Keith handed her back her arrows and sauntered away.

Marren turned and ambled to the solarium. She didn't know what she'd tell Lady Ophelia, but she had to come up with something derogatory so her lady wouldn't keep Robina in the running. In the solarium, an open area had been set up for their supper. Lady Ophelia set a romantic table with candles and an elegant table covering. How she envied Robina.

"Were you able to join them?" Lady Ophelia asked as she clipped a newly bloomed rose from an early-blooming bush. She set the rose on the table and turned to her.

"I wasn't near enough to hear them but it appeared they got on amply well."

"Oh, this pleases me. Perhaps this romantic supper will inspire love."

Marren thought she'd be ill over her honeyed words. "I shall let you know how their evening goes." Before she left, she stood by the lady. "It would do well to have Eedy moved to another bedchamber. The woman is unkind to Iona and the lass is a wee bit sensitive. Eedy was rather mean to her earlier."

"If you deem I should, I shall see to it immediately. We cannot have discord between them."

"They compete for Keith's attention and there is likely going to be rivalry amongst them, but still, her brashness was unwarranted. It also doesn't give Eedy the right to be unpleasant to anyone."

Lady Ophelia nodded. "You're a kindhearted lass to take that into account. I will handle the matter posthaste."

Marren was glad her dealings with the prim and proper

Eedy would be limited. She felt sorry for Keith because when he courted her, he was bound to affront the woman. There was no way around that because everything seemed to offend Eedy.

There were only a few minutes to see to her matters and return to the solarium for the wretched 'romantic' supper Lady Ophelia planned for Keith and Robina. Marren entered the great hall, ate a quick supper, and returned to the solarium.

She hurried so she would arrive before the 'happy couple' appeared. Marren hid beneath her table and tried to shift the covering to afford a view of the table. A few minutes later, Keith arrived. He looked so handsome and she wanted to call out to him, but didn't. He paced around the table and appeared tense. He had nothing to worry about because Robina was a fortunate woman if she was the 'chosen one.'

Robina arrived a few minutes later but hadn't changed her overdress. The woman didn't bother to comb or arrange her hair either. If she was interested in Keith, wouldn't she have at least attempted to beautify herself? That gave Marren hope she wasn't interested.

"Milady," he said and held out the chair for her.

She sat and was quiet.

Marren sighed wistfully at the woman's feigned smile.

They ate and Robina spoke of nothing but weaponry and asked questions about his soldiers. Keith plied her with all sorts of questions: those about her experience at caring for a keep, how close she was to members of her clan, to when she wanted to have bairns…

Robina seemed to be put off by his questions. "I am not friendly with many of the clan's women, but my da's soldiers allow me to sometimes take to arms with them. As to the keep, my ma has many servants and leaves the care of our home to them. There are plenty of servants to see to the matters. I am unsure when or if I shall want to have bairns. It's too messy an ordeal to consider. My ma only had me and said it was a difficult birth."

Keith stood. "I enjoyed the evening. Here," he said and handed her the rose and a bottle he must have gotten from Wynda's.

"My thanks, Laird Sutherland, for the gifts. May we practice arms again on the morrow?" Robina asked with a honeyed tone to her words.

He helped Robina rise from her chair. "I'm unfortunately unavailable on the morrow, lass. Perhaps I'll arrange something in a few days." Keith didn't elaborate and appeared disgruntled that she asked.

She didn't remark on her displeasure, but Marren got a glimpse of her besmirched face. They left the solarium, and Marren stayed beneath the table. She grew morose that he would find one of the lasses acceptable enough to marry, even though she prayed he didn't choose Robina. His happiness meant a great deal to her, but it would bring about her overwrought sadness.

Marren wanted his contentment, but she wanted him to be happy with her. How wretched to be betrothed to someone else. She considered asking Lady Ophelia to intercede on her behalf with Laird Mackay, and perhaps sway him to release her from the pact. Yet if the lady was unable to, Marren might have to leave. Then she wouldn't have to witness the interaction between Keith and the lasses. And her heart wouldn't break each time, if she had to observe him with another. A wretched thought came and she wondered what would happen once he wed. She doubted she'd be able to stay when his wife would be the lady of the keep.

Someone approached and she heard their footsteps getting closer. They stopped at her table and she held her breath. A pair of worn-scuffed boots peeked under the tablecloth.

"Come out, Marren. I know you're there."

She crawled out from under the table. "How did you know I was here?"

"I heard your breathing." Keith flashed a grin at her.

She laughed. "That's nonsense. I don't make a sound

when I breathe."

He grinned and revealed a slight cleft on his chin, one she'd only just noticed.

"I have excellent hearing. What were you doing there, spying on me? Or were you hiding from Aunt Philly again?" He leaned against the table and settled his arms over his chest in wait for her answer.

Marren fiddled with the tie of her overdress, and was completely abashed at being found by him. "Nay, I had hoped to escape the lasses and when you arrived—"

"You never have to hide from me."

She nodded. "Aye, I do."

"Why, lass?"

"Because I don't like seeing you with them especially after what we…"

"We shared a moment."

She scoffed. "It was more than a moment and you well know it. It distresses me and I should leave before I say something I'm bound to regret." She turned to leave, but he stopped her.

"Marren," he said and took her hand and squeezed it. He wouldn't release her. "Don't go. It's my fault you're upset. Let me make amends."

She willed the tears that threatened to form to cease, but a sob thickened her throat. "Nay, I'm sorry, I should go." Marren tugged her hand free from his and hastily left the solarium. When she entered her chamber, the lasses had settled for the night. Eedy had been removed and a different lass slept in her bed. At least something pleasant happened this day and the horrid Eedy was gone.

Now if she could only cease thinking of Keith and their amorous pursuits by the stream, the silly lasses who vied for his attention, and her dastardly betrothed who had yet to make an appearance, she might get some well-needed sleep.

Chapter Nine

Forty men-at-arms trained on the field. Keith spent the morning assessing their readiness. He surmised the Mackenzies wouldn't war with the Roses forever and they'd look for a new target. He'd be damned if his clan would be their latest adversary and would do whatever was necessary to avert war. The Mackenzies were keen to raid and didn't hold what they did as immoral—if they wanted something they took it, regardless if they had the right. He'd also be damned if they sought to take something of his, and allowed their trespass or forced them to war. If they called upon him, he'd meet the Mackenzies head-on and would make certain his clan was protected.

Keith stood next to Aulay and valued his commander's dedication, but Aulay wouldn't hear his praise. It would be an insult to speak of his admiration since it was Aulay's duty to ensure the readiness of the soldiers. He understood that Aulay was not only the soldier's leader, but he was also the steward and kept things running smoothly at the keep. Without him, Keith wouldn't have time to handle the more mundane matters or even attend to the courtships forced on him.

"Laird," Emmett said in greeting and joined them at the small rise beside the training fields.

"Do you think I should set a meeting with Sidheag Mackenzie? It might be wise to find out how he feels about me being laird or if he intends to instigate us." Keith needed to confront the situation head-on and not wait for possible peril to arrive on their doorstep.

Aulay scoffed derisively. "I should slap some sense into your head, Laird. Why do ye want to go and do that? Who gives a bloody hell what Sidheag thinks of you being our laird? You don't answer to him or anyone. That ring you're wearing gives proof of that."

Keith's arm tensed and the grip of his sword tightened. He peered at the ring on his finger and nodded. Aulay was right because he was answerable to no one but his clan. "It was only a slight consideration. I want to make sure we're not ensconced in a war with the Mackenzies if we can prevent it. It's good to have peace and I mean to keep it that way."

"Peace is good, but war is inevitable. Och well, if and when the time comes for such a meeting, I'll have your back, Laird, as will all the Sutherland soldiers. We won't let Mackenzie near our borders and if he's brazen enough to invade, he'll feel our wrath with the blades of our swords."

He sheathed his sword and nodded at his commander's passionate speech. "I appreciate that, Aulay, and of your dedication to our soldiers." Keith almost chortled that he'd gotten to speak the praise he wanted to give Aulay without his notice. "I need to return to the keep."

Emmett rounded him and snickered. "There he goes back to his brood of hens. Why don't ye just pick one, Laird, and be done with it? One lass is as good as the next, especially beneath the covers and in the dark of night. Unless you don't want one of the lasses and have your eye on another?" He waggled his eyebrows and grinned.

Keith shoved his chest. "Don't you have horses to feed or manure to pitch? I should answer you with my fist."

Aulay smirked. "Cease baiting our laird, brother. He has no time for us when six lasses await his undivided attention. Best get your snogs in now, Laird, because as soon as ye wed there'll be none of that. Your kisses will be saved for your ball and chain, unless of course, she's not fond of kissing."

He had enough of their jests and marched away. On his way to the keep, he had forgotten he wanted to visit Vinn to see how he was recovering from his injury. The lane to his cottage was crowded with various clansmen and women who bid him a good morning. He nodded and returned their greetings and was pleased by their acceptance. Near Vinn's cottage, he spotted the man standing outside.

"Vinn, how are you? I heard you got sliced in a fray on the field and the injury was severe. What are you doing out of bed? Shouldn't you be recovering?"

Vinn, a tall blond-headed man, casually leaned against the wall. "Och who in the bloody hell told you that? It's naught but a scratch, Laird, nothing to be concerned about."

Keith didn't believe him. Vinn wouldn't let a wound stop him from his duty, even if he insisted he should. He waved his hand at the soldier for him to show the wound. With his leg in the air, he turned it and yanked up his tartan.

"There, ye see, it's not that bad and barely pains me."

Keith grimaced at the sight of it. "Are you serious? If you're not careful it'll get diseased. You should have it covered. Get inside, and I'll have the healer come and tend to you again. Best listen to her directions, Vinn, or you might damn well lose that leg. Why didn't she stitch you up?"

"I wouldn't let her. You deem it's as bad as that, Laird?"

He nodded. "Aye, get inside and await the healer. Let her tend to you or I won't allow you back on the field. I forbid you to take to training until your wound is properly healed. I only do this to keep you from further bed rest. Take the time now and your convalesce will be short. Do you understand, Vinn?"

The soldier lowered his head. "Bollocks, aye I understand. Send her then, the healer, and I'll let her stitch me. The sooner she tends to the wound the sooner I can get back to my duty."

Keith appreciated his loyalty. Most of his soldiers were duty-bound which certainly benefited the Sutherlands. He ambled toward the keep and found a soldier who he directed to give the message to the healer to attend to Vinn.

After, he marched toward the loch. Keith had been told this day he'd meet with the lass, Iona. Before he met her at the hall, he took a quick dip in the loch and bathed away the sweat of his toil at arms all morning. The water was cold but rejuvenated him, and he didn't stay under for long what with the water being somewhat frigid. He left a change of garments by the bank earlier and hastily redressed.

Keith shook his mane of hair and rubbed the excess water from it with his discarded tartan. He sat upon a rock and wondered what to do about Marren. He detested that he'd upset her again. It wasn't his intention. Her dismay in the solarium the day before wounded him deeply and he regretted that he'd hurt her. Why couldn't he leave well enough alone? They'd reached an accord to stay away from each other—the problem was, he missed her and he didn't want to stay away.

Although he understood why she wanted him to keep his distance, he wished to at least see her. She'd hidden again and he forced himself not to seek her out. He couldn't cease thinking about their time together at the stream and how passionate their encounter was. No woman had affected him to such a state of madness in the throes of passion, but Marren. He was beguiled, besotted, and undeniably smitten with her. And there wasn't a damned thing he could do about it.

A bird squawked overhead and brought him out of his reverie. He had to meet Iona and was late. The last thing he needed to deal with was another wounded lass. He readied the boat for the outing he had planned. A nice easy boat ride on the loch was just what he needed. It was a fine day for such an outing since the sun shone and nary a cloud speckled the sky.

Keith trotted back to the castle and found the lass waiting with Philly in the hall.

Philly glared at him with a contemptible gaze. "You're late, lad. You distressed this lass and she fretted herself to a state of worry that you wouldn't come. I told her that something important must've kept ye, which I'm certain it did."

He bowed and when he straightened, Keith smiled to allay her. "I was at the fields, Philly, and was unavoidably delayed. My apologies, Milady Iona, for keeping you waiting."

Iona appeared to be weeping. He made his excuses for being late and the lass seemed to accept them, at least she smiled now and her tears subsided.

He took her cold hand and guided Iona to the exit of the hall. "Shall we? I have a pleasant afternoon planned. Philly," he called over his shoulder, "If you'll ready the solarium for our return?"

His aunt nodded and spoke to one of the passing serving lasses. Dismissed, he continued onward and wanted to get the day's courtship over with.

Keith felt discomfited in Iona's company. She yammered on about meeting the man in charge of the hawks—the one he hadn't known they'd had. He supposed he should meet the man when he had a minute to spare, but birds of prey weren't of interest to him. He'd rather take his sword to a battlefield, or hell, even waste the day fishing than go hawking. Keith recalled his father had an affinity for hawks. When he was young, Keith was forced to attend many early morning outings. Rising before the sun had never appealed to him. Graciously, his father's leisurely pursuit hadn't lasted long. Thank the Lord for that.

"Here we are."

"We're at the loch. Why are we here? You don't expect me to go swimming, do you? It's quite chilly and I'm not garbed for swimming." Iona pressed her hair over her shoulder and peered in aghast at the water. She twisted her braid in a nervous gesture and continued to gape at the water.

"Nay, the weather is fair with the sun shining, but not enough to take to the water. There's a boat here. I thought a relaxing ride on the loch would be…ah, would give us time to talk and get to know one another." Keith turned to her and smiled. If he'd marry the woman, it would do well to get to know her, but he scoffed at the thought. The lass seemed centered on one topic and it was of the feathered variety. "If you would rather not, we can do something else, lass."

"I would like to go on the boat with you. Do you hear all the birds? The forest is filled with them and they call to one another," she said with glee in her voice and a shine in her eyes.

He would have laughed at her giddiness at being surrounded by birds, but he'd hurt her tender heart if he did, so he kept his humor to himself. Keith helped her aboard and was careful not to jostle the boat when he boarded. He sat opposite from her and took the oars in hand.

What was he thinking to bring her here? She was completely mesmerized by the winged creatures and he doubted she would notice him. Who would've ever thought he'd have to compete with birds to win a woman's companionship or favor? The entire situation made him want to laugh and yet it was daunting.

Keith turned the boat about so he might take them farther out in the water. As he rowed the boat, he spotted Marren standing near the bank. She watched them from beneath a large willow whose leaves recently sprouted. How beautiful she looked in a light blue gown with her hair flowing over her shoulders. If only he could call out to her…if only she sat opposite of him…if only he could kiss her again.

"Do you know any bird calls?"

He shook his ruminations of Marren aside when Iona spoke. Keith scowled at the question because he'd never thought to be asked such a thing. Bird calls? What man in their right mind made bird calls? "Nay, do you?"

"Oh, I most certainly do. I've studied the calls of many types of birds and have learned all their calls." She proceeded to whistle and cupped her mouth to make her calls louder.

Keith frowned and rowed the boat out farther still. He got to the middle of the loch and pulled the oars inside the rim of the boat. A light sound of the water lapping the boat soothed him. The boat moved with the current, but not too speedily and they wouldn't get far. He gawked at Iona who continued her bird calls and he tried to think of questions to ask her—things that had nothing to do with birds or the like.

A large bird which he took as a white-tailed eagle flew overhead. Iona whistled and shielded her eyes from the sun to get a better look. He didn't like that the large bird flew above them. Eagles were known to be protective of their territory and would defend it at all costs. The feathered beast's talons could do much damage to a man or woman.

"They hear me. Are they not beautiful? What type of bird do you think it is? I vow to take a trip to the east so I might see other species. My da says there are all sorts of different birds there and he promised to take me."

He could give a flying shit about what she spoke of, but Keith tried to be amiable and interested even though it took a great will to be so. The woman was maddened. Who obsessed over birds no less? Keith couldn't see himself wed to her and there was absolutely no romantic attraction between them whatsoever. Iona was pleasant enough and she had a bonny face, but he figured if he didn't have anything to say to her about birds, she'd find him rather dull.

He shrugged his shoulder in answer and peered above. After an hour on the loch, he was ready to retreat to his nest. The humorous thought made him grin. One hour was enough time spent with the exasperating woman, but at least he'd made an effort.

"We should return soon." Keith took the oars and started to turn the boat about.

"Oh, not yet, I have yet to see a puffin bird. Have you seen them? I've heard they are a beautiful species with large bills. Father told me they perch in the northern lands and we are far north, are we not?"

Keith nodded. "Aye, I've seen them but they stay mainly by the sea. You won't see one of them here, we're too far inland. They usually perch on small isles."

She pointed upward. "What are those, hawks? Look at them; they're so graceful...the way they soar above as if they're floating. They are watching us."

They watched them alright and were probably affronted at their intrusion. He only hoped the eagles kept to the sky and didn't attack them. "Nay, they're not hawks, but eagles. Do you see its white tail?" He almost rebuked himself for giving her more reasons to speak about the winged creatures.

Keith glanced above and now there were two of the white-tailed eagles. It was unaccountable because they were solitary creatures. They were large birds and he'd seen them near the sea. The white-tailed eagle was an opportunistic hunter and often stole food from the weaker, smaller birds. He had seen an extremely large eagle once fly over the waters and hovered over the surface. The bird snatched a large fish from the sea as if it took little effort.

It was strange to see the eagles at this time of year because they often were inactive. Still, he didn't much care for birds unless they sat on a spit over his fire for his supper. His stomach rumbled with a pang of hunger and reminded him the midday meal approached. As he thought that, the birds flew lower and their droppings speckled his shoulder. He gave a cross look at the mark on his tartan and muttered an expletive under his breath.

Twice more they'd targeted him, but Iona sat as pretty-as-she-pleased without a speck on her garments. He was irked because his tartan was ruined and the mark would be difficult to remove. There was nothing to do but toss it. Damnation and it was his favorite tartan too. He gripped the oars with annoyance and rowed with vigor to reach the bank.

"Oh, we cannot leave yet." Iona stood and raised her arm.

"Lass, sit down before you topple—"

The boat tipped over and they both ended up in the water with a huge splash. Keith felt the swishes of water near him. Iona panicked and thrashed her arms and sent waves at him. The upended boat bobbed near them and he hoped it didn't strike her. Although a good knock on her head might get her over her strange obsession for birds.

He grabbed hold of her overdress and pulled her to the surface. With Iona in his grip, he yanked her upward and she coughed harshly when she took a breath.

"Worry not, lass, I have you." Keith swam to the loch's bank and helped Iona from the water.

On dry land, he shook at the chill that his soaked garments brought to him. He would've offered his tartan to Iona but it was useless to warm or dry her.

"You… You are a knave!"

When he tried to take her arm, she swatted him. He stepped back confused by her hostility and the dour look on her face. "Don't you have enough sense not to stand up in a boat, Lady Iona? It's your fault the boat toppled over, not mine."

"And you affront me too? I have never been treated so horribly," she nearly shouted. She slapped his face hard, growled at him, turned, and marched away with enough force to shake the ground.

Keith yanked the tartan from his upper body and tried to wring out the excess water. The material was heavy and wouldn't be wearable. He dropped it when someone startled him. Laughter sounded behind him and he narrowed his eyes at Marren. Keith wanted to be irked with her, but he could imagine how humorous the entire situation appeared, especially from her vantage point. And her sweet laughter eased him.

"Aye, so you find my almost drowning with the bird-lass comical?"

She bent over and held her stomach and then pressed her eyes to abate the laughter tears. "I'm sorry, Keith, but aye.

You should've seen your face. I vow I never saw you look so disgruntled and Iona was so angry. You're fortunate she didn't strike you harder."

"My face begs to differ. That lass has a hard slap. Is my cheek bright? It feels so and is warm. Come, feel it," he dared her. The thought of her touching him again made him warmer than his reddened cheek.

She giggled. "You tempt me, but oh, nay, that's just your blush at ending up in the water."

"Cease or I'll toss you in the loch." He grinned at the thought of her having to disrobe her wet garments too.

"You wouldn't dare." Marren stepped backward, turned, and fled.

Keith caught up to her quickly and snatched her in his arms. The moment was froth with the tension of his desire for her, but he shook it away. He strolled back to the loch where he had dropped his tartan. She wiggled in his arms and he almost groaned at the pleasure of her body against his.

"Please, don't throw me in the loch. I vow, I didn't mean to tease you."

He grinned. "I wouldn't do that to you, lass." Keith allowed her to slide from his hold and her body caressed his as she stood on her feet. She stepped back and he took a step closer. He wanted to take her in his arms and kiss the sweet breath from her.

"Are you hurt besides your reddened cheek?" She smiled widely. "Perhaps your vanity is slightly bruised? Worry not, I'll tell no one what happened."

"I'm unharmed except for my soaked garments. It's good to see you. Are you still wrath with me, lass?"

She sighed and picked up his soaked tartan and handed it to him. "I suppose not, but we shouldn't see each other."

He set his wet tartan over his shoulder but let it slip off when he took her hand. "Why not? Regardless of what happens, I don't ever want you to have to stay away from me."

Marren gripped his hand and walked beside him. "I don't

want to stay away. When I see you all I want to do is kiss you."

He stopped her from walking ahead. Keith pulled her into his arms and she embraced him. He nudged her chin upward so he could look into her bonny eyes. "I want to kiss you too." Keith lowered his head and took possession of her lips.

Their kiss turned torrid within seconds but Marren pulled back. "Keith, please, you make me want more than just kisses. We are promised to others."

He wouldn't let her flee and kept her in his embrace. Keith hugged her and she settled her head against his damp chest. "I know we are. Bloody hell, this is difficult."

"You're making it so. Please, let us try to be friends." Even with her declaration, she held on to him as if she was unwilling to let him go.

He surmised she didn't mean what she said. Keith held her face and nodded. "I'll try, lass, but I don't think it's possible."

Chapter Ten

Marren couldn't sleep. Her mind turned over the conversation she had with Keith by the loch repeatedly. They couldn't maintain a friendship, not with sensual longing tugging at them both. She struck her pillow and tried to settle again. Her attraction to him grew tenfold in the last days when she was supposed to keep her distance. To glimpse him should have been enough to appease her, but it wasn't. What she wanted, she couldn't have. Why did his body beckon her touch, and his lips beckon hers? She sighed again, tried to shake the sensual thoughts from her mind, and rolled to her side and squeezed her eyes closed.

If only she could ask Lady Ophelia to find someone else to spy for her and watch over the lasses, she could hide in the solarium or go to the village when Keith courted them. But she couldn't bring herself to ask the lady to release her from her promise.

A moan sounded across the chamber. Someone wailed and groaned. Marren slunk from her bed and followed the noise of whichever lass had the malady. Iona shivered and moaned.

She pressed a hand on her head but Iona wasn't hot and didn't seem to have a fever. "What's wrong? Do you have an ailment?"

Iona opened her eyes. "Aye, and my skin is itchy. I cannot breathe and I deem I'm going to retch." She pressed her lips together and moaned again.

Marren found an empty chamber pot and set it beside her bed. "Use this if you need to. It's almost morning. Someone should be up. I'll have the healer fetched."

Iona groaned and seemed to worsen. She flailed about the bed and rambled incoherently.

Marren hastened from the bedchamber and found Lady Ophelia in the hallway. She startled and hadn't expected anyone to be there. With a hasty greeting, she tried to pass.

"Wait, lass, Robina is ill and needs the healer. Will you send for her?"

"I was on my way to fetch the healer for Iona. She ails too, but I don't know what's wrong with her. It's a strange malady. She says she itches and is having difficulty breathing."

"It's the same for Robina. Hurry, lass, and return when you can." Lady Ophelia reentered the bedchamber where Robina slept.

Marren had pulled on a robe to cover her nightdress, but there was no time to properly dress. She reached the outside and hadn't come across anyone she might send for the healer. The woman who healed the clan lived too far from the keep for her to traipse there herself in her robe no less. Someone was always on duty at the gate and she thought to check there.

As she approached, her eyes widened with shock at the sight before her. Cassie stood with Marc by the stone gate tower and they embraced and kissed passionately. Their affection alluded to a romantic encounter. Marren smiled at their show of affection, but then Cassie always adored Marc and she shouldn't be surprised to find them in such a position.

She harrumphed and tried to signal them that she was there. "I hate to interrupt."

They pulled apart quickly when they heard her and she'd startled them. Marc glared at her and wasn't pleased to have his affectionate display witnessed. She would have laughed but she was on an important errand, one of which wasn't humorous at all.

"Marc, there are two lasses who are ailing at the keep. Can you please fetch the healer?"

"Aye, Milady," he said nothing more and trotted off.

She flashed a grin at Cassie. "How long has this been going on and why didn't you tell me? It's unlike you to keep secrets from me."

Cassie linked her arm with hers and walked along with her. "I tried to tell you several times, but you were busy."

"I'm sorry and I didn't mean to avoid you, but I am happy for you. So you've caught the elusive Marc, have you?"

Her friend's face flushed. "I cannot say I've caught him yet. We've only kissed a few times and he hasn't professed love or anything of the sort yet. I vow he will and he'll be mine."

Marren grinned at her boast. "I'm gladdened for you. Many ladies will be disappointed he's no longer available. I've been distracted of late and haven't spent much time with you, but now I see you've been otherwise occupied." She laughed lightly.

"What's going on at the keep? Who ails?"

"Iona and Robina. They came down with a strange malady during the night. Will you help tend to them? Lady Ophelia is with Robina and could use your aid. I'll see to Iona."

"Of course, I'll be glad to help. I shall heat water and bring clean cloths."

"We will need them. Iona complained that her skin itched. Have the kitchen servants bring a tub to both chambers and ask them to make certain the water is warm, not hot. Perhaps they came in contact with a plant or something to cause their sensitivity?"

"A warm bath should help then." Cassie left to do her bidding at the entrance of the castle and she reverted around it to the kitchens situated behind the keep.

Marren entered and hurried to her chamber. She noticed Iona tossed about the bed. There was little time before the servants came and she hurried to dress. Once she was properly attired, she reached Iona and helped to undress her. She stripped the bed coverings and placed Iona's garments in the bundle by the doorway for washing in case whatever ailed her was contagious.

Iona continued to shiver but Marren didn't consider it a symptom of her illness. She set a thick bed cover around her and bid her to hold it closed. The lass was distressed and perhaps her unease caused her to shake. Moments later two lads arrived with the tub. They left and returned with buckets of water and filled it. When all was ready and the servant lads had left, Marren helped Iona into the water. She noticed a rash on her neck and arms and thought to remember it and needed to tell the healer when she arrived.

After she bathed her, Marren helped Iona into a freshly laundered nightrail. The healer finally arrived and while she looked over Iona, Marren remade her bed. The healer attended to Iona and dabbed her rash with an oily salve. She checked her eyes and mouth and made smirks whilst she went about her tasks.

"I deem the lass has been poisoned given her reaction. The bath should have helped the rash and the salve will as well. I'll leave a dram left to help her breathing. Now I must go and see to the other lass."

Marren helped Iona back to bed and tucked the bed covers around her. "Rest easy now, Iona. You'll be well in no time. Is the salve helping?"

Iona nodded, closed her eyes, and she appeared to have calmed.

The lass she hadn't met yet, Eedy's replacement, approached. "I shall sit with her. You must be exhausted. Go and have your morning fare."

"My thanks… ah, I'm sorry I don't recall your name." Marren hadn't remembered seeing her arrive either and thought she had come when she'd gone to put out the flame she'd left on in the solarium.

"We haven't been introduced. I'm Trulee Macleod." She curtseyed and smiled.

"I'm Marren Macleod—"

"Oh, everyone knows who you are," she said with a scrunch to her eyes. "Lady Ophelia speaks fondly of you. She told us to follow your example. I'm pleased to finally meet you."

Marren hadn't meant to gasp when she spoke her name, but the lass was a Macleod. "We share the same surname. Where are you from, if you don't mind my asking?"

Trulee placed a stool next to Iona's bed and sat. "I don't mind. I'm from Dunvegan. We don't live on the mainland with the rest of the clan. Oh, Iona rests comfortably now, thanks to you. You were kind to help her."

She nodded but wanted to know more about her. "Who is your family? I might know them because I'm also a Macleod. Although I haven't been with my clan since I was a young lass."

Trulee scowled but quickly turned her expression to a softer mien. She was about to answer when the door opened and Lady Ophelia called to her.

"I must go. Thank you for sitting with Iona. If she worsens or you need me, come and find me." Marren headed for the door. She stepped from the chamber and didn't give her discussion with Trulee another thought. Concern for the lasses worried her and that they'd been poisoned greatly troubled her.

"The healer says Robina was poisoned."

Marren sighed woefully. "She said the same about Iona. The question is how or why? I don't think it was from something they ate since they ate everything we had. And their symptoms are mild and they have rashes. If they'd swallowed poison, it wouldn't have caused a rash, would it?"

Lady Ophelia shook her head. "I don't think so. And their breathing is affected. I must think further about this and speak more about it with the healer. Keith has taken Lady Eedy for a morning ride. Will you find him? He should be made aware of what's happening here."

"I will, Milady." Marren left her and strolled to the stables. She hoped they hadn't left yet, but as she approached, she didn't see them.

Emmett, the stable master, stood outside the wide entrance and brushed the mare she'd ridden the day she'd gone to the village with Keith.

"Good day, Emmett, will you saddle her for me? I need to find Keith, ah, Laird Sutherland."

"Our laird rode off with 'lady-thinks-she's-a-queen' a few minutes ago." He grinned with a devilish look in his eyes. "Aye, why do ye need to find him, so you can disrupt his courting?" He guffawed and winked. "I think not, Milady. You should leave him be."

"You don't understand."

He chuckled. "Och, I understand alright. We see the way ye look at him and how he looks at you. Aye, me and Aulay discussed it. You're not available, lass, to our laird or any of us, remember? Lady Ophelia declared it to one and all."

"But—"

"Nay, you won't easily sway me with your bonny smile the way you do our laird."

Marren settled her hands on her hips and scowled at him. "Emmett," she said with a bite to her words, "several of the lasses are ill and Lady Ophelia asked me to fetch Keith, ah Laird Sutherland. And you have no business sticking your big nose in my affairs. What I do or how I look at someone is of no concern to you. And what your laird does, shouldn't concern you either. Perhaps I shall tell him that you mean to interfere in his matters."

He appeared completely crestfallen. "My apologies, Milady, I'll saddle the mare right quick. But perhaps ye might want to take a different horse. Keith's horse has been testy around this one lately."

"Just saddle her and be quick about it," she snapped. She wasn't about to wait for another horse to be brought from inside the stables.

"I'll be but a second." He disappeared inside the stable and returned with a saddle. Emmett appeared contrite for his diatribe and he didn't make further disparaged remarks.

Marren was completely affronted by his insults. How dare he tell her what to do? Or that he'd insinuated…what she'd actually had done. But she didn't have time to deal with him now or dissuade him from making such assumptions even if they were true.

"You're all set, Milady." He walked away without another word to her and stood by the entrance. Emmett was miffed with her given his glare.

Once she was seated on the horse, Marren asked which direction they had ridden.

"The laird mentioned he would show her some of the Sutherland land. He could be anywhere. I wish ye luck in finding him." He laughed with a bellow and entered the stable.

The man was irksome and a pain in the arse. Fat lot of help he was. Marren groused under her breath and rode off. She rode toward the loch but saw no one. As the minutes passed, she kept a swift pace and headed to the open fields beyond the keep. She got close to the sea and spotted them ahead, where the land ended and the cliffs began. With a kick to the horse's haunches, she bid her mare to go faster. When she neared them, she tried to slow her mount, but the mare had a mind of her own and galloped toward Keith's horse.

Keith sat upon his horse and was close to Eedy who sat like a queen on her mount. He peered at her and said something to Eedy to which she couldn't hear. Keith's horse reared and brought his forelegs upward. He held on, but the horse bucked and bumped Eedy's horse. She fell off and cried out when she hit the ground.

Marren regained control of her mare, dismounted, and rushed to Eedy's side. She held her arm and lay upon the ground. "Eedy, are you hurt?"

Keith led his horse away from them and tethered him to a nearby bush. He hastened back to them and knelt next to Eedy. "Lass, did you injure yourself?"

Eedy wailed and continued to hold her arm. When her cries lessened, she scowled at them. "I am Lady Fraser…not lass or Eedy, to the likes of you. And what do you think, Laird Sutherland? Aye, I'm hurt. Can you not see the distress I am in?"

Keith shared a quick glance with her and Marren leaned forward to help Eedy up from the ground. She took her good arm and lifted as she stood.

Once Eedy was on her feet, she shoved her away. "Don't touch me."

"Come, we'll help you back to the keep. Hopefully, the healer is still there," Marren said.

"Healer? Why is the healer at the keep?" Keith asked and took Eedy's injured arm and secured it with his upper tartan. "That should help until we get back. Can you ride?"

Eedy huffed at the pain and gritted. "I shall walk."

Marren quickly told Keith about the possible poisonings and that the lasses were ill. "We need to hurry back. I'm afraid we cannot walk back to the keep. It'll take too long and Lady Ophelia wants Keith, ah, Laird Sutherland to return quickly."

Eedy pulled from Keith's hold and grimaced. "I care not how long it takes. We shall walk back. I'm not getting back on another horse for any reason."

The walk back to the keep was tormenting for Marren. Keith's gaze on her flushed her cheeks. They tried to be helpful to Eedy but her high-almighty attitude kept them from doing so. By the time they reached the stables, she was beyond tired, especially since she'd gotten little sleep the night before and had taken care of Iona most of the morning. Marren yawned but tried to hide it from them.

As they dismounted the horses, Marc shouted for Keith. "Laird, Aulay says he needs to see you about an urgent matter. He awaits ye at the gate."

Keith glanced at her and gave a nod. To Eedy, he said, "Will you be alright, Lady Fraser?"

Eedy scoffed and didn't answer but strolled toward the castle, holding her arm.

Keith ambled away with Marc and left her at the stables.

Marren caught up to Eedy and walked beside her. As soon as she settled Eedy in her chamber and had the healer fetched yet again, she hid in the solarium. When she arrived, she noticed no table had been placed for the romantic supper Keith had prepared for the previous lasses. But then Eedy likely broke her arm and he probably hadn't had time to ask Lady Ophelia to see to it.

She had to admit she was glad they wouldn't have their supper in the solarium. That he used the place for his romantic endeavors had ruined the peaceful mien of the sanctuary for her. Marren couldn't stand the thought of being witness to such a farce either because it was doubtful Keith would propose to Eedy. There was something to be thankful for this day, even though she saddened that Iona and Robina ailed. At least they were on the mend.

Of the lasses that remained, that left Caroline, the lass who liked to cook, and Lindsey, the lass who blended in the shadows. There was also Trulee, the waif as Cassie had described her. As she thought of her, Marren needed to speak to her further about her family. The lass might have answers to the questions she had about her clan and why she'd been sent away. Perhaps she'd finally learn the truth of the matter.

Chapter Eleven

Keith followed Marc to the gate. There, the gate watchman left him by the tower entrance and shouted at the lads on duty. Marc was the best man to assign to keep the gate secure and the lads at their duties. He was obstinate, fierce, and a man who wouldn't be easily swayed to give entrance to visitors without cause. Keith didn't worry so much about their protection with Marc on guard.

Marc shouted at a lad who leaned over the stone ledge where the guards posted, "Ye blighter," he said and grabbed the lad's tunic. "If I find you sleeping at your post again, I'll give ye a job that'll keep you on your feet for a fortnight."

He gave thought that Marc might be the perfect man to train Dain. The squire might make a good gate watchman, but it would take a good bit of time to train him. Perhaps he'd wait to suggest it because Marc wasn't in an agreeable mood at the moment.

Keith didn't see Aulay nearby and considered searching for him. "Where's Aulay? You said he needed me at the gate. Why is he not here?"

"He said he'd meet you here. He'll be along shortly."

As he kept watch for Aulay, he paced on the lane and considered the lassies. Who would poison them? What would the miscreant gain by hurting them? None would benefit from their demise except... He shook his head at the deplorable thought. But then he ruminated over the fact that Marren spent a good amount of time with the lasses.

He and Marren had somewhat of a relationship, if he could call it such. She all but professed to care for him. Did she poison the lasses so he wouldn't marry any of them? His mind balked at the idea of her being culpable. Marren wouldn't hurt anyone, least of all innocent lasses. That he considered her harming them brought a lurch to his gut. A sense of guilt plagued him for even rationalizing she'd be capable of such foulness.

"Laird?" Aulay set his hand on his shoulder and drew him from his reverie.

"Oh, Aulay, I didn't hear you approach."

"Nay, you were deep in thought. What troubles you?"

He shrugged his shoulders because he wouldn't voice his unfounded idea. "Nothing. Marc tells me you wanted to see me. What goes?"

Aulay pulled him aside and away from the gate lads who were now focused on their duty.

Keith stood next to his commander. "Your news must be grave."

"The sentry reported in an hour ago and told me they spotted a handful of Mackenzies on our western border. I'm going to head out and ensure they have left. I thought you might want to come along."

"Aye, I'll ready my horse and will meet you here in a few minutes." Keith didn't give him a chance to retort. He trotted off and found Winddodger still saddled and ready.

Emmett stood beside his horse and handed him the reins. "Worry not, Laird, I'll keep watch over your lasses whilst you're gone." He snickered in jest.

That gave Keith pause because he shouldn't leave when they had been poisoned and could very well be in danger.

And he was certain poor Eedy had broken her arm. He should make sure she was well and tended to. But he also had to ensure the Mackenzies wouldn't traipse his lands without repercussions. Being tugged in different directions, he wasn't sure what to do, but he was laird and the safety of his clan won out over the care of the lasses.

Even though he suspected Emmett jested with him, he said, "I'd appreciate that." Keith quickly explained the situation. "Assign others to the stables for now. I want you to stay at the keep. Be watchful of anyone suspicious."

Emmett appeared taken aback by his command. "Are ye certain you want me to? Others would be more suited to the keep than me."

Keith shook his head. "There's no one I trust more than you to see to the lasses' protection whilst I am gone."

His comrade pressed his face and grinned. "I won't let ye down, Laird. The lassies will be safe under my watch."

He thanked him and set off to meet Aulay by the gate. He had faith that Emmett would make certain the lasses would be protected until he returned. They might not appreciate it though if Emmett stood too close to them because the man stunk. When he returned, he'd suggest Emmett take a long dip in the loch to wash away the smell of horses and the stable.

At the gate, he continued onward and Aulay rode in silence next to him. The few soldiers that joined them rode mutely behind. He was surprised to see Vinn, but he must have recovered from the wound on his leg, although he wore breeches instead of his tartan. He thought to chastise him since he forbade the soldier from taking to duty until he'd given him leave to do so. But they were already on the trail and Vinn appeared capable of performing his responsibilities.

As they rode toward the western lands, Keith kept his thoughts to himself. He didn't like that the Mackenzies trespassed on their land. His reflection to meet with the Mackenzie laird might be prudent if he intended to keep his clan from war.

Throughout the ride, they saw nothing or no one out of sorts. Their horses were trained to make little noise and none snickered or snorted. The men didn't speak and remained attentive on the trail. Near the border, they focused on the woodland sounds and listened for signs of their foes.

A noise of a horse's steps alerted him that someone was there, lurking. Keith signaled to Aulay and he took a few men and reverted to thrust the interloper out of the woods from the opposite side of the copse of trees. Two soldiers including Vinn followed him. He got closer to the sound of the horse whose snort was near.

Keith pulled his sword free and made ready to defend himself should the person be an enemy. The forest darkened with the oncoming night. Little shadows remained from the sun which had lowered beyond the trees. The woodland seemed eerie as if the devil himself lurked there. He rounded a tree and saw a man standing with his back to him. Keith quietly sheathed his sword and pulled a dagger free from the belt at his waist.

He motioned to the soldiers to remain quiet and lightly stepped toward the man. When he reached him, he grabbed him from behind and held the blade of his dagger at his throat. The man gained his release and shot away from him. He stood two feet from him with a fearsome scowl on his face.

"What the bloody hell...? Oh, it's you, Keith. Why in God's good name are ye sneaking up on me? Ye scared me witless. I about pissed myself."

Keith stepped closer but lowered his dagger when he recognized Grady's uncle. "Chester, what are you doing out here in the middle of nowhere? I could've slain you."

"What am I doing here? What are you doing here? I am on my way to the Sinclairs. You haven't heard the news, I suppose?"

He shook his head. "What news?"

"Callum's wife bore him a son two days ago and I thought to visit to pay my felicitations. And I thought to visit

Eric and have some of his fine brew."

Eric, the Sinclair smith, made a potent drink that inebriated a man with few sips. He could use a bit of that brew too to ease him from the distressed situations he found himself in of late.

Keith grinned at the joyous news. Callum was a good comrade, one he'd known most of his life. He was pleased he'd been given a son and with his heir born, the Sinclairs future was secure. "This is good news, Chester, and Lady Violet? How does she fare, well?"

Chester bobbed his head. "Aye, she does from what I hear. I deem Callum must be thrilled since he was surrounded by females. An heir is a sign of God's blessing. Will you join me?"

"Nay, as much as I'd like to, I must—"

"Och, before I forget, I should tell you, I saw a small regimen of Mackenzies in the woods a few hours ago. They looked to be passing through. I deem they're long gone by now but I thought ye should know."

Aulay found them, dismounted, and stood next to him. "Well, if it isn't the know-it-all-Mackay. I should've known it was you we tracked."

Keith would've laughed, but Chester wasn't pleased to be the jest of his commander. "Join us, Chester. Lads, make camp and get a fire going. We'll settle here for the night and return to the keep on the morrow, unless you're in a hurry to reach Sinclair land, Chester?"

"I could use a rest," Chester said, "and company."

A fire was built and lit within minutes and the soldiers went hunting for their supper. Keith placed his tartan near the fire and sat on it across from Chester who set his bedroll. The man rarely went home to the Mackay keep and frequently visited the many clans in the north. Often, he was their only source of news, and many clans counted on his visits. He wasn't fond of his brother Simon, Grady's father, and for good reason. Thinking of his comrade reminded him to ask after him.

"Have you heard any word from Grady yet?"

"Nay, the lad has gone underground and hasn't been seen. I'm getting a wee bit concerned."

Keith was too, but he wouldn't admit it. "Worry not, Grady knows how to take care of himself and will return when he's ready."

"That's for certain. How is life at the Sutherland keep? And Lady Ophelia, does she fares well?"

Keith almost grinned at the mention of his aunt and the lovelorn look in Chester's eyes. "Why don't you stop by after you visit the Sinclairs and find out for yourself? I'm sure she'd appreciate your visit and news. She's always looked forward to your visits." He withheld the urge to laugh because he was positive the man was smitten with his aunt given the rosiness that now flushed his cheeks.

Chester nodded. "Aye, I might do so, that is if you're offering a warm bed and good food."

"Of course, you're always welcome at our keep, Chester."

The soldiers returned and began cooking the few hares they'd hunted. Soon the crackle of wood and scent from the meat allayed him. Keith hadn't eaten all day and was ravenous. He was handed a good portion of meat on a stick from Aulay.

While he ate, he relaxed back and regarded Chester. "Our sentry reported the sighting of the trespassers which is why we're out here. Tell me about your run-in with the Mackenzies."

"It wasn't a run-in really, but a crossing. I spoke briefly to Kieran Mackenzie, the laird's son."

Keith glared at hearing the man's name. From what he knew of him, Kieran was reputed to be an arrogant warrior who stopped at nothing to defeat his foes. He was as ferocious in arms as his father was and a feared adversary of many. "What did he have to say?"

"Not much, he wasn't one for many words. He knew who I was and didn't deem me a threat which is probably why I walked away with my life. They're a fearsome group, the Mackenzies. I doubt they ever stay inside or take advantage of their home."

Aulay remained quiet and listened to their discussion.

Keith was interested to learn more about his enemy. "Why do you say that?"

Chester swallowed his food and swiped a cloth over his mouth. The man was careful of his appearance even out on the trail where it mattered not. "Their garments were soiled and tattered as if they hadn't changed them in a good long time. They must've been out on the hunt for the Roses for a fortnight or more."

He chuckled because if there was one thing Chester detested it was soiled garments. There was never a speck of dirt on him and his clothing was miraculously wrinkle-free. "They're at war with the Roses so I suspect that might be true…that they have no time to care for such matters."

"Aye, and they looked like they'd just come from battle and could use a bath in the loch."

"I don't like that they came upon my land without my permission."

Chester grunted. "I wouldn't worry too much over it. The Mackenzies battle with the Roses has escalated and they have time for little else. It's shameful how the Roses have been weakened by their losses but I fear the Mackenzies won't cease until every last Rose is defeated."

"Which is exactly why I mean to make sure that doesn't happen to us." Keith finished his fare and pitched the stick he held into the fire.

"I tell ye this though, Kieran Mackenzie is as bloodthirsty as his father. I don't fear many men, but he is as terrifying as Sidheag. Strange too that I thought you resembled him."

Keith couldn't help but grin at that. "You don't need to fear me, Chester. I'm not one to intimidate unless it's necessary. But when I take my dagger to someone, he should be wary."

He chortled. "Nay, that's not what I meant, although you are fearsome when you wish to be. I didn't mean with your manner but in your appearance. He and you could pass for brothers if one didn't know ye came from different clans, different fathers and mothers."

"What do you mean?" Keith scowled in the wonder of why Chester told him that.

"I vow I was looking at you when I glimpsed him. He has the same shade of hair and eyes. His body build is the same as yours and his face; it was like seeing you, only it wasn't you. I almost made the mistake of calling him by your name when I first spotted him."

Keith chuckled. "Many in our parts have similar features and blond hair and blue eyes, Chester. It's our Norse roots that give us our looks. You make more of the resemblance than you should."

Chester grunted again. "If ye say so, but if you had a twin, it'd be the knavish Kieran Mackenzie that's for certain."

"Bollocks. I have no twin and Kieran Mackenzie shouldn't trespass on my land. I mean to tell him so with the edge of my sword when I get the chance."

"Aye, ye see, you even share the same terrifying arrogance."

Chapter Twelve

Two days had passed since Iona and Robina were poisoned. No other lasses came down with a malady. That relieved Marren a great deal. She helped to care for them while they convalesced. Both were well enough to leave their beds after a day of rest. The poison must not have been too potent, or deadly. She wondered who would want to harm them though. The only thought that occurred to her was that one of the lasses wanted to lessen her rivals.

Who amongst the women had the gall to be so brazen? She could count out Iona and Robina since they were targeted. Eedy might be the culprit since she seemed not to have compassion for anyone but herself. Trulee was too sweet-natured, as was Lindsey, to cause harm to others. She didn't know Caroline well enough, but the lass professed to be a good cook. She could've been the one to poison them. Her deductions didn't help to figure out who the wrongdoer was.

Marren cleaned the bedchamber and noticed Iona folding her garments. She had her satchel open on the bed and appeared to be packing her belongings. "You're not leaving us, are you?"

Iona clasped the satchel closed and turned to face her. "I am. I don't like it here and the laird won't choose me for his bride, not when I struck him. Laird Sutherland didn't seem interested in me anyhow and I shan't waste more time trying to win his favor."

"Oh, I'm sorry, Iona. I wish it wasn't so, but I believe you might be right."

"I shall leave when my father's soldiers come to collect me. I've sent him a missive and expect them this day."

Marren took her hand and clasped it lightly in hopes to solace her. "Can I do anything to help or to make you feel better?"

"There's nothing to do. I accept my choice. But I must go and explain my reasons for leaving to Lady Ophelia. I fear I'll upset her, but I cannot pretend to be interested in the laird when I am not. He has no care for my interests or me that was evident. I shall meet the falconer after the morning fare and spend the day outside."

"I'm certain that will make you feel better and perhaps bring you some cheer." Marren nodded but glanced at Trulee across the chamber who gazed at her with a peculiar look.

She wanted to finish her conversation with Trulee and had many questions about the Macleods. Marren sat upon the bed and faced her. "I'm not interrupting you, am I?" She quickly spied the words she'd written on the parchment: *To the deepest part of my heart I admit...* But Trulee closed the journal before she might catch more words.

Trulee looked up and smiled. "I was writing my thoughts. It's become a habit to write down my secrets and dreams. You should try it because it does wonders to relieve one's soul."

She loved that Trulee was a dreamer. The lass was surely a waif, one that had her head in the clouds, but she was sweet and appealing. "Perhaps I should write my thoughts. It might help to clear my head. I have much on my mind these days. I wanted to ask…"

Trulee set aside her journal and leaned close. "Did you hear Iona is leaving us?"

"She just told me."

"That's one less lass the laird must court."

Marren shifted her sitting position and smoothed her hands over the length of her skirts. Her words struck a chord in her. Trulee was pleased that she had one less rival. But it was unaccountable. The lass didn't seem capable of such treachery. "What of you? He has yet to meet with you."

Trulee smiled and set her hands in her lap. "It matters not to me who the laird chooses. I have no choice in who I marry. My father told me so and bade me to follow orders and do as Lady Ophelia bids. If the laird selects me then I must agree or suffer my father's wrath."

Marren's shoulders tensed at Trulee's dejection. She seemed nonplussed about the arrangement, although, Marren commiserated with her because she was in the same position. She had no choice in whom she married and her husband would be selected for her. With a dejected sigh, she tried not to appear as crestfallen as she felt. How wretched that most women didn't have much of a say in who they married or in their life choices.

"I wanted to speak to you because you mentioned you hail from Dunvegan. I recall living on Dunvegan as a wee lass and I was born there. My da was laird of the Macleods then, but he and my mother died when I was quite young. What is your da's name, might I know him?"

Trulee pressed her lips together before she spoke, "He's the laird now and his name is Duncan."

Marren gasped when she heard Trulee's father's name. "Duncan. He's my da's brother and my uncle. I remember him well. That makes you my cousin. We're family."

Trulee clapped her hands. "Oh, how exciting to meet you. I didn't know about you and my da never mentioned he had a brother or that I had cousins."

"When my parents died, he sent me away. I wasn't aware of you either."

"How dreadful. You must have been young since I don't remember you."

"We are a few years separated, I suppose. I hoped you might tell me why I was sent away. Your da didn't speak about me or mention my father?"

Trulee shook her head. "Nay, not once. But you can ask him about it yourself. He means to come in a fortnight to see how I fare here on his travels. I doubt Laird Sutherland will choose me for his wife so I shall probably leave when he comes."

"Why do you say that? You're certainly pleasing and beautiful. I'm certain Laird Sutherland must think so." Marren's heart went out to the lass because she seemed dismayed. She was uncertain if it was because the laird wouldn't choose her, or that her father would make her leave.

She appeared to consider her answer and gave her a strange look. "The laird won't choose me. I am not as interesting as the other lasses, but I'm not upset by it. You see, I hope to find love with the man I marry. My parents are not fond of each other and it makes for an appalling existence. My poor ma is at the mercy of my father and exists only to please him. I want love and happiness and for the man I marry to want to please me too. I doubt I shall have such with the laird."

"As do I... I want to find love as well." Marren thought she was sweet and any man would be pleased to marry her. She was beautiful but not in an overly vain way. Her pretty brown hair had touches of golden strands woven throughout and her eyes were brown but with touches of green in them. Trulee was unique and had an intriguing spirit about her.

"My father will probably make me leave when he arrives and I dread having to travel with him. He often visits the king and other nobles. Their courts are filled with vexing, self-absorbed women who seek to win favor, and the men are just as bad with their political unrest or conquests."

"I have never been to such courts and I'm thankful for that. We should get down for the midday meal. Lady Ophelia expects us." She left the chamber and Lady Ophelia stopped her in the hallway. She stood in the doorway of the other bedchamber the lasses occupied and appeared upset. "Good day, Milady, we were just on our way down for the afternoon meal."

"Join me, Marren. Lady Trulee, you may leave us. We shall see you in the hall." Once Trulee left the hallway, Lady Ophelia pulled her to an out cove and frowned. "I'm distressed, Marren. Robina has sent a missive to her father to come and retrieve her at once. She says she doesn't find Keith to her liking. Have ye ever heard of such a preposterous thing?" Lady Ophelia tisked. "Imagine that, a lass rejecting a suitor who her da would approve of? And Keith is the most chivalrous, handsome man in these parts. She could do no better."

She almost chuckled out loud at the lady's assessment of her nephew. Lady Ophelia was completely impartial in her view of him. Yet she had to agree because he was noble, kind, handsome, and a marvelous kisser. A blush warmed her cheeks because the remembrance of their time together at the stream would add to her list of his merits. Fortunately, her lady wasn't aware of why she'd blushed or of her and Keith's involvement.

Marren didn't think an answer was required but she shook her head to appease her lady. "There are several lasses who remain. Keith still has possibilities. I'm certain he'll find one of them acceptable and will make his choice soon."

"Lord I hope so. Heaven forbid I need to reach out to other clans."

She smiled to allay her. "Worry not, Milady, all shall be remedied soon."

Marren entered the chamber to offer her assistance to Robina, but she scoffed and ignored her. She would be pleased to see the last of Robina. The lass was just about as unpleasant as Eedy Fraser. As she thought of the irritable, exceedingly haughty woman, she entered the chamber. Eedy wore a wrap on her arm and she acted as though she'd been mortally wounded.

"Make yourself useful and bring me a trencher of food. I wish not to eat in the hall. My arm hurts and I shall need you to fetch it for me. Be quick about it."

Marren wanted to tell her where she could stuff the trencher, but the woman was hurt and needed her compassion. Eedy could have asked more kindly, but she wouldn't expect her to be cordial. "I'll have one of the hall's servants bring you a trencher. Is there anything else you need?"

Eedy waved her hand at her as if she was a lowly maidservant and shook her head.

She smirked at the woman's absurdity and hurried to the hall. Once she retrieved food for Eedy and directed a maidservant to deliver it, she returned to the hall and sat next to Cassie but didn't speak. The day was getting away from her and she hadn't visited the solarium in days. Marren hoped to make a new concoction with the wild Marygold flowers she'd discovered by the keep's wall. She itched to get at her tables and take her mind from her troubles, but alas, that wouldn't be.

With Keith being away, Lady Ophelia implored her to entertain the lasses, and Marren had no notion how to fill the day. Fortunately, Cassie suggested they ask the minstrels to come and play for them. After the midday meal, they practiced the dances, mainly the caroles that were expected of a lady who might visit the king's court or a wealthier lord's keep. Such entertainments never really appealed to Marren because she didn't care for dancing and it was doubtful she'd ever visit such a keep.

At least the dancing brought a bit of merriment to the lasses' solemn mood and to hers as well as she watched them fumble their way through the steps. That is until Marren spotted Keith who watched them from the threshold of the great hall. He gazed at them with no expression. She wondered why he appeared indifferent or perhaps his manner was more of intrigue.

She left the lasses, joined him by the doorway, and leaned back against the stone wall. He faced her from the opposite side and she smiled. "You have returned, I see. Was your journey successful or troublesome? You left hastily and your aunt was quite displeased with you. I made certain the healer tended to Lady Eedy. She didn't break her arm, but only strained it. She's well enough even though she gripes about her pain most of the day."

He kept his expression devoid of emotion or interest. "I thank you, lass. You're enjoying the afternoon, I see."

"The lasses were bored with you being gone so I thought music might enliven us. I have news. Both Iona and Robina are intent to leave us this day. You might want to speak with them before they depart and soothe their wounded hearts. Their families are on their way to fetch them."

His shoulders slumped a little and she wondered if he was bothered by their departure.

"I will be sure to speak to them before they go. What about you? Will you soon leave me too?" His words were spoken low and with the music playing loudly in the background, she barely heard him. He kept his gaze on her, but he didn't smile.

Marren grimaced. "You know I must."

"I don't want you to leave, lass. This is your home."

"Not my home, but only a place I exist until I am sent for." A sob thickened her throat. As much as she wanted him to beg her to stay, when she was called by her betrothed for her marriage, Marren had no choice but to leave him. Even if she might stay and be his—only in his thoughts and in his heart, she'd never truly belong to him.

"Marren?"

"Nay, Keith, this is too difficult and my heart weeps at the sorrow of it. I can't bear to see you kiss others. You have probably kissed them all, haven't you?"

He grabbed her arm to keep her from leaving. "I have only kissed you. You're the only lass that I want to kiss. If I could kiss you right this second, I would. I want to badly…"

Keith practically pressed her against the doorjamb with his hard, hot body.

"You shouldn't say such things. You must wed to remain laird and I won't come between you and your duty. There's no hope that we can ever be together and I cannot bear to see you with another. Please, don't make this harder than it has to be." Marren didn't want to cause him upset, but he appeared so. Tears shimmered in her eyes and Keith pressed his thumb beneath her eye to wipe one away.

"You won't have to bear it much longer. You cannot leave me. I won't allow you to go." He gently squeezed her arm as if he tried to tell her something without actually saying it.

"Don't ask that of me. I must go soon before you take one of them as your wife. Cease looking at me like that. You see, that is exactly why I must go. Your wife wouldn't be pleased to see you gaze at me as you're doing now." Tears sprang to her eyes and she wouldn't allow him to see her weep like a bairn. Marren fled before he could stop her. She went to the one place that solaced her, the solarium—her precious sanctuary.

Chapter Thirteen

Keith wanted to follow Marren and embrace her and perhaps soothe her disgruntlement. He wanted to ease her distress and he chided himself for being the cause of it. Marren's tears were akin to a sword thrust in his heart. He felt wretched for causing her woe. She was right though. He had to marry if he was to remain the laird. As much as he cared for her, he couldn't put her above his sacred duty. The dilemma sat like a rock on his chest and threatened to cease his breath. It was killing him not to take her to his bed and do the things he'd dreamed of.

When she gazed at him with her smoldering passionate eyes, he wanted to appease her and declare that he wouldn't marry any of the lasses. He almost had and was about to make promises he was unable to keep—that she wouldn't have to suffer seeing him with others when he intended to refute each lass. He practically begged her to stay and that unsettled him.

Perhaps it was best if she left. Then he wouldn't be tormented with seeing her or being unable to kiss and hold her as he wanted to. Why did God punish him and disallow him from being with the one woman who he most cherished? Was it his penance for staying away from Sutherland land and shirking his responsibilities? Whatever the cause, he was anguished by it.

Dain signaled to him from down the lane and Keith turned and headed in the opposite direction. He didn't want to hear the lad's complaints. Still, he hadn't found the right position for the young squire, but he certainly didn't want the lad underfoot.

"Laird, ye look like you carry a great boulder on your shoulders."

He shot a glance at Marc who walked next to him. Keith hadn't noticed his approach and had been caught in his reflection of what to do about Marren. "The boulder is about to get a wee bit lighter."

With two lasses leaving, his choice of wife dwindled. And he intended to speak to Philly about Marren. It was time to send her back from whence she came. Not only was Marren unhappy, but he also didn't need the distraction. It was the last thing he wanted, to cause her to be woeful. Even though it would be the most difficult thing he'd ever do, he'd have to send her away.

The day darkened with thick gray clouds. The rain came first with sparse drops but it grew heavier by the minute and a torrent was unleashed. Keith paid no attention to the heavy rain and walked along in complete dumbfounded misery.

Marc pulled him to stop beneath a pine tree. The densely branched tree kept them somewhat dry. Keith peered at his comrade and scoffed. "Are you ever going to don a tunic? You must be freezing your arse off."

Marc chuckled. "The cold doesn't bother me. I vow if I could forgo my tartan and boots too, I'd do so. Garments don't make the man. It's his actions that claim his standing. When are you going to uncover yourself, Keith, and reveal your true nature? Ye hide beneath your unruffled demeanor, och I know deep within is a man who wants to fight."

He was perplexed by Marc's words. Was he referring to

his garments or something else? "There's nothing to fight for."

Marc grinned. "Are ye sure about that, Laird? From where I'm standing, I see one thing that deserves ye to take a stand. If you want her, you will have to fight for her. She's worth the effort, is she not? Stand up to the elders and declare your rights. If you're man enough to do so and are willing to lay your heart on the line, they have to accept your choice." He shoved his shoulder and marched off and had no concern for the rain that pelted his unclad body.

Keith shook his head. Marc didn't understand the full weight of his problem. Hell, he barely did. Was his affection for Marren evident to all, or only Marc? He grimaced because the woman put him in a mire of a situation. On one hand, he didn't want her to leave him, and on the other hand, if he was to take a wife, he couldn't bear her to be in his presence.

To want something that remained close, but he couldn't have… It would cause misery for all involved. He wanted his wife to be pleased with him, not ireful at his gaze of another. Keith doubted he'd be able to withstand the temptation to look at Marren with desire in his eyes.

As Keith reached the entry to the castle, he stood on the steps and regarded the carriage that stopped in the courtyard. He'd almost forgotten the lasses were leaving, but he couldn't allow them to do so without offering his gratitude. It was the least he could do, to give them a wee bit of solace before they returned home.

Iona stepped through the threshold with his aunt who gave him a cross look. Philly motioned to him to step forward and he hurried to stand beside the lass. Iona wouldn't look at him but kept her gaze at her feet.

"Give us a moment, Philly?"

His aunt nodded and backed through the threshold.

"Milady Iona, I understand you're leaving. You won't change your mind?"

She shook her head. "There's no reason to."

"I'm sorry to see you go and for what happened at the

loch. I didn't wish to cause you upset or to displease you. And I'm disheartened you became ill here, but you appear to be recovered?"

Her chin raised and she appeared ready to weep. "I have and am well. You have nothing to be sorry for, Laird Sutherland. It is I who should apologize to you for striking you, but it's obvious that you shan't offer for me, and so I shall leave. I don't hold you in disdain and hope for your happiness with whichever woman you choose for your bride."

"I appreciate that, lass. You have my thanks for coming. It was a pleasure to meet you and I'm sure a man will find you more than pleasing as a wife. I wish you well." That was if the man loved birds as much as she did.

She swiped at the tears that fell from her eyes and hastened forward. Keith pulled his tartan from his chest and used it to keep the rain from soaking her on her traipse to her carriage.

Before she entered, she turned to him. "Whoever you choose as wife is fortunate, Laird Sutherland, and I wish you well too." She embarked on her journey and the carriage rolled toward the gate.

"You shall regret that, my lad."

He raised a brow but scowled when he realized his aunt was displeased with him. "Philly, the woman was obsessed with birds. Could you honestly see me wed to her?"

Philly laughed. "I suppose not, but the Frasers would have brought us a great alliance. 'Tis a shame it wasn't meant to be."

Keith could only nod, but his marriage wasn't required to gain them an alliance, or was it? Perhaps there was more to the elders wanting the security of him staying. He needed to speak to Samuel and find out what the real intent of his marriage was. Surely they weren't using him to make a pact with another clan. If that was the case, such matters would better be handled with a meeting and a discussion. Yet, his shoulders slumped when he considered many marriages were placed to align clans.

Another carriage careened forward and entered the courtyard.

His aunt set a hand on his shoulder. "I shall fetch Lady Robina. I suppose you'd like another moment?"

He nodded but sighed. Robina would've made a prized bride except she probably would have forced him to spar with her. He didn't mind the thought of a scuffle with his wife, especially if it led to an amorous makeup session in bed afterward. But he envisioned the bout with her would be with weapons or harsh words, and not with romantic notions. If Robina had her way, there'd be no show of affection afterward either. He envisioned himself bloodied and her grin wide at her accomplishment of bringing him low. Keith shook the horrid image from his imagination.

The black-haired beauty joined him on the steps. Her eyes flashed ire at him. Keith didn't want any lass to detest him or be angered with him. Chivalry was important to him. As part of his dedication in training as a knight, he'd taken a vow to uphold nobility toward women regardless of the situation. He sighed and stepped in front of her to prevent her from leaving without having a word with him.

"Milady Robina, I don't want you to leave without allowing me to apologize."

She lowered her gaze to the wet steps. "What have you to apologize for? We don't suit and someone tried to hex me, I'm certain of it. I refuse to stay here a moment longer. I don't mind having to compete for my husband if he has an interest. But you don't, do you?"

He wouldn't speak falsely, but had to carefully choose his words, "Nay, I'm sorry and I'm confounded why someone would…hex you. You are lovely and some man will be fortunate enough to win your hand and…affection."

"Perhaps, Laird Sutherland." She flounced off without a farewell.

Keith hadn't even had time to use his tartan to protect her from the rain. He waited for her carriage to disappear before he entered the hall. He sat next to Philly and scowled. The great hall was empty save for his aunt. He was glad for a moment of privacy.

"She was a bonny lass, wasn't she?"

He nodded but wouldn't voice his words of what he thought of the lass. At least there was no real loss there because the Robertsons weren't a clan who brought fierce arms as an ally. Their numbers had decreased in recent years and their soldiers were young.

"Aunt..."

Philly leaned forward. "Oh, you never call me aunt. Something tells me that you're about to say something dreadful. Go on then, speak it."

He sighed deeply. "I wanted to discuss Marren."

"Marren? Why? There is naught to discuss about her."

"Aye, there is. I detest admitting this to you, but she and I... I fear I might upset you. You seem to care for her but I... I wish her to be sent back to her guardian. Who is he?"

Philly scowled and sat back as if she tried to make sense of why he was asking such a question. "What is it you wish to admit? You didn't say? She and you what? I hope it is not unfavorable, my lad, because you know what your duty is. Need I remind you that your sacred duty is to lead this clan and to do so, you must take a wife? Now I've given you six fine lasses to choose from..."

"Who is her guardian?" he asked in a sterner voice.

"I'm certain I mentioned it. I told you, did I not that her guardian is... She's the ward of Laird Mackay. He shall one day choose her husband. I had thought he would take her for himself, but alas, he has not called for her."

Keith's voice shook a little when he spoke, "Mackay, Grady's father, Simon Mackay?"

"Aye, the one and the same. Chester brought her here and told me that Simon bade me to see to her wifely training when she was young. I assumed Simon would take her for his wife eventually, but he never sent for her. I deem he's either forgotten her or he doesn't want her. I had thought to write to him to inquire what he intended…but things have been quite busy here of late and with your return, I haven't had a moment."

Keith felt as though he was struck in the gullet. Simon Mackay was Marren's betrothed? The thought of her married to the fiend sickened him beyond sense.

"Why do you ask about her? I told you she is unavailable to you. You haven't done anything untoward, have you? Tell me and be truthful. God, I hope not."

He couldn't speak the truth now and had to consider what his aunt told him. Keith shook his head and kept his face devoid of the anger that heated him like hot iron.

"Good, I remind you that you have four lasses that vie for your attention. Your time would better be spent courting them than in worry about a lass who has no importance to you."

No importance? His aunt's words tensed every part of him. He pushed his trencher of food away and had lost his appetite. Keith didn't retort to his aunt's directive because he knew what was required of him. Yet he couldn't help but be despaired at what Philly told him.

Grady's father, Simon Mackay, was a knave—worse than a knave, and perhaps had the blood of the devil in his veins. He was a brute who had no qualms of hurting those weaker than himself, and that included women and children.

Keith had heard firsthand the accounts of the man's brutality, and somehow, he had to tell his aunt to refuse the Mackay when, or if he called for Marren. The thought of her being married to Simon Mackay coiled his gut, but there was nothing at the moment to be done. When he could think of a way to explain the situation to Philly, he would. Until then, he'd give it extreme consideration.

The reason for the delicacy on the matter was strictly because he'd promised Grady he would never divulge his secrets or about his father's mistreatment. If he had to advise his aunt on Simon's behavior, he'd be breaking his pledge to the one comrade who meant more to him than anyone, who was like a brother to him.

"Lad, did you hear me? This day, you shall meet with Lady Lindsey. I have set up games by the hearth for you to enjoy. It's the perfect day to spend indoors by the fire what with the heavy rain."

"Aye, I need to see to a few matters first and will return in an hour. Will that suit you?"

"Don't dally and remember your duty."

"I don't need to be constantly reminded, Philly. There are clan matters I must attend to that are just as important as what you deem my sacred duty." He left the hall without another word to her.

She had to know he was irked with her badgering, but he might have been a wee bit brash. He supposed another apology was in order because he didn't want his aunt upset with him. He'd already made more apologies this day than he had in his entire life.

Before he'd meet with Lindsey Gordon, he needed to check with Aulay. The soldiers' regimens needed to be enforced and their training hours lengthened. If the Mackenzies threatened them, they'd be ready to face their large army. Fortunately, the Sutherlands had at least four-hundred men and a good number of allies who would take up arms in support of any war they participated in.

After he spoke with Aulay, he stopped at the gate and took a few missives from the gate watchman. Marc insisted he send Dain to another location for training and that the lad was too young to join the lads who guarded the gate. Keith grimaced because Dain was indeed young, and perhaps too wet behind the ears to put in a position with others who earned their way. He'd have to give the wee squire a bit more thought.

Keith tucked the missives inside his tunic and hastened to the stables. Winddodger had been affable when he'd ridden him on the search for the Mackenzies. But now back in the stable, he was sure Winddodger caused Emmett a wee bit of hell. He entered the darkened domain and heard

Emmett's shouts. The stable boasted at least sixty stalls and were three lanes wide. He listened to the voices which led him around the last corner and he found two lads trying to rein his unruly horse.

As soon as Winddodger saw him, he reared and bucked to get loose. Keith waved the lads away and took the reins and led his horse from the stable and let him loose in the corral. Winddodger galloped away and ran at full force around the pen as if his tail was on fire. He regarded his horse and stepped to the center. When his horse tired, he ambled to him and snorted.

"Ah, you're displeased in the stable, aye? What has you so riled, I wonder? Is it a winsome mare or are you irked with being penned in?"

Winddodger whinnied.

"Your horse is going to hurt someone if we don't curtail his aggressiveness."

Keith patted his horse's neck and turned to Emmett. "Aye, I agree. Best keep him here in the corral until I figure out what troubles him."

Emmett chortled. "He wants the mare, the one Milady Marren rode to the village. But she wants nothing to do with him. Mayhap I'll put her in here and let him have his way. She gives him a wee bit of torment, that can't be helped. Perhaps in time, he'll win her over."

Keith's eyes narrowed at his comrade. It was as if he spoke of his situation because he too wanted a female he couldn't have and there was no winning Marren in time or otherwise.

"Do what you think is best. I need to return to the hall." Keith left the pen and hesitated to return to the castle. But he had to. He entered and found his aunt speaking with Lady Lindsey.

"Good day, ladies," he said in his most pleasant voice. As much as he dreaded spending the afternoon with the droll woman, he'd make the most of it. Keith plucked off his wet tartan and dried the rain from his hair and patted his arms.

There was no time to change his garments and he had to make do with his appearance.

Lindsey was a plain woman who didn't behold beauty as the others had. Yet she seemed kind and was gentle of heart, so he would put his assumptions about her aside. He tried to recall the traits he'd professed to want of a wife, but his head hurt from all the turmoil he'd endured in the last few days and nothing came to him.

"There you are. Lady Lindsey has awaited you. I have set up games and there is fresh mead and food on the table for you." Philly winked at him and gestured to a side table where she'd placed a rose and a bottle of the scent he had wanted to gift to Lindsey.

He nodded. "Shall we, Milady?"

She stepped to the table and sat far from him.

"Come and sit next to me. I don't bite, lass, and we can't play droughts if you're down there." He stood and held out a chair close to his and waited.

Lindsey joined him. "I do like this game and often play it with my ma."

"Aye? I haven't played the game since I was a young lad. I think I remember the rules."

She proceeded to tell him the rules and began the game with a simple move. For the next hour, they played the game on the checkered board and he'd tried to let her win. It was only chivalrous of him to do so, but the lass wasn't too keen on the strategic moves necessary to win. She intended to put him to sleep with her incessant chatter about some nonsense. He hadn't paid much attention to what she spoke of. Still, it took all his will not to trounce her and his competitive nature urged him to make moves that would surely win him the game.

In the end, he withstood his desire and she finally moved her pawn to defeat him. It was a good thing too because he was about to rip his hair out in frustration of waiting for her to make a decent play. Or he would've fallen asleep with the drollery of her conversation.

They switched to a game of cards and again she didn't seem to know how to execute her moves properly. They played maw which was equivalent to the English version of cribbage and easily mastered. He grew bored and several times he tried to abate a yawn but tried his best to appear interested. Several times, he tried to strike up an easy exchange, but she appeared not to converse easily and appeared timid.

As the day wore on, she became less inclined to talk. That suited him, because who wanted a wife who yammered on? Still, she should be more vocal in her desires or at the very least be interested to know more about him as he was of her. How would he discern if she was the right woman for him if she didn't tell him what she was about?

She'd spoken little about her home life, but that too bordered on dullness. The woman didn't have interests such as other women but spent her days following her mother, and apparently, she had a talent for listening. That wasn't such a bad quality to have in a wife, because most wives never listened. He would have laughed at his untrue thought, not most wives, but some. Their marriage, if he chose her, would be froth with mundane life and absolute drollery. He'd grow old quick out of sheer boredom.

Still, she had spoken of nothing that sparked his interest. And he admitted after being in her presence for several hours that there was undeniably no attraction between them. She kept her eyes averted and didn't appear to hold him with any sort of desirous longing. He sighed woefully because he'd hoped to feel something akin for her, even a wee spark of a romantic notion. Keith had professed to want a wife who not only cared for him but also desired him.

As the minutes trickled by in a grueling, bored-to-death, agony, Keith's one thought was that if he married her, his life would be a tedious never-ending existence. He imagined he'd spend a good deal of time away from the keep if she was his wife. He wanted his wife to draw his excitement, to make him lust after her, and to muddle his thoughts with nothing but her. But it wasn't to be with this lass.

Keith yawned again and pressed his hands over his face to try to liven himself but it was useless. The hour, fortunately, neared the supper hour and he was relieved the ordeal was over. He couldn't tell her yet that their courtship was at an end. Until he could name the lass he intended to marry, it was best he kept to himself what he planned to do.

He rose and retrieved the rose and scent and set them before her. "For you, Milady, for spending an enjoyable afternoon with me." Keith almost blanched at his falsely spoken words, but he wouldn't cause her tears which would surely fall if he told her the truth. "We should make ready for supper, and I'm sure all will join us soon." Keith ordinarily didn't tell falsehoods, but to keep from hurting her tender feelings, he'd complimented her.

"Oh, how lovely. I thank you, Milord. Shall I see you then, at supper?"

"Aye, you shall." He bowed to her and set off. Without giving it much thought, he went in search of Marren. Every encounter with Marren was more exciting than that of his courtships thus far, especially with that particular lass. There was no way in hell he'd ever marry Lady Lindsey. When he found his aunt, he'd tell her so.

Chapter Fourteen

With spring in the air and warmer days to be had, most of the clansmen spent their time on the farm fields or on boats in the sea. That left the women mostly alone during the day to attend to their chores. Even the castle was quiet during the day.

Marren tried to keep busy and had made several varieties of fragrances to sell at Wynda's. She had yet to revisit the village and thought to do so soon. Her last visit brought both happiness and sorrow to her because she'd been with Keith in a way she'd always dreamed of, but it also brought her despair because they'd never be together again.

The day was too pleasant to spend inside or to ruminate over such disparaged thoughts. Nor was it a day to spend in travel to the village. With the sun shining so, her day would better be spent enjoying it. She dressed in a lighter fabric overdress and instead of her warm boots, she wore slip-on shoes. Her hair was pulled into a coif at the base of her nape and tied securely with a ribbon.

When she reached the great hall, she sat at the table and joined Trulee, Caroline, Lindsey, and Eedy. Cassie wasn't about but was probably seeing to Lady Ophelia's bedchamber, or with Marc doing what she longed to do with Keith. Marren ate quietly and listened to their conversations. Lindsey chattered on about her afternoon spent with Keith the day before and sounded rather poised.

"I vow I'm beginning to care for him and I have hope that he shall ask for my hand."

Eedy shot Lindsey an annoyed glance. "I wouldn't be so assured if I was you. You don't know how he feels about you unless he's told you. Has he?"

Lindsey shook her head. "Well, nay, not yet, but I vow he will."

Eedy laughed derisively. "I doubt he has the same sentiment for you and why would he? You're an unaccountable lass. What have you to offer him? Drollery? Aye, if he wants to be bored to tears every day, you might win him. But remember, you're not the only one vying for his proposal."

Caroline scoffed. "Don't say that. None of us knows what the laird is thinking. He might care for her. Lindsey, don't listen to her. She's envious because your day with him went better than hers. You should be confident if you deem you got that sense from him."

Trulee had been quiet up till now but put her view in, "Until he declares his care or love for one of us, we shall wonder. But I don't fault Lindsey for having hope if he's what she wants."

Eedy scoffed loudly. "It's up to him. Whether we have a care for him or not doesn't much matter. I shall wed a laird and if it's not Laird Sutherland then I will find another. One man is as good as the next, as long as he provides, what else could a woman want?"

Trulee set her goblet down and frowned. "Do you not care if the man loves you? Surely you want your husband to have affection for you. Does it matter what his title is?"

Eedy raised her haughty chin. "Of course it matters, unless you want to marry a low-ranking noble or a lowly soldier, or even, God forbid, a farmhand. Love is unnecessary. Marriage is but an agreement between two people. It is best to keep sentiment from it if it's to be successful."

Trulee sat back with a frown. "I don't agree or believe that. Love is all that matters. Marriage should be the joining of two souls and hearts. I will only wed a man who I love and I shall know who he is when I meet him."

Lindsey patted her hand. "Does that mean you have no interest in Laird Sutherland? If so, then that only leaves Eedy, Caroline, and myself in the running."

Marren thought their discussion was useless and she focused on eating her morning fare. But she couldn't help overhearing their conversation and winced at their conjecture. How would she assure he'd end up with the right woman when she deemed none of them acceptable? She liked Trulee, but the lass was a waif who wore her heart on her sleeve. As to the other lasses, they had no appeal and as far as she was concerned, did not suit Keith.

Trulee pressed the length of her dark hair behind her shoulder and smiled. "I am uncertain how I feel about Laird Sutherland. Since I have yet to spend time with him, I shall get a better sense when I do. He never looks at me when we're in the same room, so I doubt he finds me as appealing as others," she said and glanced at her.

Marren raised her brows at her look. She couldn't ask her what she meant by it, not with the others present.

"Well, I have spent time with him. He's a rather stern man and had bored me to tears during our ride. When I fell from my horse, he was downright unsympathetic. He could be a little more gallant if you ask me," Eedy said.

Caroline snorted a laugh. "You only say that because his horse bumped yours and you fell from your horse and broke your arm. That wasn't the laird's fault. I am supposed to spend the evening with him and Lady Ophelia gave me the use of the kitchens this afternoon. I shall make a meal for him. I vow it will be romantic." She pressed her hand over her heart and sighed. "The way to a man's heart is with a well-cooked meal. At least, that's what my ma always told me."

Marren hadn't ever cooked a meal a day in her life and she envied Caroline's talent. The more she thought about it, the more she realized she had no wifely talents at all, besides her ability to grow flora and make scents. The one thing that would aid her when she married was her ability to direct the servants and see to the household.

Eedy scoffed. "You need not know how to cook to gain a husband, Caroline, but must employ a good cook. A laird only wants a wife to warm his bed, bear his heirs, and see to his needs regardless of how it's obtained. Is that not true, Lady Marren? You've been tutored by Lady Ophelia in wifely duties, and surely she's directed you in such matters in her fostering. It's a shame you have yet to snare a man."

Marren's gaze shot to Eedy and she wasn't sure if her words were meant to wound her, or if she wanted her to agree. She only nodded and wouldn't join in the debate or give credit to her blasphemous reasoning. But Eedy had somewhat of a point. A man did want a wife to warm his bed, have his children, and see to his care. What else was needed?

"Let us be about our day," Caroline said and left and probably headed for the kitchen.

Eedy rose. "I shall go and rest my arm."

She hastily left the hall and Marren was gladdened because the less time she spent in 'prim-and-proper' Eedy's presence, the better. Marren was a wee bit envious of her because Eedy didn't let her heart rule her as she had. Eedy would make a match one day and be settled even if there was no love betwixt her and her husband. The woman would never have her heart broken that was certain.

Only Trulee and Lindsey remained. The hall's servants came to clean away the morning meal. They bustled in and had the hall cleaned within minutes and then absconded as quickly.

"There is a chance the laird will ask for my hand, is there

not?" Lindsey asked suddenly with forlorn.

"Of course there is," Trulee said and patted her hand, and she gave another strange look at her.

Marren didn't want to discourage Lindsey, and until she spoke with Keith, she didn't know what he thought of her. She had to admit though, the lass was rather dull, and…well, she was kind and gentle-hearted. Marren tried to list the lass's other qualities but came up nil.

Lindsey pressed her eyes but couldn't stop the tears from flowing. "I think I love him. What shall I do if he doesn't feel the same? I shall die from heartbreak."

Marren clasped her hand to comfort her but recoiled at her misbegotten fervent declaration. Lindsey was overzealous in her emotions. "You cannot be despaired. If Laird Sutherland doesn't love you it would be his loss. And besides, you shall find another to love you. Don't give up though, Lindsey, he hasn't made a decision yet." She commiserated with the lass and she shouldn't encourage her, but the lass's tears brought on her empathy. To love a man and not have the sentiment returned was heart-wrenching. She knew that firsthand.

"I need to be alone," Lindsey said and wiped her eyes. She stood and fled the hall.

Trulee smiled after her. "She's going to have her heart broken."

"Perhaps." Marren rose and was about to leave when Trulee called to her.

"Marren, what are you doing this morn? Are you up for a walk? I long to be outside."

"I was going to go in search of blooms in the woods. You're welcome to join me."

"I would like that. It's better than sitting here in the keep awaiting my turn with the laird. Or listening to them speak of affection for Laird Sutherland. Let me get my cloak and we shall go."

Marren reached the exit. "You don't need your cloak. It's warm this day." She grabbed the basket she intended to take with her on the trek and led Trulee from the castle.

Outside, she walked toward the gatehouse and was eased in the lass's company.

"I have never been outside here and their land is enchanting. It's not as beautiful as the isle I live on. At home, I'm never inside. The clan's people seem kind here."

Marren was glad Trulee asked to walk with her because she hoped to ask more questions about her uncle and to find out why she'd given her strange looks at the table. "They are."

"And the men are easy on the eyes. Oh, look at him. He's like a statue I saw once in the king's gardens."

"You visited the king's keep?"

Trulee nodded and kept pace with her. "Aye, my da is one of King Robert's faithful council. He spends much time at Dundonald Castle in Kintyre. He comes home but once or twice a year. My da is keen to retain the king's aid in his wars with the MacDonalds."

Marren hadn't heard much about the goings-on between the clans or the king's business. As much as Trulee appeared to be a waif with her head in the clouds, she certainly was educated in such matters. "I heard the king ails and it's rumored he'll soon die."

"I heard the same. There's bound to be a scuffle over who will be king again. Many vie for the crown. Who is he?" Trulee asked and tilted her head at the gate watchman. "Do all the men go unclothed?"

"That's Marc. He never wears a tunic even in winter."

Trulee giggled. "With all that muscle I suppose he doesn't get cold. The view is pleasing though."

Marren laughed. "Aye, it is and my good friend Cassie thinks so too. She has her heart set on winning him. Lady Ophelia always chastises him for forgoing his tunic, but he refuses to clad himself."

"I won't complain, that's for certain. The women here are fortunate in their scenery."

Marren chortled. "Perhaps we are."

They reached the woods and Marren searched along the higher brush for heather and bluebells. While she did so, Trulee traipsed past the trees. She had walked about ten steps ahead when a roe deer stood before her. Marren was in awe of the animal whose antlers were wee and numbered to three, but still, he was impressive. The roe didn't run off but stood there and stared at Trulee who held out her hand and the animal butted his head against her palm.

"You're quite a handsome fellow. Go on," Trulee said.

The roebuck backed away and tilted his head as if he bowed to Trulee. Marren had never seen anything as incredulous. The lass had a way with animals.

"How…?" she couldn't form the question she wanted to ask as she watched the roe scamper off.

"I have always had a connection with animals. It's a feeling I get and sometimes I can sense their emotions like I know what they're thinking. He was a sweet roe and had a peaceful demeanor."

"How is this possible?" Marren was astounded by her ability.

"My great-great-grandmother was the princess of an ancient tribe that had natural abilities. They revered all the land had to offer. My ma's mother told me tales of their heroics and mystic allure. I have some of their gifts, I suppose. I wish I'd been born in that time, to practice such gifts without being termed a heretic or witch. None know of my gift. Please, don't tell anyone."

"I promise to keep it a secret. Still, it's amazing the roe let you pet him. They're usually skittish."

"I've always had the touch and animals seem to find their way to me."

"We should return before the watch sends a search for us." Marren had almost filled her basket and there was enough flora to make a good scent.

They walked along in silence back to the keep. Marren wished she'd grown up with Trulee. She liked her and would've enjoyed her childhood traipsing the outdoors.

Instead, she was forced to spend those tender years at keeps where the men were feared which also gave her trepidation. Regardless of what Keith decided to do or whom he chose as his wife, Marren wanted to retain a friendship with her cousin. Trulee was the only family she'd ever known or had.

"Oh, will you look at that?"

Jarred from her thoughts at Trulee's words, Marren glanced ahead. Keith's horse caused a ruckus and was ornery. He continually butted his head on the mare's side and whinnied loudly. The poor mare tried to flee from his attack and backed several times. Her cry sounded and her eyes beheld fear.

"He's a beast. Come, we should go. Emmett says he means to give them time to acclimate to one another. Apparently, the warhorse is smitten with the mare."

Trulee shook her head. "Nay, I don't think so. That's not affection on his part." She grabbed her sleeve to keep her from walking away. "I cannot leave. There is trouble. That horse is disturbed. He wants nothing to do with the mare and she's beyond frightened. See how wide her eyes are. We should call the stable master and have her removed immediately before he hurts her. I fear for her."

"But—"

"He's angry," as Trulee spoke, Winddodger bucked and broke a rail of the corral.

He went maddened and continued to bray and the sounds of his whinnies were fearsome. He bucked again and lifted his forelegs and broke another rung of the rail. The poor mare snorted and ran along the other end of the corral as if her life was in great peril.

Marren stepped closer and reached her hand out to soothe the beast. "There, there, what has you so riled?" She glanced back at Trulee. "He just needs a wee bit of coaxing to calm him."

"Nay, Marren, don't—"

Winddodger used his body and broke free from the pen and tromped forward. He knocked Marren aside and her body was propelled against a cart that sat a few feet from the pen. She fell forward and smacked her head on the ground and gasped. Marren held her hand on her head and was stunned by the stoned ground and she lay still.

Trulee ran to her and knelt beside her. "Don't move. I'll get help."

She panted at the pain in her side and the throb in her head. "Nay, I'll be alright. Give me a moment."

Trulee tore a piece of her underdress and gently pressed it on her head. "Hold still. You're bleeding and the wound is deep. I need to get help. Can you hold this?"

Marren groaned and held the cloth at her head. "I cannot breathe." She rasped and couldn't catch her breath. It was as if someone sat upon her chest and constricted her.

"Breathe easy, that's right. Slowly now." Trulee turned and peered behind her. "Oh, you must be the stable master... Thank God. Marren has been hurt."

"What happened?" He scowled fiercely and peered down at her.

"There's no time to explain. Get help and send for the healer. Be still, Marren, we'll get you help."

"Don't leave me," she grated. The pain in her side all but took her breath away. Her vision blurred as she watched Emmett saunter off. She closed her eyes to resist the urge to retch, and her body grew heavy. Marren drifted into a dark comforting place...

Chapter Fifteen

'Another day of grueling hell and courtship' that was Keith's first thought upon waking. If he knew how wretched his day would be, he might have closed his eyes and stayed abed. He lingered in bed and ignored the knock that came every half an hour. Finally, he was awake enough to find out what the person wanted. He hoped it wasn't the squire Dain who constantly pestered him for tasks. The lad needed a task befitting a squire, but Keith couldn't think of one, or any that he needed of Dain. So far he'd come up nil to keep the lad busy and out of his way.

"Come in," he shouted. The knock persisted and he muttered under his breath. Keith tugged a tunic over his head and secured a tartan around his hips with his belt. With heavy steps, he reached the door and yanked it open. "Bollocks, what is it?"

"Keith, do you deem to linger in bed all day?"

"I pondered it, Philly. It's early and the sun has only been up for a few hours."

"Don't be brash, lad. This day you'll meet with Caroline. She has planned to cook all your meals this day. With the first being the morning meal. The maids will bring it soon."

"Aye, alright, I'll get about my duty then and will seek her later."

"You're bound to be impressed. I'm told she has a talent for making delicious meals. I've even given her use of the kitchens."

He nodded but didn't give in to his aunt's ploy to discuss the lass. Come mealtime he'd join her and hoped she cooked as good as she proclaimed.

"Has any of the lasses appealed? You have been tight-lipped about them and I'm eager to hear your thoughts."

He narrowed his eyes. "Do you intend to badger me on this subject every morn?"

Philly grinned. "Aye, of course I do, that is, until you give me a reasonable answer. So is there a lass who is in the forefront? Don't keep this old lady in suspense."

He knew well not to humor her. If he named a lass, she'd spend the afternoon planning his wedding. "There might be," he teased. "When I'm firm in my decision, you'll be the first to know."

She swatted his arm. "You're a vexing lad. A decision must be made soon."

"I still haven't met all the lasses and until I do, I won't choose. Give me another fortnight."

Philly groused and set her hands on her hips. "You have a week, that's all. Samuel has asked repeatedly for the name of your intended bride. I have put him off but must give him an answer soon. The lairdship depends upon it."

"Yet again you remind me. I'm well aware of the time constraint and what's expected of me." Keith's impatience rose because he wasn't ready to name his bride. Of the lasses he met so far, none stood out as a possible wife. Since Robina and Iona left, he'd only met with Eedy, but she was too prudish and proper. The woman had no sense of humor and brought no merriment to him. She also didn't seem capable of caring for the keep or being concerned for the clan's people. A life with her would be difficult and severe.

"I must go. You're not the only one who has duties. After your meal with the lass, come to my secret garden and we'll discuss your thoughts of her."

Keith nodded and considered his time with Lindsey Gordon the day before. She was sweet enough but bored him to tears when he'd spent the afternoon with her. He had yet to meet with Caroline Gunn or Trulee Macleod and hoped one of the lasses suited. Then he'd be done with the dreaded courtship and could put the affair behind him.

He finished his morning ritual and left his chamber and didn't await the maids with the morning meal. He'd grab a bite to eat on his way to the training fields.

Outside his door, Dain stood and jumped to attention. "M'laird, do you need anything?"

"Nay, lad, go and fetch yourself something to eat."

He swiped back the long bangs of his dark hair and pouted. "But I already ate, early this morn. Do ye want me to shine your armor or mayhap brush your horse?"

Keith stepped aside when a maidservant passed them. "Nay, lad, stay away from my horse. He's ill-tempered of late. If you want to make yourself useful go and help Emmett with the other horses. I'm sure he could use help in the stables."

Dain scampered off with a smile on his face. He seemed pleased by his request and Keith thought perhaps the lad had an affinity to care for horses. He shook his thoughts of the squire away and descended the stairs.

The great hall was empty and the servants had removed the morning fare. On the sideboard, there was a jug of mead and he helped himself to a small helping. He wasn't fond of mead, but it was the only drink on the sideboard. Next to the jug sat a small trencher of bread and sweetcakes. He snatched a hunk of bread and ate it as he left the keep.

"Laird," Marc called. "There you are. Two crofters are in a disagreement over a pig. Each of them claims the right to it. Ye might want to come and settle the matter. It's getting heated and they might come to blows."

He followed Marc to the gate and when they got there,

two men wrestled on the ground. Several men shouted wagers and others whooped when one got in a good strike. Both men were braw and skilled with their fists. Neither would desist in throwing punches. Keith stood aside and waited for them to tire. That was something he'd learned from Emmett. When a horse was full of vigor it was best to let him run himself out. The men got to their feet and began their persuasive argument of how the pig belonged to them. Their speeches did not indicate who the animal belonged to.

When he heard enough, Keith raised his hand. "I have made a decision. Since you both claim to own the pig and there's no proof of ownership, I will have the animal taken and used for the next clan gathering. That way all will get to enjoy the meat."

A cheer rose amongst the spectators. The men grumbled and wanted to further argue his ruling. But Keith raised his hands for them to remain silent, and the men stormed away. The matter was easily resolved, now if only he might find an easy solution to his marriage situation…

Keith stopped by the training fields and watched the soldier's paces. Their skill with the sword, pike, and maces, improved since he'd last inspected them. As he was about to leave, Samuel, the clan's elder, approached in a march that bolstered his anger.

"Laird," he said with a curt nod.

"Samuel," he returned the greeting in kind.

"Ophelia tells me you have yet to decide on your bride."

He nodded. "That's right. I still have two lasses to meet and won't decide until I've met them all. Are you set on this? I don't need to take a wife to ensure I'll remain here. Haven't I proven I mean to take my duty seriously? I wear the Sutherland ring, is that not enough?"

Samuel set his hand on the butt of his sword that he wore on his hip as if the conversation was casual. "Och so far ye have. The ring can be easily removed, lad. But how long do you plan to stay? Another month, a year mayhap? I cannot allow you to up and leave when ye have a mind to."

"This is my home and my clan. There is nothing that calls me away and I plan to stay until God takes me. But I need time, Samuel. Choosing a wife shouldn't be rushed. It is an important decision and there is more than my happiness and my vow to the clan to consider. Being wed to the laird, a bride must also have a care for the clan. I will not marry a woman simply because you expect me to do so. I mean to make certain she not only cares for me but all those within the clan."

Samuel stared hard at him. "I hadn't thought of that, lad. Let me consider this further and I will let you know my decision. You will still meet with the lasses."

He nodded and was pleased he'd spoken to Samuel. Maybe his reasoning would sway the man to forgo the edict. What he'd said was the truth. Keith didn't want to wed hastily or marry a woman because he was forced to. And he didn't want to be saddled with the wrong woman. When he took a wife it would be for the remainder of his life. Such a vow was sacred and he wanted to get it right from the start. Regrets would plague him for the rest of his days if he decided hastily who the woman would be.

Before Samuel left, he turned and grunted. "You're wearing the laird's ring, are you not?"

He nodded. "I am, but why do you ask this? I already said I was…"

Samuel chortled. "I have hope, lad, that you'll figure out what I mean."

He wanted to ask what he'd meant, but he shook his head and ambled away from the man. Samuel aged and perhaps his mind was soft. He certainly made no sense. Keith hoped to buy more time—time he desperately needed if he might free Marren from her obligation to Laird Mackay. He might be able to marry her after all. It was a sound plan, but he needed to figure out how to approach Simon Mackay.

Where the hell was Grady? He sure could use his counsel on the matter of his father's involvement with Marren. What baffled him about the situation was that he couldn't see

Simon wanting to marry her. The man was aged and he'd detested women. When Grady's mother died, he forbade any women from entering his keep. Did Simon plan to use Marren in a scheme to lure Grady home? He sure hoped not because his comrade had pledged never to again set foot on Mackay land.

Keith left the fields and entered the hall. Caroline had set the table for two and there were four covered platters in the center and an array of candles. No one else attended the latter-day meal and he thought it strange. Caroline still wore her hair wrapped completely in white fabric. The only hint he had as to the color of her hair was the darkened hue of her eyebrows. She was a dainty lass and much too thin for his liking, but nonetheless, he smiled.

"Good day, lass."

She curtseyed and motioned to him. "Laird, please sit and join me. Did you enjoy the morning fare I had sent to you this morn?"

Keith hadn't waited for the maids to bring the meal when he was in a rush to get to the fields, but to appease her he said, "Aye, it was tasty. My thanks."

"We shall enjoy the midday meal together. I worked all morning on it and I hope you like it." Caroline uncovered the platters and beamed at him.

An unpleasant odor reached his nose. He peered at the platters in wonderment of what she'd cooked. Whatever it was didn't appear tasty and nor did it smell pleasing. She served brown bread which was a wee bit hard and over baked. The center platter had two seared salmon fish in the center, but they were charred and overcooked. He thought the fish was salmon, but he could be mistaken. With it, she served a green mushy substance which he took for peas. The ale was the only thing that looked appealing and enticing enough for him to try.

She scooped a helping of the green mush and plopped it on his trencher. With that, she placed a piece of fish and a hunk of bread. "Go on, taste it," Caroline said proudly.

He took his supper dagger and jabbed the fish. If it was cooked properly it would've fallen apart, but it was solid and came in one piece on the blade. His shoulders slumped because he liked salmon, but he suspected it was as dry as sand on the inside. He set it on his trencher and cut a portion. As he was about to place it in his mouth someone shouted for him. Keith set down his supper dagger and gazed at the door, giving gracious thanks to whoever interrupted him.

"I'm sorry, lass, but it sounds important. I must go," he said and rose and hurried to the door.

Emmett reached him and his breath hastened. "Laird—"

"I'm glad you called me. I was about to eat something awful. It probably would've killed me. I just hope that lass doesn't weep for the rest of the day…" He glowered at Emmett and wondered what bothered him. "You look as though you ate some of what that lass just tried to serve me. What's wrong with you?"

"Laird, it's milady… Marren… She's been hurt."

Keith's chest tightened and a teneness rose to his shoulders. "How? Is she hurt badly?"

Emmett nodded. "She hasn't come to yet. The healer is being fetched."

He rushed past Emmet and reached the stables within seconds and spotted a crowd gathered. As he approached, he heard their talk.

"Aye, she's dead alright," a woman said.

"The poor lass is not moving at all," a man holding a shovel said.

"She's lost a lot of blood…," came from a young maiden.

"Someone should have a box readied," one of the elders said.

"Father John should be fetched," an old woman said and crossed herself.

Keith's heart thronged in his chest and until he reached her, he wouldn't believe Marren was dead. When he was able to get through the crowd, he knelt next to her. He pressed his hand gently on her chest and was relieved to feel the thump of her heart. Her eyes were closed and she remained still. She appeared to be asleep and her face beheld an expressionless mien.

"Emmett, we need to get her inside. I'll carry her."

"Nay! Don't move her." Trulee pressed between his men and glared at them.

Keith glowered at her and was affronted by her tone. "Why not, lass? She needs to be seen to."

"She complained that she couldn't breathe. We must keep her still until the healer comes."

"Marren must be taken inside, lass. We cannot let her lay on the ground. We'll handle her with care and won't move her much. Emmett, find something to carry her on."

"I have a wide plank of wood I was going to use to fix Winddodger's stall."

"Get it and be quick." From his initial view of her, he was uncertain of her injuries. It appeared as if she was fast asleep and dreaming pleasant thoughts except for the blood. As he waited for Emmett to return, he gently pressed the dark strands of Marren's hair by her forehead aside and winced at the gash on her head. Marren's face was pale and the gash had sullied her hair and neck. There was a fair amount of blood on her garments too.

Emmett returned and Marc stood with him. Marc took a step forward and said, "Och the poor lass. Just look at her, she looks like an angel, a wee wounded one. Let us get her inside, Laird. We'll be gentle."

Keith stood aside and allowed them to shift Marren's body onto the wood. They carried her to the keep and he followed Trulee who instructed them at their task the entire way.

"Take her to my chamber," Keith ordered.

Both Emmett and Marc raised their brows at his command.

"It's quieter there and private." He motioned them forward and when the healer arrived and once Marren was placed on his bed, she slammed the door in his face. Emmett and Marc stood in the hallway with him and were as disgruntled as he was.

Trulee stood next to him with a great look of concern on her bonny face. "Laird, if you'll allow me inside your chamber... I'll help the healer."

He nodded. "Aye, go on."

She entered and quietly closed the door behind her.

Keith tensed with worry and he paced the hallway in wait for word of Marren's condition. He stopped near Emmett. "How did this happen?"

"It was my fault, Laird."

Keith gripped his tunic and shoved him against the wall with force. "I'll bloody kill you."

Marc rushed forward and set his hand on his to get him to release Emmett. "Hold on, Laird, he doesn't mean that. It wasn't his fault. The lasses were near the corral and Winddodger went crazed. He broke out of the pen and ran Milady Marren over. Trulee witnessed it and said Marren crashed into the cart and fell and hit the ground."

"God Almighty." He paced again and the image of his horse knocking Marren down and her dainty body hitting the cart brought a grimace to him. He groaned and prayed she wasn't hurt too badly. "I'm worried that she hasn't awakened."

"She must've hit her head hard," Emmett said.

"Don't say that," Marc shouted. "Can ye not see how distressed our laird is?"

Emmett chuckled but ceased when he gave him a sharp look. "Aye, and if I didn't know better I'd think he might love the lass."

"Of course he does. Let us leave him." Marc shuffled Emmett from the hallway.

Quiet abounded which wasn't necessarily a good thing. It gave him time to think. If he lost Marren it would crush him. Perhaps he did love her as Emmett boasted.

His aunt came a few minutes later. "I just heard what

happened to Marren. Is she going to be alright?"

"I know not. The healer hasn't come out yet and still tends to her."

"The poor lass. She's the sweetest lass and I admire her. Marren is a lot like I was at her age."

Keith needed something to take his mind off of what was happening inside his chamber. He leaned against the wall and almost grinned at the fact that his aunt admired Marren. He wondered if that was what appealed about her…that she reminded him of Philly. "Why didn't you ever marry, Philly? Were you ever smitten with a man?"

She took the space beside him and leaned back and was silent for a moment. "I loved a man once, a long time ago when I was a lass a few years younger than Marren's age. He asked my da for my hand and my father gladly gave it, willingly. He knew how much I loved him. But unfortunately, the man's brother, his laird, forbade him from marrying me. That was the end of that. I never found another man to my liking."

"Not even Chester Mackay?"

Philly's cheeks brightened.

"Oh, it's him…he's the man you loved. You were in love with Chester Mackay?" Keith was astounded. He'd suspected Chester had feelings for his aunt, but he'd never guessed there was something between them or that they had a history.

She nodded but didn't verbally confirm his assumption.

Keith set a hand on her thin shoulder. "He never married either and whenever I see him, he asks after you. I deem Chester might still love you as well."

"Oh, shush, he does not. Besides, as long as his brother lives, he can't come to me. His brother forbade him from marrying me. I gave up hope long ago."

Keith pulled away from the wall and hugged her. "You've waited all these years for him?"

"I might have. Love never dwindles, Keith." Philly squeezed him. "That's all I want for you. It's what your da had with your ma. Find love in your heart, lad, and it will always be there."

Keith sobered at her words. Was there love in his heart for Marren or did he just enjoy being with her? The thought of her in pain brought him intense grief. God wouldn't take her from him when he had accepted the truth—that she mattered a great deal to him.

"Milady Ophelia," Eedy called from a door down the hallway. "It's Lady Lindsey, she ails."

"What now?" Philly sighed. "Stay here, lad, and let me know how Marren fares. Remember what I said, once you love it shall be forever."

"I'm beginning to understand that," he said and nodded after her. He closed his eyes and envisioned Marren's smiling face. Keith had to admit what he'd refuted, but to do so would only cause him distress when he couldn't do anything about his love for her. His aunt had lived a life of pining for a man she loved, would he do the same and pine for Marren for all his days?

Although he was concerned for Lindsey, Marren's situation was grave. Keith was disheartened at Winddodger's temperament of late. Something needed to be done about his horse. Winddodger was a danger to his clansmen and women. His next thought brought further dismay. His horse might need to be put down unless he figured out what troubled him. Perhaps he didn't care for the mares but only wanted freedom or to run with the wind. He'd have to ask Emmett for his view of the matter.

Chapter Sixteen

Throughout the night, Keith stood in his chamber and paced alongside the bed, to the door, and back again. Marren hadn't stirred once. As the hours passed, he grew more pensive about her condition. Her face had drained of its color and her lips decreased in hue. She appeared gravely ill and at death's door. The agonizing sight of her stiffened his shoulders and tensed his chest. He'd never felt so tormented.

"Why won't she awaken?" Keith finally tired and sat beside the bed, solemn, and full of dread.

Trulee hadn't left Marren's bedside and leaned against the wood of the window casement. "The healer says there's no reason she doesn't wake. Her bump is not severe and she stitched her wound. She has bruises on her body, and the healer says she broke two rib bones which is the cause of her breathing difficulty. She wrapped her tightly so it will be uncomfortable for her when she awakens. Marren will heal."

"Where is the healer, I want to question her?" Keith waited for the healer to tell him of Marren's injuries, but the woman was in great need.

"After she looks over Lindsey, she'll return and leave

medicinals." Trulee rattled off the list of injuries the healer had told her Marren endured.

He almost wept as Trulee continued to name her injuries. Marren's face was scraped and the bruises turned dark with a tinge of blue. A lump formed in his throat at the thought of her suffering. He held himself culpable because it was his horse that caused her wounds. Anger pressed him too that she'd senselessly neared the corral. What was wrong with the lass? She wasn't dimwitted and he'd told her about his horse's surly nature of late. Then he derided himself because it wasn't Marren's fault his horse had gone mad.

"You care for her, do you not?" Trulee sidled next to the bed and sat on a stool.

"Of course I do. I have known her most of my life."

"It's more than knowing that brings you dismay. You love her. I noticed it right off, the way you look at her. When she's in the same room as you, you look at no other with such affection."

He remained silent during her reflection.

She reached across Marren's body and took his hand. "You never intended to take one of us for your wife, did you? And you delay telling your aunt."

He glanced up at the lass and gave a slight nod.

"My cousin is a fortunate woman, to have a man who loves her." She released his hand and took a cloth from a bowl that sat near. Trulee gently pressed it on Marren's face. "I deem she cares for you as well."

"If she dies…"

"She won't."

"How do you know that? Her breathing is shallow and she barely takes a breath."

"Marren is a Macleod and we are fighters. She will survive this. Have faith."

But Keith didn't have faith. He willed Marren to open her eyes and to glare at him with her bonny blue eyes, but her dark lashes remained still. "Has she spoken of me to you?" he asked and hoped Trulee could give him insight as to what

Marren thought of him.

"Nay, but we only recently met and she hasn't confided in me. She asked me questions about my home and my da. She has memories of when her parents were alive. I cannot fathom why my da sent her away. What would cause him to make her leave when she was just a wee lass and no danger to anyone?"

Keith took Marren's hand in his. More questions needed answers before he confronted Laird Mackay about Marren and how she came to be his ward. But then he thought of someone who might be able to shed light on the matter.

"You should go, Laird, and get something to eat. I will stay with her until you return. The moment she awakens, I'll have you fetched."

He hesitated to leave her, but as laird, he was expected to do his duty regardless of his want. "Very well, lass, but I want to be notified the moment she comes to." Keith left his chamber and ambled down the stairs in a daze. He strolled toward the stables tense and dismayed, but he needed to speak to Emmett. As he neared, he gazed at the broken wood of the corral and scowled fiercely at the damage. His beast of a horse had destroyed it.

Emmett sauntered through the stable entrance and stopped short when he noticed him. He held the reins of a horse and sidled next to him. "Laird, how is Milady Marren?"

"She hasn't awakened."

"I blame myself," Emmett said woefully. "I should've kept watch over the horse because I suspected he was ornery. It's my fault she was injured."

Keith set his hand on his shoulder. "Nay, it's mine. I should've seen to Winddodger and made certain he was kept away from everyone. Has he been found?"

"Marc said he barreled through the gate and galloped into the woods. Aulay has sent the sentry in search of him."

"Mayhap it's best we leave him be for now."

"Och he's your warhorse," Emmett said astoundingly.

"No longer, Emmett, because I cannot rely on him when

I'm in battle. I'll get another horse." Keith sighed because it had taken him months to gain Winddodger's trust. Once the horse trusted him, training came easier. There hadn't been an issue with the horse until now.

"Aulay said not to worry about the soldiers or the keep. He has all in hand."

"I should seek him out and get his report."

"Is there another reason you came by?"

"I thought to…never mind." Keith shook his head. He couldn't leave the keep, at least until Marren awakened and he was assured she would be well. "I need to pay the Sinclairs a visit, but must wait."

"Do you want me to go in your stead? I can take a message or send one of the stable lads."

"I must go in person." Keith turned and headed back to the keep. He had hoped to visit his comrade's keep for several reasons, namely to question Chester Mackay about his brother's involvement with Marren, and for another, to see his longtime friend. He hadn't yet wished him felicitations on the birth of his son.

When he entered the keep, Philly called to him. She sat alone at the table. "Come, lad, you should try to eat something."

"I'm not hungry."

"I understand you're upset about Marren's injuries and that you hold guilt because your horse caused it. The lass should be of no concern to you. She's my responsibility and I shall make certain she's cared for. You should be more concerned with your courtship. And the poor lass, Caroline, has been weeping all day. She says you didn't even try the food she'd made for you."

His throat tightened at the thought of it. "If you could've seen what she prepared, you wouldn't have eaten it either."

"You should have appeased her and at least tried her food. Now she won't cease weeping and there's nothing more disturbing than a sobbing lass. Lindsey is still bedridden and the healer says she too was poisoned, the same as the other lasses. What is going on, Keith? I like not these disturbances or peril within our home."

"That's a good question, Philly. Does the healer say what the poison might be?"

She rose. "Walk with me to the solarium. I need to ease myself and I find solace there."

He allowed her to take his arm and he led her to the gardens. There, his aunt strolled along the plants and removed some of the dead leaves.

"Spring is almost gone. This is usually my favorite time of year. It's when all is renewed and fresh sprouts give the promise of beauty." She plucked a bloom from a bush. "I should save this for Marren. She'd love it for her scents."

The mention of Marren's scents furrowed his brows. He'd forgotten she made scents. "You didn't answer me, Aunt. Does the healer have a notion of what poisoned the lasses?"

"She deems it might be something they were exposed to." Philly continued to tend to her plants and disregarded him.

"So it wasn't something they ate?"

Philly shook her head. "That's highly unlikely. Perhaps it was the soap they use."

"But they don't all use the same soap."

"Nay, they do not. What about the scents you gave them? Do you think that might be the cause? Perhaps they reacted to it."

Keith narrowed his eyes as he glimpsed Marren's table. *The scents.* His suspicion that Marren had something to do with the lasses poisoning sunk his shoulders. He wouldn't believe her responsible. There had to be a reasonable explanation, but it was plausible that the scents he'd given to the lasses caused their malady.

He stared ahead and thought of who had come down with the poisoning. Robina and Iona, both of whom he'd given a jar to. Then there was Eedy, but she hadn't come down with the malady. Then he recalled he hadn't given her a jar because she'd fallen from her horse and he'd been called away. Lindsey, the wearisome lass was the last to be affected, and he'd given a jar to her after their never-ending afternoon of drollery at the games. He groaned at the realization that the gift he'd given them was poisoned. But what bothered him more was the fact that Marren made the scents. It was her jars that poisoned the lasses.

"I shall remove the containers of scents immediately."

"That might be a good idea, Philly, and until I figure out the mystery, I won't give out another."

"That might be best. Only Trulee remains. Perhaps on the morrow, you might make time for her." Philly ceased her speech when he shook his head.

"Trulee is acceptable, but alas I doubt she has a care for me." Keith wasn't about to relate his discussion with the lass. She was privy to his feelings about Marren. There was no sense in pursuing her now.

"Does this mean you're through with the courtship?" She grinned with a shine to her eyes. "Might you have a name for me? It's time to make a decision."

"I don't know what it means, but you're right the courtships are at an end. I spoke to Samuel and he is considering allowing me time to search for a wife. This haste…makes it harder for me to settle on a lass when none of them…" He wasn't about to tell her he had no interest in the women she'd selected for him. "The courtship is not going as well as you planned, Philly."

She handed him a yellow flower and smiled lightly. "I'm sorry, lad, about that. I had great hope one of the lasses would suit. Apparently, they do not. I am surprised that Samuel agreed to allow you more time since it was at his behest that you marry at the soonest."

"I will speak to him again and gain his answer and acceptance." Keith thought about what Samuel told him, but he needed to figure out his cryptic comments. What did he mean by *you're wearing the laird's ring*, and *I had hope you'd figure it out*. Did he imply that because he was laird he should stand up to him? Samuel was his elder and he respected the man, not only because he was a great warrior, but he gave good counsel when it was needed. Yet Samuel was correct in that he led the clan. He alone had control over his destiny, not the clan. Now all he had to do was assert himself and demand that his view be acknowledged.

Cassie ran into the solarium and stopped before his aunt. "Oh, Milady, I don't mean to interrupt," she said and bowed, "Marren has awakened and Lady Trulee sent me to fetch you, Laird Sutherland."

Chapter Seventeen

Marren lay still and drew steady breaths. It hurt to breathe and she couldn't fathom how she'd ended up in Keith's bedchamber. She only hoped she hadn't done something she'd regret—like spent the night with him. But she was certain she'd remember if she had. His touches were unforgettable.

Lady Ophelia entered and stood next to Trulee. They fussed over her. Keith came a moment later and appeared concerned. His handsome face was shadowed with a beard and his brows drew together as he peered at her. She didn't like the despair in his eyes. Something dreadful caused it. Marren realized it was she who drew his woe and forlorn manner. She sighed and the breath sent a stitch to her side.

"The healer says you'll recover but it will take time. You cannot move, lass, from that bed. She's wrapped your middle well and good to keep you from hurting yourself further. I shall go and bring you something to eat," Lady Ophelia said. She left her alone with Keith and Trulee.

"You worried me so. I'm sorry, Marren, and I should have warned you not to get close to the corral..." Trulee pressed the bed covering around her.

Keith approached the bedside and set a gentle kiss on her forehead. "You had me worried, too." He turned and glanced at Trulee. "Will you give us a moment?"

She nodded and reached the door. "I shall make certain you're not disturbed." Trulee closed the door quietly behind her.

"Did I drink too much wine again? I feel wretched."

Keith chuckled. "You don't remember what happened?"

She tried to, yet nothing came to mind. Trulee gave her a clue when she'd said she got too close to the corral. Given Keith's remorseful demeanor, she must've instigated his horse, but she didn't recall Winddodger harming her. When she didn't answer, he leaned forward and gently kissed her lips.

"I thought you would… I worried that you wouldn't…" He didn't seem to know what he wanted to say.

Marren took a slow shallow breath and flinched at the pain in her side. "I'm sorry and didn't mean to cause anyone to worry. What happened?"

"My horse trampled you," he said and continued the explanation.

She narrowed her eyes and a vision of his horse flashed in her mind, but she didn't remember falling or hitting the cart or anything that came after.

"I will have him put down as soon as he is found."

Marren gasped and moaned as a pain throbbed in her side. "Oh, Keith, nay, don't do that. He didn't intend to harm me. Winddodger just wanted out of the corral. It's not his fault that I got in his way. You should speak to Trulee. I recall her saying there was something wrong with him before I…ah before I was hurt."

"I'll speak to her, but he's a danger and I must think of my clan's safety. Now, I wish you to stay here in my bedchamber until you are recovered."

She frowned and decided she shouldn't stay. It would bring untold troubles if she did. "But—"

"I won't hear your argument, lass. You need to rest and it's quieter here. Your chamber is occupied. I insist that you recover here."

"Where will you stay?" He certainly couldn't stay in his chamber too.

"I must leave for a time. I'm not sure how long I'll be but I want you to stay here and mend."

She nodded when he gawked at her as if she disagreed, he'd be ireful. "Very well. Where will you go? You won't be gone long, will you?"

"I must visit my comrade Callum and I've put it off because..." He took her hand.

Marren squeezed his fingers. Her head slightly throbbed. "What? What is it, Keith?"

"I feared you'd die and I couldn't bear it. Marren, I need to be truthful."

"Now you're worrying me. What is it that makes you scowl so?" She reached out to touch his face, but he drew back.

"Nothing, lass. I should tell you that Lindsey was also poisoned."

"Oh, nay. Will she be alright?"

"She's recovering and it appears the poison didn't cause her as much discomfort as it had the others. Philly and I discussed the situation and we concluded that... We think the scents I gave the lasses caused their ailment."

"The scents? You believe they reacted to it?" Marren shifted her position and grimaced at the difficult movement. "I could see one reacting, but all?"

"That's my thought exactly. You supply Wynda with scents, do you not?"

His stern gaze disheartened her. Marren tried to keep still because it hurt too much to move, but she wanted to stand to confront him. "What are you implying? Do you deem that I had something to do with poisoning them?"

"What else am I to assume? You make scents and we are involved..."

"Involved?" Marren drew a harsh breath and flinched again. "We are nothing but friends. That you would think that of me makes me ill at ease. How dare you accuse me of such wretchedness?" She growled low in her throat and flashed an ireful glare at him. "Leave me."

"Lass, we need to discuss this—"

"There is nothing to discuss. If you can believe me capable of such foulness or think that I'd ever do something so cruel—"

"I didn't mean that and what I said was wrong. There is more than friendship betwixt us. You cannot deny that. Who else would want the lasses gone?"

"And you reasoned that only I would?" Marren tried to abate the burning tears that gathered in her eyes. "I never expected or wanted to be with you, Keith. Nor would I harm others to try to win your favor. Please, go. I cannot look at you when you deem me so lowly to cause harm to the lasses," her voice rose, "Get out."

Keith reached the end of the bed and turned. His voice hardened as he asked, "Just tell me you had nothing to do with it."

"Nay, I won't tell you that. Think what you want. I care not and as soon as I'm able to leave this bed, you can have your chamber back."

"Marren, I don't want to leave with you being angry. We should—"

"Get out, Keith. I cannot look at you," she shouted and pain stitched her side. Marren wanted to weep and as soon as he left, she'd cry her heart out.

Trulee opened the door and peered inside. "Is everything alright in here? I heard shouting."

Marren gritted her teeth and shot a loathsome glance at Keith. "All is well. Laird Sutherland was just leaving."

"Marren, you're being unreasonable."

"Unreasonable? You accused me of it… Perhaps I am unreasonable, but I would never allege you of doing something so heinous. I wish not to see you ever again."

Keith fisted his hands and paced at the end of the bed. "I shall go then."

"Farewell."

He left and Marren wept quietly. How could he reason she'd hurt anyone? But as she gave his accusation more consideration, she had to agree that the scents Keith gave the lasses might be the cause of their malady. She needed to investigate further, but as she was bedridden it would have to wait.

Lady Ophelia returned with a trencher laden with all sorts of foodstuff. Marren felt sick to her stomach and couldn't eat a bite.

Trulee left but returned in a short time. "The healer left this for your pain. You should drink it, but only take a wee bit. It's potent and shall make you sleep though."

"That's exactly what I need." She hastily took the dram from her and drank a small sip. Marren wanted to sleep and to forget her discord with Keith. Her heart ached and she regretted sending him away with her heated words.

Trulee sat in the chair next to the bedside. "I received a missive from my da. He writes that he shall come in a few weeks. I am certain he means to drag me all over Scotland before he takes me home."

Marren clasped her hand. "Mayhap you'll be saved by a proposal from Keith."

Trulee laughed, but it was more of a snort. She eyed Lady Ophelia across the chamber and leaned close. She whispered, "We both know that is not a possibility."

Chapter Eighteen

Keith ambled through the stables and assessed the horses as he passed the stalls. He needed a sturdy horse for his trek. As he inspected each animal, he didn't find one to his liking until he stopped in front of Aulay's horse. He reached his hand over the wood and petted the warhorse. The bustle and noise of the stables didn't intrude as he reflected on what happened in his bedchamber. He drew a deep sigh and had gone about his discussion in the worst way. Keith hadn't meant to accuse Marren, but he had. He couldn't blame her for being irked with him.

Still, it was a consideration. The lass made scents and sold them to the hawker where he'd purchased the containers from Wynda. He and Marren had grown close since his homecoming and she was privy to the edict of his marriage. He had to be reasonable even though he detested admitting she might have had something to do with the lasses poisoning. But if she didn't poison the lasses with her scents then who did?

Emmett approached and stood next to him. "Laird, what brings you in here?"

"Saddle him," he said and tilted his head at Aulay's horse.

"But that's my brother's horse."

"Aye, and he won't need his horse. Ready him. I'll tell Aulay I'm taking him. Have him readied by the time I return." Keith trotted to the fields and motioned to Aulay who stood on the expanse of grass with several soldiers. But his commander held up a finger for him to wait until he finished his instruction.

Aulay reached the incline and stood next to him. "Are ye here to watch the soldiers? We're doing hand-to-hand combat this morn."

He shook his head. "I must leave this day for a short trek. I'm taking your horse." Keith hadn't meant to be blunt, but there was no sense in sweetening it.

"But I need him. I'm going to head out this night to train a new sentry and we have yet to find your horse."

"Find another mount, Aulay. I'm leaving now."

Aulay stood in front of him and prevented him from going. "So that's it? You're giving up? You are still wearing the ring though. Shouldn't ye leave it behind for...the new laird?"

He muttered a curse. "You got it wrong. The ring is mine and I will never take it off. I am not giving up on anything, Aulay. I am going to the Sinclairs for a short visitation and will return. I won't be gone long."

"Och, then aye, Laird, take my horse. Is there a reason you're running away...even for a short time?" Aulay bellowed a laugh.

"I'm not running."

"You fool no one, Laird. Safe travels to ye then. Oh and you might want to take Vinn with you, and Dain too. The lad grumbles and complains that you give him nothing to do. Mayhap time away from the keep will do them both good. Vinn is irked that I won't let him take to arms because you forbade him from doing his duty. I'm not saying you should permit him to train with arms again. He still heals and needs to rest his leg for a time."

"Send someone to fetch them and have them meet me at the stables." Keith set off and returned to the stables. He found Aulay's horse ready and waiting. Within minutes, Vinn and Dain came. They headed out on the trail to the Sinclair holding in the late afternoon.

The journey took them a little more than a day. Keith tried not to revisit his conversation with Marren but failed. He never should have accused her of such treachery. The lass was sweet and wasn't one to be mean-spirited toward others. He'd made a grave mistake and couldn't think of a way to remedy it.

As they approached the Sinclair gatehouse, he tried to recall the last time he'd been there. It was the day Callum married Violet. What a festive time they had. He envied his comrade. Although, before he married Violet, Callum's life was full of disorder and torment. Keith was pleased all had settled and peace came to the Sinclairs. If only he could attain such. But peace wouldn't prevail until he married one of the lasses or found a way to refute Marren's betrothal.

The watch, a lad named Peter, grinned and waved him onward.

Keith dismounted and handed the reins of his horse to Dain. "See him settled."

Vinn greeted some of the Sinclair soldiers and strolled off.

Keith left and ambled toward the keep. Callum's home was comfortable and the ambiance full of a woman's touch. He searched the great hall and found Callum sitting in the lone chair by the hearth. The hearth sat dark with the weather warm enough to forgo a fire. His comrade pressed a finger against his lips to signal him to be quiet. In Callum's arms lay his bairn who slept soundlessly against his chest.

Keith kept his voice low when he asked, "Is Chester Mackay here?"

Callum nodded and pointed to the door.

He retreated and found a man outside who directed him

to the smith's cottage. Eric, the smith, often entertained Chester when he visited. Inside the smith's hut, several fires lit, and the bellows were in full use by the apprentices. The lads tirelessly struck the forge and made an array of objects. Keith considered purchasing a well-made dagger for Bain before he left. It would do well as a gift when he announced the lad's fostering in arms.

Chester sat in the makeshift office. There was a full jug of brew on the table. They sat back with their feet propped up as though they had nothing else to occupy their time.

"Do you have another cup? I could use a drink."

"Well now, seems ye changed your mind and decided to visit." Chester leaned back and snatched an unused cup from a shelf. He poured a wee bit of brew and tried to hand it to him.

"I said I needed a drink, not a sip." His glare induced Chester to fill his cup to the rim.

"What brings ye here? You finally came to see the wee Sinclair? He's a handsome lad."

"I saw Callum but didn't get much of a view of his bairn. He was sleeping."

Eric grinned. "He's a fussy one and has as much angst as his da."

Keith laughed. "I also came to see you." He nodded to Chester.

Chester grunted. "I just saw ye a few days ago in the woods. What's so important to bring ye here to see me?"

Keith took another gulp of brew and eased at the good burn that came to his chest. He nodded to Eric and gave the signal that he wanted privacy.

"I should check on the lad's progress," Eric said when he'd gotten the hint and absconded.

"Something troubles you." Chester eyed him curiously. He set down his empty cup with a bang and Chester refilled it. "It's not like ye to be silent. What troubles you?"

Keith sat back and regarded the man. He didn't know how much Grady had told him about his relations with his da, Chester's brother. He suspected Chester was privy to their discord, but his comrade didn't want pity and hadn't told anyone about his da's mistreatment.

"Lad, you're worrying me. Spit it out. Is it about Grady?"

"Nay, it's not about Grady. Are you aware of your brother's ward?"

Chester's brows rose. "Ah, his ward? There was a lass, supposedly his ward, who stayed at our keep a long time ago…years past. Simon never told me who she was. He said she was the key to our future though. I thought he intended to marry her since his wife died. But the lass was young and not even ten in years, too wee to marry."

"She was sent to my aunt to foster."

Chester nodded. "Aye, my brother couldn't stand the sight of another female in his home and so he bid me to take her to Lady Ophelia to foster."

"Has your brother changed his mind about marrying her? Does he still intend to do so?"

"I see you're troubled by this." Chester seemed to consider his question. "I am uncertain what he plans because Simon has never spoken of her, or what he intended since the day I took her to the Sutherlands. My brother despises women so I doubt he wanted to take her as his wife. Who knows what he plans to do with her. He tells me little and I don't ask questions. I'm rarely there anyhow and traipse about the Highlands."

"Do you think he'd care if she married another?"

Chester chortled. "So that's what this is about? Ye want the lass for yourself?"

"I do, but I don't want to cause Simon Mackay to war with us."

"He might do, but my brother is not in good health these days. I doubt he shall last the year. He's in no condition to marry anyone. If ye want the lass, you shouldn't let my brother stop you from taking what you want. He wouldn't let a war dissuade him from taking a woman if he was inclined to."

"I'll think about it." Keith took the jug, poured, and drank the remaining brew. "This is good and allays me."

"Eric makes the best drink in these parts. Why do ye think I sit this close to the bellows when the weather is hotter than a poke?"

He laughed and returned his cup to the shelf. "I suppose you haven't heard from Grady?"

Chester shook his head. "Nay and it's worrying me to no end. Where could the lad have gone? When I find him I'm going to give his ears a blister and hell for taking off. He should've told me where he was going."

Keith grinned. At least Grady had an uncle who cared for him. "I should return so I can greet Callum properly." He left the smith's domain and entered the castle's hall again and found Callum holding his son in the air.

"Don't get too close. The bairn needs to be changed."

Keith scoffed and held out his hands. "Give him to me."

Callum handed him over quickly and left the table.

He eyed the babe and smiled at the resemblance between father and son. The babe wailed and had the same disposition as his comrade too.

"I need to fetch Violet. She's in the garden with the lasses." He left him alone with the bairn.

Keith rocked him and drew little breath. The bairn needed to be changed, that was certain from the stench that overtook the hall. "What did they name you, I wonder?"

"Clive," Violet said as she entered.

Keith's brows rose at the name they chose for their son. He was surprised they'd named him after Callum's cousin, the man who murdered several Sinclair clansmen. But Clive had done so out of retribution for Callum. He was a noble man even if he'd done the heinous crimes.

At that moment shrieks rang his ears. Callum's daughters ran into the hall and his comrade followed. Keith handed the bairn to Violet and eyed the wee lasses. "Look at you two weeds. You've grown."

"Uncle Keith, you should see me pitch a rock," Dela

said, "Da taught me and I can almost throw it as far as he can."

Cora stood quietly next to her ma. She was a coy lass and sweet. He pressed a hand on her head and smiled. "I've missed you minxes."

Callum placed a kiss on Violet's face. "He needs changing." He turned to the lasses and said, "Go on with your ma now." When the hall emptied, he set a tankard of ale on the table. "Did you find Chester?"

"I did, but he wasn't as helpful as I'd hoped he'd be."

"What's this I hear about you courting six lasses?"

"Make that seven," Keith said and grinned.

Callum spit out the sip of ale he'd taken and coughed. "You're a glutton for punishment, my friend. Seven lasses? No wonder you left your holding and came here."

He smiled at the lightness of his friend's mood. Callum was a completely changed man and appeared well pleased. It gave him hope that he too would find peace and happiness. "You speak the truth."

Callum refilled his drink and took a sip. "So how long do you plan to stay?"

"How long will you let me?" Keith grinned again when his comrade guffawed.

"With seven lasses, I don't blame you for wanting to escape."

"You don't know the half of it. My aunt found the most confounded...far be it for me to insult them, but they don't suit. All but one, that is."

Callum sat back and smiled. "Then the answer is easy. Marry her."

He quickly told him about the clan's edict and his aunt's ploy. Keith also told him about his father's abdication and his travels and Marren's betrothal. "I would marry her if I could, but she's angry with me. I've mucked it badly and I should stay away right now. It's more complicated than I care to admit."

"Love, my friend, always is complicated."

Keith spent a month at the Sinclair holding. He didn't want to return to face Marren's wrath or his aunt's badgering, hell, or Samuel's demands. Why had he mentioned the lasses poisoning or accuse Marren of causing it? He had no proof of her guilt. And now Marren probably wouldn't forgive him. He couldn't bear to see her angry eyes. As each day passed, he wondered how she fared and if she'd healed. Lord, he missed her.

There was also his aunt's disgruntlement to deal with when he returned. Surely she was also wrath with him for leaving the holding when he'd promised to court the lasses. He hadn't told Philly that he was leaving but he hoped Aulay told her. And what of the lasses? Had they also left? He should have been there for their departure. They'd come to the Sutherland keep for him and he'd left without giving thought to their feelings. The least he could've done was to thank them and be considerate.

For days, he spent his time with Chester drinking Eric's brew. Chester hadn't revealed more about his brother's ward, and his hope to sway Simon Mackay to release Marren from their betrothal was a futile effort.

Callum shouted for him from outside the smith's hut. "I knew I'd find you here. There's someone at the gate for you."

"Who?"

"What am I, your messenger? Go to the gate and find out." Callum walked with him but remained closed-mouthed on who had come.

When they reached the iron postern, Peter raised it.

Keith walked through and found Emmett and Aulay on the other side.

"Laird," Aulay said with a bite to his tone.

"What are you doing here?"

His commander stepped forward. "Lady Ophelia sent us. She said to bring ye home even if we have to tie you to your horse to do so."

Emmett chuckled at his brother's speech. "I came to assist."

Callum laughed. "If you need help, lads, I got a good rope."

Keith glared at him.

Callum shrugged his shoulders. "What? You know well that you're hiding here. It's time to face the music and her."

Aulay's face was staid and he didn't find their discussion humorous in the least. "You shirk your duty as our laird and Samuel said if you don't wish to return, you're to hand over the ring." He held out his hand. "I shall return it to him until another laird is named."

Keith grimaced. "I mean to return. Stand down, Aulay." He motioned to Dain. "Ready my horse and find Vinn. We'll leave at the soonest since I have no choice but to return."

Emmett stood aside with a big smile on his face. "Are ye going to ask about her, Laird?"

"I'll do so if only to appease you. How is my aunt? Is she wrath with me?" Keith grinned because he knew who Emmett referred to but he wouldn't entertain him.

"Your aunt has faith that you'll return and she is not irked by your absence," Aulay said, "But she says it is time for you to come and get back to your duties."

Emmett drew him with a press to his shoulder. "She's not the *her* I meant, Laird."

His sigh raised his shoulders. "Very well, Emmett, I'll bite. How is Marren?"

All stood about, even Callum, who was more interested in the conversation than he should be.

"She left your bed."

Callum's brows rose. "Your bed, Keith? What the hell was she doing in your bed?"

Keith wouldn't let his comrade bait him, but to his stable master, he said, "And?"

Emmett continued the telling, "She's her old self and heals well. All keep their distance though because whenever you're mentioned, she cries."

His shoulders slumped. "She cries?"

"Aye, a more sorrowful sigh I've never seen. She walks around with a sad look on her bonny face. Even the lasses have tried to squelch her melancholy, but fail."

"The lasses are still there?"

Aulay scowled. "Your aunt won't let them leave."

Keith pressed his eyes to allay the tension that throbbed in his head.

Emmett groaned and shoved his shoulder. "What are ye going to do about it?"

"About what?" He took the reins from Dain and frowned at his stable master.

"About milady's distress? The way I see it, Laird, you caused her grief and now ye must fix it."

"I would if I knew how."

Callum bellowed with laughter. "Well, this is certainly a quandary I never thought you'd find yourself in. Go home, my friend, and cease dragging your feet. You have a lass to woo and a wedding to plan."

"It'll take more than wooing to get her to forgive me."

The men laughed and seemed to enjoy his discomfort. But he agreed. Nothing would stop him from loving Marren. He had to woo and win her heart…somehow.

Chapter Nineteen

Keith was lost in his despair on the ride home. He'd sent his clansmen ahead and took his time on the trek. He needed time to ponder what he'd say to Marren and he didn't need his friends' banter or distraction. Behind him, Vinn rode with Dain and hadn't intruded on his thoughts. He hadn't come up with anything plausible to say to her. Marren was honorable and wouldn't hurt anyone, least of all the lasses. She'd gone out of her way to aid him and had befriended some of the women even though he suspected it must've been difficult for her to do so. Keith had been a fool to even suggest she had anything to do with their ailment. But how could he make amends?

An hour before he reached the gate, a fury of early summer rain came heavy upon them and flooded the travel paths and lanes. He didn't mind the rain so much and was used to being soaked through with the typical seasonal weather. The dismal effect of the day didn't wear on him and he felt remarkably alert. The closer he got to Sutherland land, the more he realized he couldn't live without Marren. Somehow he would make her understand that.

At the gate, he dismounted and handed the reins to Dain. "Settle my horse." To Vinn, he said, "You'll both report to Aulay and you will look after the lad. Ensure he trains with the younger soldiers. You have my permission to train with arms." He had yet to figure out what to do with the lad and had no need of a squire or even a man to look after his possessions. But the lad pressed him for something to do. He'd forgotten to ask Callum's smith for a blade, but he'd find one amongst his possessions to give the lad.

Vinn compelled Dain onward with a shove to his shoulders. "Aye, Laird, do not worry about the lad, I'll take care of him. I'll have him strengthen his muscle before I allow him to use weaponry."

"Keith, you're back."

He gave a quick glance and nod to Marc. "How goes the keep? All is well?"

"It is. Why wouldn't it be?"

As he walked toward the castle, Aulay approached and walked with them. Neither he nor Marc spoke a word. Something had their tongues mute. They wore disgruntled frowns and hardened faces.

Keith continued on his way. "Your report, Aulay?"

His commander broke into a litany of everyday mundane topics from how many sheep they now had, to the planting of the crops, to the injuries sustained by the soldiers. All was a muddle in his mind. Being home tensed him beyond and he barely listened to his commander's chatter.

Keith stopped him and regarded him for a moment. Aulay didn't mention Marren and that had given him concern. "That's all?" he asked in regard to the report. "What about my aunt and the lasses? They fare well?"

Marc bellowed a laugh. "You know what he's asking, Aulay. Best put him out of his misery and tell him."

Aulay peered ahead when he answered, "If he wants to know about her, he should find out on his own. It's not my place to tell him..."

"What in bloody hell does that mean?" Keith stuck his

arm out to keep his commander from proceeding ahead. "Tell me what?"

"What's that noise?" Aulay shot his gaze toward the keep and trotted off.

He and Marc quickly followed. Keith pressed through the crowd gathered at the edge of the courtyard and stopped short. The sight before him rendered him speechless and astounded.

Marc grinned. "Well, will ye look at that?"

Aulay chuckled. "There's nothing more pleasing on the eyes than two women brawling. Och but in a mud puddle no less?"

Keith glared at Lindsey and Caroline who were covered with mud. The puddle was deep and wide and just outside the keep's entrance. The women continued to fight and pulled hair, slapped, and rolled around. Their grunts and shrieks urged on the onlookers, as well as the effect the rain and mud had on their garments. The material covered their bodies and gave all indication of the size of their womanly features. The men hooted, cheered, and jeered at the entertainment.

Emmett approached and grinned when Caroline took a fist full of Lindsey's hair and shoved her face in the mud. The lass gasped and flailed her arms.

"Will you three cease standing there? Break them apart and get them inside." Keith wasn't at all impressed with their row, but he wasn't about to get near them.

Emmett pouted. "But I didn't get to place my wager yet."

Keith glared to get them to follow his order. They broke up the fight and separated the women. Both lasses shouted at each other and he couldn't make out what their row was about. He could guess, but wouldn't. Their yelling was muted by the fanfare of the men standing about.

His aunt stood on the step of the keep and scowled with a shake to her head until she spotted him. To the lasses, she said, "Get inside and clean yourselves. When you are finished, come to me in the garden and we will have a word about your behavior this day."

The lasses appeared contrite for their debauched display and hurried away.

Philly waved him forward. "You have returned."

"I have."

The crowd dissipated and all left him except his comrades.

"We need to talk."

"Aye, we do," he replied.

"But there's no time now. I must meet those lasses and give them my disapproval. Lady Eedy is leaving us in a few minutes. I have asked Aulay to have five soldiers escort her home. She will not await her father's men and insisted upon a proper escort." Philly stepped aside as the woman paraded through the exit of the keep.

"Lady Eedy," he said and bowed his head.

She growled low and stood next to him. "You are a knave, Laird Sutherland. Aye for calling me such, and for leaving me here with those wretched lasses."

"I apologize, Milady."

"It's obvious you don't intend to ask for my hand."

"Nay, I do not," Keith said.

She growled again and started to walk away with vigorous steps when he called to her. Eedy stopped and turned to face him.

"Eedy, I'm sorry you came here and…that we didn't suit. If you're hoping to marry a laird, you might want to seek Kieran Mackenzie. I hear he's looking for a wife."

Her growl went from low to a shriek. She turned and marched onward when a cart, driven by a farmer passed and the wheels hit the puddle. A large splash covered almost the entirety of Eedy's garments.

She gasped and muttered. "I detest this place and you, Laird Sutherland."

His soldiers stepped forward to offer their assistance. Keith was gladdened by the lass's departure. She was a haughty woman and one he certainly wouldn't marry. He imagined his life being a living hell if he'd wed her.

"Why'd ye tell her about the Mackenzie?" Aulay asked.

Keith grinned. "They deserve each other. Besides, if I can cause him a wee bit of trouble, it's the least I can do to suggest she consider him for a husband."

Emmett snorted. "They might suit, Laird, but did ye think that instead of facing one enemy, you'll now face two? Together they'd be a force. Seems she's mightily peeved with ye. She'd probably insist the Mackenzie bring her your head."

"Bollocks, I didn't think of that."

"Laird?"

Keith turned and found Samuel standing behind him. The elder man wore a harsh gaze on his face. He appeared disgruntled. The time to face him drew near, and as much as he didn't want to upset the man, he needed to stand up for himself. Samuel wouldn't like what he had to say on the subject of the chiefdom, his intended bride, or about the clan. But Keith wasn't about to back down. The discussion had been delayed long enough.

"I need a word and it cannot wait."

He nodded and motioned for the elder man to enter the keep. "Then let's get out of this rain."

Aulay and Emmett rushed forward to assist Samuel, but the man flapped his arms. "The day I need your help is the day I'm lowered into my grave."

His comrades retreated with looks of affront. Keith almost laughed at the surly nature of his clansman, but he resisted and followed Samuel inside.

At the table, Keith removed the wet tartan from his upper body and bid Samuel to sit. The man shook his head in decline and the dampened wisps of his white hair shook in the breeze of his movement. He continued to glare at him and the moment was more awkward than Keith gave credit to. Keith wouldn't own to be fearful of the man, but he was his elder and he sorely hoped to win his approval.

"I came for the name of your bride or the return of the laird's ring. Which will it be, lad?"

Keith strolled to the side table and hoped there was a strong drink available. Nothing sat on the buttery though and he was disappointed. The conversation he would have with the man was cause for a strong drink, one that would've given him the resolve to speak his peace.

"Your answer?" Samuel prodded him.

He turned to face him. "I had hoped you considered giving me time to find a bride, but I see that is not so. I will not marry any of the lasses my aunt brought here. I will marry Marren Macleod."

"She wasn't part of the bargain."

"She wasn't, but I don't give a damn. I want her and no other. If that displeases you, Samuel, then I suppose I will have to deal with your displeasure. I will not give you my father's ring either. I am laird and will choose Marren if she'll have me and if not…" he couldn't stand the thought of Marren rejecting him. Somehow he had to win her forgiveness and acceptance. "If she doesn't agree to be my wife, I won't marry at this time."

Samuel glowered but didn't speak.

"I wear this ring and in doing so I rule this clan, the clan does not rule me. That's my decision." He waited for the man's rebuff but Samuel stood there in silence. The standoff didn't last long.

Samuel grunted. "Well, it's about time ye acted like a laird, lad. I never thought you'd take the bait, but it seems you realized your error in dealing with me. If this is your decision then I suppose I must accept it. The ring is deserved and should remain where it belongs." The man ambled away before Keith could retort to his approval.

Keith drew a sigh of relief at his elder's acceptance. Had that been Samuel's goal since he'd been named laird? For Keith to stand up for what he believed instead of letting his elders make demands of him? His lesson spurred a renewed faith in his ability to lead his clan and to win Marren's hand. He wouldn't fail in either quest. He left the hall without a word to anyone and went in search of Marren.

Chapter Twenty

The sound of the rain hitting the loch soothed her. Marren loved to sit by the water on a rainy day. Most detested the foul weather, but the sound and beauty of it eased her. She'd heard Keith had returned and she wasn't ready to see him. Countless times she'd gone over in her head their last encounter, what she could remember of it. Her words had been harsh and she regretted yelling at him. She was still irate that he accused her of such treachery, but she missed him.

Marren sat upon a rock and held her hand out to catch the raindrops in her palm. The rain came heavy and she was soaked through. Something caught the side of her eye and she turned to see Keith's approach. For a moment, her breath ceased. He looked handsome but tired. Concern riddled his brows and he wore a most serious expression. His face had a sparse amount of whiskers, but she could tell by the set of his mouth that he was dismayed by something.

"It's you."

"Aye, it's me. I looked everywhere for you."

She kept her gaze on the water because it hurt too much to look at him. "You found me."

"Can I join you?"

He didn't wait for her reply and sat next to her. She was forced to move aside to give him room and he practically touched her body with his. "Why are you here?"

He took the locks of her hair and set them behind her back. His hand gently caressed her shoulder, but he kept his gaze on the water as she had. "You're still angry?"

"You accused me of the foulest deed."

Keith took her hand and rubbed his thumb over her knuckles. "I was a fool to think…that you had anything to do with the lasses' poisoning. There is no one with a gentler heart than you. I was confused and tried to reason why—"

"Don't you have lasses that await your courting?" Marren pulled her hand free and tried to abate the woe that tightened her chest.

"They're gone. Well, Eedy left, and the others will leave later this day. I will speak to them before they go, except for Trulee who awaits her da. She and I don't suit."

"How wretched for you. Will you lose the position of laird?"

"I told Samuel I wouldn't wed any of the lasses my aunt foisted on me."

Marren peered at her lap. "You say that because they left and you've been abandoned."

Keith stretched his legs out and appeared as if he would stay put. Marren was fast losing her composure. She couldn't be so near to him without wanting to kiss him or embracing him. With all her heart, she wanted to forgive him.

"I told him that before the lasses left."

"Well then, I suppose that's settled."

"I still plan to marry."

Tears threatened to fill her eyes to the brim. She couldn't listen to his awful plans and rose to stand by the loch's bank. To abscond now, he'd think her cowardly and she wouldn't allow him to think so lowly of her.

"Marren, I—"

She wouldn't face him or allow him to continue. "I wish

you well, Keith. There's nothing more to say and I don't want to cause you further trouble. It wasn't my intention to come between you and the lasses and I'm sorry if I did. I should return to the keep." Marren turned and bumped into his hard body. He stood directly behind her. His arms embraced her and she had nowhere to go. If she stepped backward she'd end up in the loch, and he prevented her from stepping forward.

"Lass, you're the only woman I want to marry."

She peered into his alluring blue eyes and sighed. "You are impossible. This entire situation is impossible."

He lifted her chin and his face neared. She needed to abscond before her heart shattered.

"Not impossible. I'll grant it's complicated but attainable."

"But—"

He set his mouth on hers. His kiss evoked her passion. Marren put her arms around his neck and held him tightly. Keith kept his mouth against hers and his hands persuaded her to return the kiss. When his lips moved to her neck, she drew a light breath. He ignited a yearning she thought was long gone or at least she'd hoped had abated. Marren smoothed her hands over his muscular chest and moaned softly at the desire building within her.

"Lass, what you do to me…" His lips moved over her skin and his hands caressed her body.

Marren wanted him, but not just for a moment of pleasure. She pulled away. "I cannot do this."

He kept hold of her waist. "If you're still angry…"

"Nay, it's not that. It's you…if we cannot be together this means naught—"

"I love you."

Tears sprang to her eyes. Emotion clogged her throat and her voice lowered to barely a whisper, "You say that because—"

"Because it is the truth, Marren. I love you. I have always loved you. The happiest moments of my life are the times I spent with you even when we were wee and troublesome."

"But—"

He pressed his finger on her lips and smiled. "I don't want to lose you, not now or ever. Even as a wee lass you tormented me and no one has caused me more trouble than you."

"That's not how I remember it. You pulled my hair and tripped me."

"Aye, how else could I get your attention? Marren, I do not say I love you because I want your body or because I find you appealing. I say it because no other woman makes me feel like you do."

"I want to be with you, but we cannot." She caressed his face and gazed at him. His words affected her, but she wouldn't allow him to hurt her again. "I am promised to another."

Keith pulled her against him and kept her in his embrace. He leaned his chin on the top of her head and sighed. "You might be promised to another, but that doesn't mean you need to keep a vow made by another. Refute the betrothal."

"What are you saying?"

"Marry me."

She pulled back in awe of his declaration. "I cannot, can I?"

He held her face tenderly and his expression most staid. "Why can't you? Do you love me?"

She stared at him in wonder of how to answer. "Aye, I always have."

"Then it's simple, lass. Marry me. Together we will face the consequences. But nothing, not even the Mackays declaring war against us will stop me from being with you." He pressed a light kiss on her forehead. "Say it, Marren, and tell me what I want to hear."

"I love you too."

He lifted her in his arms and kissed her passionately. She tightened her hold on him and returned his fervor. Keith set her on her feet. He glided his hands on the fabric of her overdress and bared her shoulder. Marren helped him to remove his tartan and tunic and pressed her hands over the confines of his bared muscular chest. She couldn't take her eyes from his. He was about to help her remove her gown when she spotted a glint from the other side of the loch.

"Someone is there."

Keith turned and glowered at the trees. "It's just Aulay, Emmett, and Marc. They have nothing better to do than to annoy me." He clasped her hand and grinned when Aulay shouted.

"It's about bloody time, Laird."

Marc whistled.

Emmett made childish whooping calls.

"Be gone, all of you. Get back to your duties."

The brush shook as they retreated.

"We're alone now." He removed her gown and kissed her shoulder. "You're lovely and pleasing to look at. How I've missed you, lass." Keith continued kissing her body and reignited her passion.

The rain fell heavier and drowned out any sound but that of it hitting the loch. Droplets wet their bodies as they caressed and kissed.

"Don't make me wait." She was eager to join with him again.

"I won't, lass." Keith tugged her hand and he sat upon the rock.

Marren straddled his hips and sat upon his lap. She clasped his shoulders and he lured her desire with his lustful touches. She writhed against him and thought she'd scream if he didn't take her. He lifted her thighs and she pressed onward until he found his way. The movement of his body nearly shattered her. She focused on his thrusts and was awed by the sensations until all clashed her heart. A mindless aura swept over her and she called his name repeatedly. He couldn't save her from the overwhelming peril of losing herself.

Keith moaned and set his head against hers. "I love

watching you succumb. Aye, it's a bonny sight." He pressed his hands on her face and pulled her forward for a gentle kiss.

The ecstasy abated but still, Marren felt the twinges between her legs. He thrust and caused her to gasp. The sensation built again and she held on for dear life as their bodies dueled for dominance.

Keith's arms shook, but he continued to help her maintain her position and held her thighs. He moaned and kissed her as he propelled her body. When he released her mouth, he growled and closed his eyes. His culmination spurred hers and she joined him in the surrender of their desire.

Marren kept moving as he lost himself. The pleasurable twinges subsided and she placed her head on his chest. His heartbeat clashed and his breath rasped. Loving Keith was astounding and burst her heart with love for him.

They lay lethargically on the rock, and both listened to the sound of the rain. How magical the moment was. She touched his face to get him to look at her. "I will marry you, Keith Sutherland, and to hell with my betrothal."

"I will force Laird Mackay to agree to our marriage. His son is my good comrade and I'm certain there is some way to remedy the situation. But no matter what, Marren, we will be together." Keith leaned forward and kissed her gently.

Chapter Twenty-One

Morning light shone through the window casement in a stream of dust. Someone knocked at Keith's bedchamber door several times already, but she ignored it until the banging came heavier and more persistent. Marren awoke and shook Keith, but he grumbled until she pressed his lips with a kiss. He clasped her body with one arm and yanked the covers.

He burrowed them beneath the bedcovers and moaned. "It's too early to arise, my love. I should warn you, I am not pleasant in the morn."

She flashed a sweet grin at him and dislodged the covers. "Tell that to whoever keeps knocking."

"Damn. It's a good thing I locked the door."

Marren giggled low. "You better go; otherwise Lady Ophelia will force the door lock."

He laughed. "You might be right about that." Instead of leaving the bed, he sidled next to her and pressed her back upon the bedding. "I'd rather stay here and kiss you." He pressed a loving kiss on her lips, but another knock came and Lady Ophelia's voice. They shot their gaze at the door.

"Keith, lad, I know you're in there. I shall wait here until you open this door."

He groaned. "She means what she says," he whispered, "I should see what she wants."

"Who are ye talking to? You need to rise. Open the door now."

Marren set her mouth near his ear and whispered, "You cannot let her know I'm in here. I don't want her to see me."

"Ah, in all your naked glory?" He almost laughed aloud, but she pressed her hand on his mouth and shook her head. "Very well, I'll go. Stay abed. I would if I could." Keith threw his legs over the side of the bed and reached for his garments. Once clothed, he pressed another kiss on her lips. "Until later?"

She nodded and was thankful he closed the door before Lady Ophelia could barge inside. Marren wrapped a cover around her body and hastened to the door to listen.

"I haven't seen ye since yesterday, lad. We need to discuss your marriage. All the lasses have gone except for Trulee. Now, what are we going to do? Unless you have decided to offer for Trulee's hand? She would make a fine wife for you and is quite my favorite of the lasses that came. Her father is soon to come and we would do well to offer him a good bride price."

Keith's voice was barely audible through the heavy wood of the door. "I already spoke to Samuel and we agree."

"What have you agreed upon?"

Keith's voice grew farther away and she couldn't hear his reply. He'd told her that he intended to tell his aunt about their forthcoming marriage. Marren grew pensive about it because she didn't know how Lady Ophelia would react. Would she be angry with her? And what would she say about her negating the Mackay's betrothal pact?

Marren hurried to dress and reached her bedchamber. She quickly closed the door behind her and found Trulee inside. She held a pillow on her lap and appeared to be writing in her journal.

"And where did you spend the night? Never mind, I can guess." Trulee smiled widely.

Marren grinned but didn't confirm Trulee's suspicion. "I must dress and head to the village. Would you like to join me?"

"I would, but I promised to spend the morning with Cassie."

She pulled on a freshly laundered gown and yanked on her boots. With the rain the day before, the ground probably was full of puddles. After her morning toiletry, and ensuring the jars of scents were secure in the sack, she left the chamber and was about to take the stairs when Lady Ophelia called to her.

Marren flinched and turned. "Good morn, Milady."

"I had thought to spend the morning in the garden and I would like you to attend me. There's much we need to discuss." Lady Ophelia didn't show discord in her expression and neither smiled nor frowned.

She wondered where Keith had gotten to, but he must've gone about his duties. Marren hoped to speak to him before she met with her lady. She needed to know what he'd told her and how she might gain Lady Ophelia's consent to marry him. "I cannot, Milady, because I need to go to the village. Wynda expected me yesterday and with the rain..."

"Later then?" Lady Ophelia called over her shoulder and left the hall.

She had no time to ask her what she wanted, but she imagined Keith revealed their plan. How would she explain? Marren didn't want her lady to be angry, but until she spoke with her, she wouldn't know her feelings on the matter of their marriage.

Outside, the rain had moved on and the ground dried overnight except for a few puddles in gullies and holes on the lane to the stables. She strolled along and sighed happily at Keith's declaration of love. How could she not forgive him after he'd given his heart to her? Marren felt the same and the thought of spending her life with him was all she'd ever hoped for. They had a few hurdles to overcome before she would allow him to call for Father John though. The first hindrance was Lady Ophelia. Marren wanted her approval and didn't want to cause the lady's displeasure.

She moseyed at a slow pace to the stables, lost in her musings. When she reached the corral, she found Emmett who whistled as he went about his tasks near the water trough.

"Good day, Emmett, I need a horse."

"Ah, Milady... Did you enjoy the loch yesterday?" He beamed at her with a shine in his eyes and retrieved the mare that grazed at the grasses which grew by the corral post. Emmett held on to the reins and patted the mare's neck.

She smiled sweetly, but wouldn't let him bait her. "I did enjoy the day. I'm in a hurry and must get to the village. Wynda awaits me. Will you tie my satchel to the saddle?" She handed him the small sack she'd put her scents in.

Emmett appeased her and hastily did as she asked. "The laird hasn't been here yet this day. I wonder what kept him busy this morn? I imagine he had his hands full?" He raised a brow at her as if he suspected what transpired between her and Keith.

"You will have to ask him." She took the reins from Emmett and walked away. The man was nosey and couldn't keep himself from prying. When she reached the gate, she hurried by Marc, but he stopped her when he shouted her name.

"Milady, where are ye off to? Do you need me to escort you?"

She shook her head and rode through the gate. Marren had been on the lane for almost ten minutes before Keith caught up to her. When he sidled next to her, she smiled and so wanted to touch his face, but he was too far from her.

"Where do you think you're going, lass?" He pulled her from her horse and settled her on his lap. Keith didn't bother to saddle his horse and it gave them room and was comfortable. He enclosed her in his arms and set his face against hers.

"I am off to the village. Wynda awaits me and I have new scents for her."

"Aye and we should ask her about the scents I purchased from her. Mayhap she can explain what caused the lasses' ailments." He reached for her mare's reins and attached them to his horse's bridle. "Let us onward then. I want to see if Jumpin' Joe has heard from Grady."

"You worry about him, your friend?"

"Aye, I do. He's been gone longer than usual. I just hope something didn't happen to him, like him getting himself injured or killed."

"He's a good comrade then for you to be so concerned?"

Keith set his arms around her waist and rode forward. "He's my closest comrade. I have known him since we were lads and I trust him more than anyone."

"I hope he turns up soon."

"I hope so too. Grady is Laird Mackay's son, and I had hoped he might tell me about Simon's intention. But he's probably unaware of his father's plans since Grady hasn't been home in years. Do you recall him from when you were there?"

She shook her head. "I was quite young when I last stayed there. Laird Mackay sent me here to foster with Philly and I was only about eight or so in years. I don't remember the laird's son."

"Surely you met him here. He came home with me often."

Marren clasped his hand and smiled at the roughness of his hands. "You never introduced me to him. I'm certain I would remember if you had."

Keith flashed a grin. "There's a reason for that. You were too bonny and I wasn't about to let Grady see you."

She laughed at his jest. "I shall meet him then when he comes for a visit. And there is no reason to be jealous because my heart belongs to you."

"You say that now," he said and bellowed when she

elbowed his side.

They reached the village and stabled the horses at the hostler. Marren stood beside Keith as he handed her the satchel she'd attached to her horse.

"Oh nay, there's Father John. I cannot see him now. I cannot make my confession, not after what we did… He'll make my penance hell."

Keith pulled her in his arms and kissed her passionately. He pressed her against the stable wall and hid her from the priest's view. When he pulled back, Father John was gone. He laughed outright. "There, lass, I saved you from the priest's chastise."

"We're fortunate he didn't burn our ears with a harsh lecture for kissing in public."

He grinned. "Father John knows better than to lecture me." Keith laughed when she pinched him. "His sermon falls on deaf ears."

"You must be a tenacious sinner. Go on then and search for Grady. I shall be at Wynda's and will await you there."

He squeezed her hand in parting and walked toward the inn/tavern.

Marren entered Wynda's shop but she wasn't in the main room. She called for her but didn't hear a response. As she perused the shelves, she stopped at the containers of scents. Two of hers were gone which she took as sold. Next to the scents she made were other jars. They appeared to be the same as those Keith had given to the lasses and were brown, but they weren't hers.

Marren procured her jars from the smith who made them specifically for her. He used brown clay which he tinted red with a layer of lead glaze to the inside which essentially preserved the contents from seeping out.

She picked up a container and undid the wax seal and sniffed it. The scent smelled similar to that which Keith gave to the lasses. There was an odd odor to the liquid and she couldn't for the life of her discern what it was. Was Wynda the culprit behind the poisoning? There was no reason to believe so. What purpose would she have for wanting to poison Keith's lasses? Before she could reason it further, Wynda appeared.

"Oh, Marren, it's you. I didn't hear you enter. Come along, you're welcome. Do you have more scents for me? I had hoped you'd come by." Wynda waved her forward.

"I do. They are in the satchel, there. I'll take this," she said and handed her the opened jar.

"It's not for sale."

"But I already opened it. Let me at least pay you for it." Marren waited for her to hand back the container but Wynda scowled at it.

"I said it's not for sale. I shall get what I owe you. I only sold two of your scents." Wynda eyed the door and appeared nervous.

"If you're busy, I can come back later."

Wynda stood before her and blocked her exit. Marren got a strange sense from her. Something bothered the lass. They weren't necessarily on friendly terms, but Wynda always treated her kindly. There was an air of hostility in her manner which cautioned Marren.

"There are other scents in the back. Let me close up and we shall have a look at them. Perhaps there is something that better suits you." Wynda stopped at the door as if she looked through the small window opening and turned to her a moment later.

Marren shook her head. "I have no time. Keith will be here any second."

"Keith? Laird Sutherland is in the village?"

"He is and shall meet me here in a moment." Marren inched closer to the door.

When Wynda reached the table where she kept the scents, Marren hastened to the door. She pulled at the handle but it was locked. Something whacked her head and her vision blurred for a moment. She held onto the table to keep herself from falling. Wynda grabbed the opened container of scent and poured the entire contents on her.

She gasped and tried not to breathe in the terrible odor. Marren remembered the lasses had trouble breathing and had gotten a rash. Whatever was in that container must have caused their malady. As she was forced to take a breath, her throat seemed to close. Marren wheezed and pressed her hands over her to try to ease the scent from overtaking her.

Wynda grabbed her and forced her toward the back storeroom. Dizziness came and Marren tried to dig her heels in but she was propelled into a darkened room. Wynda closed the door and she heard a click. Marren banged on the door but she wheezed and her eyes watered. There was one thing she knew for certain—Wynda was the culprit behind the lasses poisoning.

She fell to the floor and peered up at the ceiling and tried to remain calm. The small area of the storeroom made the effect of the scent even more potent. It caused her senses to water and her skin to crawl with a strange aura. Wynda had poured more on her than what the lasses had used. Would it be deadly? That thought completely unsettled her and she cried out. Marren continued to bang on the door and called for Wynda until her voice gave out.

As she succumbed to the awful effects of the potion, the only thought that solaced her was that Keith would be there soon. *He will find me.*

Chapter Twenty-Two

Keith entered the tavern but couldn't approach Jumpin' Joe. His comrade was in a heated argument with his brother, Father John. He was surprised to find the Saint inside the tavern because Joe rarely allowed the priest to disturb the patrons. By the look of it, they disagreed on some matter, given the glares they gave each other. He lingered near enough to overhear some of their conversation.

"We must tell him," John said.

"Nay, it cannot be true. You're wrong, brother. There must be a mistake in your records."

John scoffed, but his back was to him and Keith couldn't see his face. "They were never married and there is no record of his birth in our parish. You have to tell him."

Joe frowned. "It won't be me who tells him and ye cannot either. It is not our place and none of our affair. Keep your bloody lips shut on the matter. Besides, what does it matter?"

"It matters a great deal," John said in a shout.

His comrade noticed him and his face brightened. It was almost as though Keith startled him. He wondered who they spoke of and why the priest was so riled.

Keith moseyed forward. "Father...Joe. What's going on? What are you two irked about?"

Joe shook his head at his brother. "Nothing important, nothing that concerns you. My brother was just leaving. Good day, John."

John dipped his chin and his eyes glared as if he wanted to say something. But he averted his attention to his brother. "I mean it, Joe. Someone must tell him and that someone should be you." The priest marched off and left the tavern.

"What was that all about? Why's he so irked? Tell who what?"

Joe took a cloth and dried a tankard and disregarded his questions. "It's none of your affair or mine. My brother would do well to keep his nose from other people's business. Here," he said and poured him a cup of ale. "If you're here looking for Grady again, I haven't seen him."

"His absence concerns me. I might have to go in search of him. It's not like Grady to go off without telling me where he's going or to be gone so long. I fear something happened to him."

Joe guffawed. "Our comrade has always been closed-mouthed about his affairs. Maybe he doesn't want to be found. I tell ye this... Grady left his belongings here. I promised to safeguard his trunks. A man does not leave his wealth behind if he doesn't mean to return. He'll be back."

Grady wouldn't leave his coins behind. He'd amassed a fortune when they'd traveled across the channel. Keith wasn't as confident about Grady's return as Joe was though. His comrade wouldn't leave for such a long period without taking some possessions or a means to support himself. Something was amiss and he sure as hell wanted to know what happened to him.

"I must go. If he returns..."

Joe nodded. "I'll be sure to tell him you're awaiting him."

Keith left the tavern and veered around Father John who stood on the lane. He didn't want to have a confrontation with the priest. He sauntered with quick steps and reached Wynda's shop within seconds. He tried to enter but the door was locked and he knocked.

Wynda hastened to unlock it and opened the door. "Keith, what brings you here? Though I'm gladdened to see you, now is not a good time." She walked with slow steps toward the storeroom and turned. She had a strange look on her face but replaced it with a quick smile.

"Good day, Wynda."

"I hadn't expected you this day. Philly told me that you were to wed. I heard you were courting some women she'd brought to Dunrobin. Have you gone and gotten yourself betrothed?" She neared and set her hand on his shoulder and affectionately squeezed him.

He raised his brows in astound that she was privy to his matters and that she was forthright in touching him. The only people who knew about his forthcoming marriage were the Sutherlands. No one would speak of his private matters to her. Philly certainly wouldn't but he intended to ask her about it when he returned home. Anger forced him to fist his hands, but he took a breath. The lass was just making small talk.

"Who told you about my forthcoming marriage—?"

"Lady Ophelia mentioned it when she was last here. She was excited and told me about the lasses and that you intended to marry. It's a shame it hasn't worked out."

How did she know about his courtship failings? He scrunched his eyes slightly at her falsehood. His aunt hadn't been to the village; at least, he was unaware that she'd gone to see Wynda since his return. Why would his aunt divulge news of his courtship to Wynda? The fact that she knew about his situation perplexed him. But Keith had no time to reason why she was interested in his matters. He peered about the small cottage and was dismayed that Marren had left.

"I was supposed to meet Marren here. Has she come and gone?"

Wynda leaned against the table that displayed the scents

and shook her head. "I haven't seen her this day."

Keith reverted his gaze and saw the pouches of scents Marren was delivering. Something struck him about it. Perhaps Marren left the scents and hadn't seen Wynda.

"Good day then." He ducked under the doorframe and hastily left. Keith walked with spry steps to the hostelry and thought Marren might have decided to meet him there. As he approached, he noticed Marren's mare was still tethered to the pole. She was still in the village. He turned about and ambled back on the lane and sought her, but there was no sign of Marren.

Keith returned to Joe's and sipped on a cup of ale. He considered why Marren would leave without a word to him. Had she walked back to the Sutherland keep? That didn't seem right. The trek was too great a distance for her to walk. Surely she wouldn't go on foot and without him, or at least without letting him know she would leave.

What concerned him more was why Wynda lied to him about Marren being in her shop? The only thing he could think of was that Marren entered the shop and Wynda was perhaps in the storeroom or elsewhere and hadn't seen her. Still, Marren said she would await him and she wasn't one to go back on her word.

"Ye look like you're troubled. If it's about Grady, I wouldn't worry so much. He's a grown man and can take care of himself." Joe took the bench across from him.

"I am concerned about Grady, perhaps more than I should be. But he's my comrade and until he returns it will drive me mad. But that's not what's troubling me right now. I'm worried about Marren. She was supposed to await me at Wynda's but when I got there, she wasn't there." He went on to tell him how the lass lied to him.

Joe tossed the rag he used to wipe the table and motioned to him. "Let's go. We'll start our search for her where ye last saw her. We'll ask Wynda straight out why she lied to you."

Keith walked alongside his comrade and they entered

Wynda's shop. The bell tinkled low and he closed the door. She stood behind a table and mixed a concoction.

"You have returned. What brings you back?"

He stood before her and scowled. "Where is Marren? I know she was here. Those," he said and pointed to the containers Marren had brought, "are the scents she intended to give you."

"I told you she hasn't been here and I haven't seen her."

Keith motioned to Joe to search the cottage and he slunk along the tables. "I know you speak falsely because that's her satchel." He picked up the satchel which only an hour before he'd handed to Marren when they reached the village. "Why would you lie to me, lass?"

As he spoke to Wynda, Joe slunk around the confines of the shop.

"Me lie to you? Why would I care about Marren's whereabouts? I should ask you to leave."

Joe reached a door and turned the handle but it was locked. He lifted a wooden beam that acted as a security measure and frowned at it. "What's in here?"

"Nothing. Stay out of there," Wynda clipped. "It's just a storage room. I want you both to leave now. You have no business here. I need to get back to my mixing."

Keith rushed to the storeroom door but before he reached his comrade, Joe used his shoulder to force the door open. He shouted to him and stood at the threshold. As he neared the doorway, Keith peered inside and saw Marren lying on the floor. She lay in the small space and her eyes were closed. He breathed a sigh of relief when he noticed her bodice rose and fell with her breath. Marren wheezed and a mass of red blotches covered her neck and face. He pressed a hand on her shoulder to try to roust her, but she didn't awaken.

"What happened to her? What did you do?"

Wynda took advantage of their inattention and left the shop. The low tinkle of the bell told them she had absconded.

Joe shot his gaze at the door. "See to Marren. I'll go after

Wynda." He rushed out and left the door open.

Keith lifted Marren in his arms and she opened her eyes. "Be still, lass. You'll be alright. I need to get you out of here and then you'll tell me what happened." He carried her to the inn and as he passed the lane, he spotted Joe. His comrade held Wynda's arms and forced her to the center of the village.

"Is my room occupied?" he asked Joe when he reached him.

"Nay. Take her there and I'll have the healer fetched."

Keith heard Joe's shouts to the villagers, but he hurried to get Marren settled. Inside the small inn room, he placed her on the bed and pressed a hand on her face. "What happened, love?"

"Wynda…she attacked me. Why would she…? I got the sense that she was angry that you and me… But that can't be right, could it? No one knows of our liaison except for your comrades. Are you aware of her fondness for you? I think she was the one who poisoned the lasses at Dunrobin."

"I'm sorry she hurt you, Marren." He pressed a gentle kiss on her head and squeezed her hand. "That lass is maddened if she thinks I'm fond of her. I have never given her a reason to believe I'm interested…"

"I don't think it matters to her. She made some odd comments."

"Rest, my love. Here, drink this," he said and handed her a small cup of water. "The healer should be here soon." Keith didn't like the sound of her breathing which rasped as she drew breath.

A few minutes later, a knock came at the door and he opened it to find the healer, an older man who had grayed on the edges of his hair. "Sir… I think she's been poisoned."

The healer passed him and assessed Marren. "Milady, all will be well. Rest easy and we'll see what we can do to help your breathing and about that rash."

Keith refused to leave her side, but after the man gave Marren a dram of medicinals to counteract the effects of her ailment, she appeared to breathe easier.

"Cease your worry, Keith. I'm alright." She gazed at him with a worrisome look and clasped his hand with assurance.

"I don't want to leave you, but I should find Joe…"

"Go on. I'm well." She released his hand.

"Do you promise?" He leaned his head against hers and sighed. "I can deal with Wynda later if you want me to stay…"

"I promise, Keith, but you should go. I'll rest here until you return." She smiled slightly and closed her eyes.

"I'll return as quickly as I can," he said as he reached the door. Keith marched to where he'd last seen Joe and stepped through the mass of the crowd until he reached his comrade. Wynda's eyes sparkled with anger as the sheriff tied her hands and bid the crowd to quiet.

But the villagers didn't heed him and shouted expletives and threw items at her.

"Joe, what has she told you?"

"She's said nothing."

Keith peered at Wynda. "Why, lass, would you harm Marren? She's your friend."

"She's no friend of mine."

"Why would you poison the lasses at Dunrobin?"

She cast her gaze at the ground and wouldn't look at him. He gripped her face and forced her to. "You will tell us why you did these unlawful things…" Keith released her and stepped back when the sheriff yanked her closer to him.

"Worry not, Milord, I'll see that the lass pays for her ill-deeds." The sheriff pushed back a man who tried to get too close.

Keith glared at her. "I demand an explanation."

"I always loved you. Always." Tears formed in Wynda's eyes.

He frowned at her admission, and his empathy was nonexistent. Keith refused to let her tears sway him. The crowd drew rowdy and demanded the sheriff sentence her.

"You were always kind to me even as children when the others scorned me because my mother was feared. But you never teased me. I love you, Keith. Please, understand... When Lady Ophelia told me that you would take a wife, I had to do something... I couldn't let them have you. You are meant to be with me."

His shoulders tensed at her words. Keith always sympathized with Wynda when they were young because the other lads teased and picked on her. They were unchivalrous. He wouldn't stand for it and had stood up for her many times. But that was years ago when he was a young lad, and he barely remembered speaking more than a handful of words to the lass in recent years.

"You hurt many including Marren. Not only did you try to poison others with your potions, but you also struck and held Marren against her will. You're as deplorable as those who tormented you, Wynda. I cannot even look at you..."

"Don't hate me, Keith."

Silence abounded in the center of the village for all the noise the people had made only moments before. All stood about and stared, mute, and in shock at the lass's deeds and words. The sheriff shouted her list of crimes and Wynda didn't try to defend herself.

Shouts of 'Witch, Sorceress, and Devil's Mistress,' came from the villagers. Some threw objects at her. As much as he detested seeing a woman in such a position, he would do naught to save her. She'd caused her troubles and would now pay for the atrocities.

Keith sighed heavily because there would be no saving the lass. There was naught he could do because she tried to murder the lasses at his keep and had hurt Marren in her outlandish attempt to... He was uncertain about what she had intended. "I don't hate you, but you are—"

Father John took that moment to intercede and pulled him back. "Condemned. Aye, this woman should be condemned for her actions. She tried to murder lasses and hurt Marren Macleod. She's used her black-magic to harm and is a witch." He waved his hand at the crowd to instigate their outrage and gain their support. "What say you, good folks? What should her punishment be: the stocks, imprisonment, or death? She must pay for her crimes. God will not forgive such treachery and sinful behavior."

The villagers shouted their judgment and Keith shook his head at John. He drew him aside and tried to speak with him, but the yells and blasphemies prevented him from trying to reason with the clergyman.

He approached Wynda and shook his head. "What you did was wrong, lass, and you should be banished. Father, she's young and was foolish, but none were gravely injured by her deeds. All recovered from her poisoning. Imprisonment and death seems a bit harsh. Aye, the stocks or banishment would be better served. I'd banish her if she was one of my clan."

Father John nodded. "It is only because she is a woman that we don't hang her in the nearest tree. You, Laird Sutherland, speak the truth. We shall banish her then. As long as she promises not to return to Wick or cause further grief to anyone."

"Keith, please, don't let them send me away…"

"You must go. It's either that or Father John will let the villagers seek their judgment and by the sound of it, you'll be executed. Be appeased that you're only being banished."

"But I love you."

He shook his head. "But I love another."

Chapter Twenty-Three

Marren spent a week recovering from her malady. The itching of her skin nearly drove her mad. She had avoided Keith's aunt and pretended to sleep whenever she came into the bedchamber. Keith visited her in the early evenings and kept busy during the day. Marren had seen little of him, but he assured her that he'd return at the end of the day after he'd tended to his duties.

She dressed and stood by the door. Marren hesitated to leave the chamber. Once she did, she couldn't avoid Lady Ophelia. It was time to face her and explain about her and Keith. She jerked the door open and hastened down the stairs. At the entrance of the great hall, she stood and watched Cassie who faced the hearth. Her dear friend had tried to comfort her, but Marren had too many questions that needed answers before she might explain why she was forlorn.

"Good morn, Marren," Cassie said and still faced the fire. "I was told to have you attend Lady Ophelia in the solarium the moment you came down."

Marren's shoulders slumped. "I suppose I need to meet

with her then."

Before she fled, Cassie approached. "Wait. Will you tell me why you were hiding in the chamber? It's been days and you recovered long ago. What troubles you?"

"It's because of me that the lasses were poisoned."

Cassie scoffed. "You don't believe that. Wynda was maddened. Keith told me what happened in the village. It wasn't your fault."

"I should go see Lady Ophelia." Marren set off to the gardens. At the entrance to the solarium, she stood and watched her lady. She delicately handled a plant she watered.

"Good day, Marren. Join me."

She hurried forward and stood by the table. "You wanted to see me? I have been remiss in handling tasks in the castle and there is no excuse for my idleness except… Well, I am recovered now and I can get back to it. Is there something you need?"

"Aye, lass, there is. How about an answer as to why—"

"He told you, didn't he?"

Lady Ophelia's brows furrowed. "Told me what? Who, Keith? I was going to ask why you haven't made any scents. You haven't been here since your return from the village. It's been over a week. Surely you want to get back to it. You shouldn't let what Wynda did affect your passion to make scents. I know how much you enjoy it."

Marren picked up a flower the lady dropped, a yellow bloom of which she had never seen. "I haven't been inspired. Scents no longer appeal to me."

"I disbelieve you. What a shame to allow what happened to dissuade you from doing what you love to do."

"Perhaps I might get back to it…someday. Is there anything else?" She wanted to leave. The aura in the garden became awkward. Lady Ophelia seemed to hesitate and focused on the arrangement of flowers she was making.

She set down the stem she held and smiled. "As to Keith, he told me about his discussion with Samuel. I'm proud he stands against the edict. He also told me that you agreed to marry him. Have you changed your mind?"

"You're not against our plan to wed then?"

Lady Ophelia smiled and placed a hand on her upper arm. "Who am I to stand in the way of love? When I was a young lass, I loved a man who I hoped to marry. We were thwarted and neither of us fought to follow our hearts. I regretted it, and have every day since. It is my hope he regretted it too. But alas, we were not meant to be together. If you are destined to be with Keith, let nothing stand in your way."

"I don't want to cause the clan to oust him as laird. If they do, it shall be my fault. Keith said Samuel accepted his terms, but I feel there are yet more problems that will come of this. And I certainly hope you are right, Milady, that he and I are destined to be together."

Cassie strolled into the garden and motioned to them. "Lady Ophelia, Trulee's father has arrived and he wishes to see you."

Marren followed them to the hall. She was most interested to meet her uncle. From her memory of him, he wasn't a bad sort. But a child's memory was often flawed. In the hall, she entered and found Trulee by the hearth, where Cassie had stood earlier. She stepped next to her as Laird Macleod spoke to Lady Ophelia.

Trulee wouldn't stand still and her hands shook when she pressed her hair away from her face. Her words came softly, "He means to force me to go with him."

"You mustn't worry so." Marren took her hand and clasped it.

"But he will make me marry someone I don't love."

Marren's heart went out to her friend. "You cannot refuse your father."

"And you cannot refuse your laird."

She realized what Trulee spoke was the truth. Her uncle was her laird and guardian even if he'd betrothed her to the Mackay. Duncan could easily change his mind, but he could also enforce his command that she marry the Mackay. Either way, she had to convince her uncle the best option was Keith.

Duncan approached and stood a few feet from his daughter. "Lass," he said to Trulee, "You're looking well. Lady Ophelia tells me the Sutherland laird hasn't offered for your hand. Tell me this is not true?"

Trulee inclined her head. "Nay, Father, he hasn't offered for me."

"How could he not want you, the fairest lass in the land? Worry not, Daughter, other more worthy men vie for your hand as a wife. We shall leave posthaste, on the morrow at first light. Now, introduce me to your friend. She looks familiar."

Trulee curtseyed and raised her face. "M'laird, this is Marren... Marren Macleod."

Marren gazed at him and regarded his manner. He didn't appear fearsome and his face was somewhat handsome. His hair and eyes reminded her of the bark of an oak tree, not necessarily brown, but perhaps a shade of brownish-gray. She wondered if he resembled her father, but her memory of her papa was clouded.

"Marren Macleod?"

"Good day, Laird Macleod...Uncle." She curtseyed but kept her eyes on him.

"How is it you are...? How have you come to be here at the Sutherland's holding? I distinctly remember, lass, taking you to the—"

She cut him off. "Aye, to the Mackays. I have often wondered why. Why would you send me away from my family?"

He scowled slightly as if he pondered her question. "I had to send you away, but I didn't send ye off to the Mackays. You'll explain why you're here and not where I left ye."

She remembered the first keep she'd been taken to where the frightening man looked at her with loathing. His face was shadowy and she'd never had a name to put to him. "How can I explain when I am uncertain where I was taken?

I was young then and wasn't aware of what was happening and you didn't enlighten me as to why I had to leave my home. If you didn't take me to the Mackays, then where did you send me?"

"You were taken to the island of Donnán, the Mackenzie fief. I made a pact with Laird Mackenzie to align our clans. But why am I explaining this to you? What did you do to cause him to send you to the Mackays?"

"I did nothing. I was but a child." She blocked him from leaving. Marren glanced about the hall and found all watching her including Lady Ophelia and Keith. "I wish, Uncle, that you would explain. If you sent me to the Mackenzies, how did I end up at the Mackay holding?"

"I know not, lass. Mackenzie and I agreed to align our clans through marriage. I offered your hand to a Mackenzie to seal our pact. Obviously, you failed me. Sidheag must've found you unworthy to marry one of his followers. Perhaps he foisted you off to the Mackays."

Emotions threatened to unleash her anger but she wanted answers to questions that long plagued her. "I was sent to the Mackays and had stayed there for a year or so before he sent me here to foster with Lady Ophelia. He has never called me back."

Duncan scowled fiercely. "It matters not to me. If the Mackenzies didn't want you and sent you to the Mackays, it has nothing to do with our pact which I intend to reaffirm. Mackenzie cannot go back on our agreement. I need their support. Our wars with the MacDonalds intensify and I mean to call on him whilst I am here in the area to remind him of our alliance."

A lump the size of an apple formed in her throat and she swallowed hard against the emotions that threatened to abound. "I am your brother's child. Did you not deem that I would need you after my parents perished? That's all I have been to you…a means to gain support for your petty war?"

"Aye, you are my brother's child and since he was gone, I couldn't look at ye. You had to go and what better cause than being the means to our safety. Now that you've botched that, lass, I suppose my daughter will further my efforts with the Mackenzies. I should take you back to Sidheag and force him to marry you to one of his clan, but evidently, they didn't want you. Apparently, neither do the Mackays."

His words stabbed her like a sharpened dagger to her heart. All she'd ever wanted was to be reunited with her family, to be cared for, to be wanted. Marren couldn't put a voice to her wishes and she stared at her uncle with fat tears blurring her vision.

Keith sidled next to her. His expression was fierce with a haze of anger in the depths of the deep blue of his eyes. The stance of his body filled with fury as he fisted his hands. "No one is taking Marren anywhere. You've come to collect your daughter. Do so and be gone."

"Who the hell are you to tell me what to do with my ward?" Duncan stepped toward Keith.

Marren feared they'd come to blows.

"I am the laird of the Sutherlands. My aunt took on the duty to foster Marren Macleod and until Laird Mackay says otherwise, she will remain here."

"I am her guardian, not Mackay," Duncan bellowed.

"You gave up your right to her guardianship when you took her to the Mackenzies and left her there. Now, there is nothing more to say on the matter. You will leave now and are unwelcome."

Marren pressed Keith back with a touch to his shoulder. "Uncle, did you not care at all what happened to me? Did you not care for my father, your own brother? Surely family—"

Duncan held up his hand. "My brother was a weak laird. He allowed the MacDonalds to trounce us at every turn. When his boat went down it was the best thing that happened to our clan. As to family, when a lass is disobedient—"

"How could I be disobedient? I was wee, a mere child, no more than seven when you abandoned me."

"You served your purpose, lass."

His words again disheartened her and wounded her

heart. Marren had been able to resist her tears up till now. All the woe she'd held in over the years suddenly burst forth like a flood. Tears streamed her cheeks. The last thing she wanted was for her uncle to see how much despair he'd caused her.

Marren fled the hall and rushed to the solarium. She paced alongside the overflowing wooden planters whose greenery was usually a solace to her. But the beautiful garden did nothing to ease her discontent. She ambled inside the solarium and stood by her table. Since her return, she hadn't had a passion to make the scents. It wasn't because of what Wynda had done. There was little sense to make the scents if she couldn't sell them in the village. With Wynda being banished, there was no other hawker who sold such items.

"Marren…"

She turned at Keith's call and wiped the last of her tears away. "I couldn't stay in the hall and listen to another word…"

"I understand." He took her in his arms and his stare was full of concern.

"Do you deem he means to take me back to Mackenzie land?"

"It doesn't matter what he means to do. I won't let you go."

"Did you mean what you said about Mackay? That until he calls for me… You intend to send me to him if he does?"

He pressed his hands on the side of her face and raised it until she looked into his eyes. "Love, if you remember, I told you that I wanted no other woman but you. And that even if I had to war with the Mackays, I would make you my wife. Nothing will stop me from being with you."

"Oh, Keith, how I love you."

He kissed her with longing and Marren eased at the dissipating shudders of her sadness. The only thing she now felt was an extreme desire for him. Keith lifted her and set her on the table in front of him. His hands perused her body as his mouth turned over hers. She was completely swept away in the allure of his passion.

Neither heard the man who entered the solarium. He cleared his throat to alert them that he was there. Keith pulled his mouth away from hers and she peered over his shoulder at the man who stood beyond. She'd never seen him before, but he was handsome with short dark hair and winsome blue eyes.

Keith smiled lightly at her and turned to find out who the intruder was. "Grady, where the hell have you been? I worried about you and thought you were in trouble."

Grady kept his position by the entrance. He leaned his shoulder against the threshold. "A better question might be… Why are you kissing my betrothed?"

Chapter Twenty-Four

Keith closed the door to his office, a place he'd avoided since his return home. The small chamber reminded him too much of his father and he felt as if he intruded when he'd entered. But his da was gone and now the only place where he'd be assured privacy was in the small confines of the area where his father had attended to writs. Grady followed him inside and closed the door quietly behind him.

"Before you explain... I will tell you this... Marren and I... We plan to marry. You recall through the years I told you about the lass who stayed here when I was a lad. It was her...Marren. When I returned, I admitted to myself there was more than a rapport between us. I love her, Grady, more than any woman I'd ever met. She needs me and I admit I need her."

Grady's eyes narrowed as he watched him round his desk. "You sound like a besotted lovesick arse. I never thought you'd confess such drivel. Since when have you become mawkish?" He bellowed with laughter.

Keith sat wearily in the chair. The day had gone to hell with Duncan Macleod's arrival and now his good comrade came and proclaimed the absurdity of being betrothed to Marren. Now Grady accused him of being overemotional. Perhaps he was, but he hadn't expected to hear his friend's declaration. When would this hellish day end?

"Do you plan to steal my bride?" his comrade said with what he hoped was feigned outrage.

"You never told me you were betrothed."

Grady nodded. "Aye, I did. Do you not recall? At Callum's wedding, I told you that my father betrothed me to a lass. Milady Violet teased us about marrying and I told you that I was betrothed."

"Bollocks, Grady, you evaded the telling. Why didn't you tell me your betrothed was Marren?"

"Why would it matter? It was the dictate of my father and the only order I ever agreed to. I swore never to return home, but I meant to take Marren for my wife. You always spoke kindly of her, but you never professed to love her."

"Och, I do."

"I cannot and won't thwart the betrothal." Grady leaned against the chair in front of the desk. His glare indicated he meant what he said. "I only agreed to wed the lass to get my da to desist in his search of me. I vowed never to return to Mackay land, and he let me be since I agreed to marry her. I'd hoped to marry and the way you spoke of her… Besides, if you marry the lass it will cause more problems than what you face right now."

"What problems?" Keith stared hard at his friend and when he remained silent and didn't answer his question, he smirked. "Why wait until now then to claim her? She waited for years for the Mackay to come to fetch her for the wedding. Damnation, Grady, and I disbelieve that Mackay is you." Keith's ire rose and he hoped to convince his comrade to cease his claim.

"There hasn't been time. I traveled with you across the channel and when we returned there was all that discord at Callum's keep. I had personal matters which called me away. What was I to do? I'm not in the position to house a wife at present, Keith, and thought to be settled before I do."

"You've been gone for months. What was so important that called you away?"

"I'd rather not say," Grady retorted tersely.

Keith had enough of his evasiveness. He reached across the desk and grabbed Grady's tunic. He yanked him over it and caused the items on the desk to scatter. Inkpots toppled and stained the desk and parchments black. The chairs tipped over and the desk shifted on the wooden floorboards.

Grady punched him before he had a chance to defend himself or to strike. But he gave as good as he got and struck Grady just below his right eye. They continued to throw fists and turned the office into a disarray of furniture and parchments.

His comrade knocked him in the jaw and he swore his teeth had loosened. Keith scowled and pressed Grady's face against the floor until his friend groaned in surrender. He shoved him away and gasped for breath as the exertion of their brawl overtook him.

Grady scooted toward the wall and leaned his back against it. "Damn it, Keith, you have no right to be angry with me."

"Do I not? You've never even spoken to the lass and don't know her as I do. I made promises to Marren and I mean to keep them. You must concede the betrothal. Do it for me."

"I'll consider it but I don't deem it a good idea. There's another reason I meant to keep my vow to wed her…"

"What reason?" Keith's breath settled and he glared at Grady. "What?"

"I agreed to wed her to keep her from being returned to the Mackenzies. Sidheag intended to either marry her or wed her to one of his clan. If we refused the agreement, the Mackenzies would've made her life a living hell."

"Worry not about the Mackenzies. If they get wind of my marriage to Marren, I'll deal with them. But hear me, Grady, I intend to marry her with or without your approval."

"Give me time to speak to her. If the lass won't have me, I'll let her go."

Keith lay on his back on the floor and groaned. "Bloody hell, you cut my lip." He licked the trickle of blood and halfheartedly scowled.

"We haven't fought like that since we were lads. I still can best you."

Keith chortled. "Aye, like hell you can. I remember our brawls. Why won't you tell me where you've been? First, you go off and don't tell me where you're going. You send no word and stay away for months. It's unlike you to be secretive."

"When you left Wick to return home, I traveled to Nigg."

"That's not the first time you've gone there. What's at Nigg, a ladylove? Jumpin' Joe said that's what you told him when you left that you were off to see your lady." Keith sat up and crawled to sit beside his comrade and leaned against the wall.

"Nay, I was not visiting a lass. I… I wanted to keep to myself what takes me there, but I suppose there's no reason why I shouldn't tell you. You'll keep this to yourself and speak of it to no one?"

Keith shoved his shoulder. "What the hell is it? Are you involved in some debauched scheme?"

Grady shook his head. "There's an order of nuns there, the order of the Sisters of Iona. The Prioress, Sister Anna wanted to make an orphanage for lads, aye a school for young ones who have been abandoned or abused. I patron her and went to ensure all was well. I often go when I am able. The lads sent there were neglected and ill-treated. Sister Anna and I vowed to help them."

"That's kind of you and I understand why you would—"

"It's important to me. When the lads are old enough, I help get them settled at keeps here in the north, some even in the south. I was blessed that your father and Callum's father took me in and it's the least I can do to repay—"

"Grady, you don't need to explain further. I commend you. I know why you seek to aid those lads. By doing so it lessens your torment, doesn't it?"

"Sister Anna does her best to tend to the lads' wounds of body and soul. I do what I can to ensure they're settled and their lives are enriched at good keeps under worthy men."

Keith kept his gaze ahead and wouldn't look at his friend. He didn't want to see the torment he'd suffered in his eyes. He'd seen it often enough when Grady had spoken of his childhood. "Has she tended to your soul or do you still carry your scars?"

Grady scoffed derisively, "I have no scars and my soul is intact. I assure you."

"Is it? You confessed to me of the pain you suffered. I believe you're still anguished."

"I am not speaking of myself. My anguish abated the day I left my da's lands. Nor do I aid the lads in some backward way of healing myself. I do it because I have the means to do so and a lot of coins for which I have no purpose. I have wished to put my wealth to good use. Do not make more of this than you should."

"You're my comrade and we've been friends a long time—"

"Which is why, you should see to your matters and leave me to mine. This discussion is finished. None are to know about my endeavor in Nigg. Sister Anna and I have an agreement to keep my name silent."

Keith sighed and nodded. He understood why Grady wanted his past kept secret. He also understood the torment he'd suffered as a lad. Although he'd told little about the wounds he'd suffered, Grady's manner and look of torment told Keith all he needed to know—that his friend had undergone tremendous hardship at the hand of his father. He decided it was best to allow his comrade his privacy regarding the matters of his childhood. When Grady was ready to speak of it, he would. Until then, he'd do what he could to support his comrade.

"Now about Marren…"

"I will meet with her and I'll let you know what I decide to do. But I'm still peeved with you, Keith. Bloody hell, who would've ever considered you'd try to steal my bride."

"There is danger in leaving and that is what you risk losing."

Grady chortled. "Just because I left her didn't mean I chose to lose her."

"Aye, but you did."

Chapter Twenty-Five

Marren spent a restless night in the chamber she shared with Trulee. Fortunately, Lady Ophelia allowed Duncan Macleod to stay the night and her dear friend needn't travel in the dark of night. Marren hadn't gone down to the hall for supper and avoided all. Someone knocked at her door but she refused to answer it. Keith had come at least three times but she couldn't face him. Not when she was confused about his comrade's sudden appearance and the fact that she was betrothed to Keith's closest comrade.

She stood by the window casement and worried about what she'd say to Keith. The last thing she wanted to do was cause difficulties between Keith and his friend. It was evident that Grady was aware of the betrothal. What confused her more was her reaction to him. It wasn't his handsomeness that drew her regard. There was a despondent look in his eyes which indicated he'd suffered a great loss. She had to wonder if that loss was her, but she scoffed at her assumption. He hadn't told her why he finally came or if he truly intended to make good on the betrothal. Perhaps his arrival had nothing to do with her.

Trulee awoke and sat on the side of the bed. Her long brown waves were in disarray and she pressed the sleepiness from her eyes. She gazed at her lap and her voice sounded sorrowful, "I don't want to leave you when I've only just found you."

"But you must." Marren sat next to her and pressed her hand against her hair. "Your father won't leave without you."

"You need me."

She clasped her cousin's hand to solace her. "I do, but everything shall resolve itself. I'm certain Keith will figure out how to convince Grady Mackay to leave off our betrothal. You shouldn't worry about me, not when you're so disheartened to have to travel with your father."

"I know you love Keith. You must find a way to marry him. You cannot put yourself in peril because my da used you to secure his war with the MacDonalds."

Marren sighed wearily. If only there was an easy solution to both their problems. "Promise you will send a missive to let me know you fare well?"

Trulee nodded and squeezed her hand. "I shall, but I have a plan to thwart my da. He means to travel to the Mackenzie's keep to reaffirm his alliance. He shall use me as barter just as he had done to you."

"How can you thwart him? He's your da and has the right to accept a marriage for you."

"I shall pretend to go along with him. Once we are well away, I will ask to take a respite and then will hide in the woods until he leaves. Once he does, I will make my way back here. If my da returns, you shall tell him I haven't come. Will you do that for me?"

"Of course I will. But your plan is risky. You put yourself in greater danger than your father's will to marry you to his ally. What if you come across a knave in the woods?"

Trulee pulled her knees up and leaned on them as she considered what Marren asked her. "It will be dangerous, I admit, to leave my da's men in the woods, but I must do what I can. I shan't marry a Mackenzie. I've heard the Mackenzie laird is beyond aged and remember… I told you I wanted to marry for love? I want the kind of love you and Keith have. I want a man to look at me the way Keith looks at you and I won't marry a decrepit old man."

"This is distressing because I only wish for your happiness. Hopefully, your father will understand when you go against his wishes. He may not and I will worry so for you. Please promise me you will keep yourself safe."

"I shall be well on my own until I make it back here. Have no worry for me. Besides, I have a great sense of direction. It will be easy. I'll find a place to hide and then will return when I'm certain my da has left the area."

A knock interrupted their discussion.

Lady Ophelia popped her head through the door opening. "Lady Trulee, your da waits for you in the courtyard and wishes to depart. You're to come at once. Don't dally." She closed the door.

Trulee made ready to leave but grabbed her arm before she could leave the chamber. "Marren… I've been thinking… You want Keith's friend to call off the betrothal right?"

"Of course I do. I wish to think of a way to make him dislike me." She'd spent a good amount of time during the night trying to figure that out, but she hadn't come up with a sound plan.

"No man wants to marry a shrew. I remind you of Lady Eedy."

She smiled widely. "Oh, you are devious, Trulee. Aye, Lady Eedy was a harridan. No man would want to be saddled with the likes of her."

"I suggest you act like her when you're in the presence of Grady Mackay. If you do, he'll be sure to release you from the betrothal. I almost feel sorry for him." Trulee snickered with laughter.

"That is if I can pull it off." Several notions came to her as she linked her arm with Trulee's and left the bedchamber.

Marren walked with her to the courtyard and she said no more about her cousin's foolhardy plan or her suggestion to dupe Grady Mackay. Desperation forced both their hands. She hoped Trulee didn't come upon trouble in her abscond in the woods. She prayed Trulee would change her mind but she wouldn't want to marry the Mackenzie laird either. From her childhood memories of the man, she recalled being frightened of him. Although she couldn't place his face in her mind, his evil nature had remained with her. God help Trulee if she was forced to marry him.

They reached the outside where her uncle gave her a cross glance and he muttered for Trulee to make haste. He rode with no more than five Macleods. Marren wanted to say a few choice words to him, to speak of his uncaring mien toward her, and of his hateful words of her da. But she wouldn't bother since he had no care for his family.

Marren waved to Trulee who wore a grimace at her departure. She stood on the step and noticed the Sutherlands lined up and stood in rows as if they protected her. Marren thought it absurd since Laird Macleod insisted she stay and follow through with his plan to align his clan to the Mackenzies, even if it had shifted to include the Mackays. She spotted Keith who held his sword in hand and appeared ready for battle.

As soon as the Macleods rode through the gate, it was lowered. Keith shouted orders for his men to take vigilance on the barbican and walls. The men hurried to do his bidding.

She hadn't mattered to her uncle and she reasoned he wouldn't care if he ever saw her again. He only cared about his precious alliance. That saddened her because all she'd ever wanted was to belong to a family, to have her family care for her, and to be loved.

Marren ambled away from the courtyard and found herself at the back exit of the keep. She moseyed through the late summer high weeds and grasses. A horse sounded behind her and she startled when she spotted the rider riding swiftly toward her. The closer he got, she recognized Grady Mackay and she slowed her pace. He dismounted and let his horse's reins loose.

"He'll run off if you don't tether his reins," she said more or less to herself. Then she remembered she was supposed to treat him disdainfully. It would be difficult because she wasn't one to be unkind toward anyone, but if she wanted him to refute her she had to be crass.

"Nay, lass, my horse obeys my commands. All I need to do is whistle and he'll return to me. I wanted a moment alone with you to speak about our betrothal."

"You shall call me Lady Macleod. I am not your lass." She put enough vigor in her tone to hopefully affront him. Marren dawdled forward and unfortunately, he followed.

Although Grady Mackay presented a strong, fearless warrior, he had a demeanor of chivalry about him. She imagined he was formidable when faced with a threat though. Muscles bulged at his biceps and legs. His chest was wide with musculature she noticed through his tunic. With his short dark hair and the day's growth of beard on his face, he appeared as a warrior who feared no one. Strangely, she didn't feel awkward in his presence.

"I didn't mean to offend you."

He stepped away and set his arms behind his back. Marren turned and saw a figure perched on the wall of the Sutherland fortification. She knew it was Keith, watching them from afar. As much as she wanted to thwart Grady, she didn't want Keith to see the row she intended to start.

Grady took hold of her arm and pulled her toward him. Before she knew what he was about, he kissed her. His lips pressed hers in a possessive manner and he gripped her face to keep her from pulling away. After a moment, she used her hands to push his chest and gained her freedom.

"I don't know what you intended to prove," she said and slapped his face with as much force as she could garner. "How dare you affront me so?"

Grady rubbed his jaw and peered at her as if he was shocked by her reaction. "Admit it, you enjoyed my kiss." He grabbed her before she could step away and tightened his hold around her. "Mayhap we should try that again?" He pressed his lips against hers again and held her face.

Marren raised her knee and struck his middle. Grady groaned and muttered an expletive. He fell to his knees on the ground and stared at her as if she'd gravely wounded him. Then she remembered Keith had been watching them from the wall. She glanced up but he wasn't where he'd been only moments before. Hopefully, he hadn't seen Grady kiss her. How would she explain?

She narrowed her eyes and lifted her chin. "I warn you to keep your hands off me, sir. You should keep your distance because I don't allow men to be so forward."

Grady laughed and rose to his feet. "Not even Keith? I saw you kissing him in the garden. I only wanted to see if there was something betwixt us."

"You affront me to suggest there is. And Keith is someone I have known most of my life. I care for him and…" She scowled as she was about to admit she enjoyed Keith's kisses. But she need not account for her actions with Keith, not to Grady when he was but a stranger to her.

"I spoke to him about our situation. He tells me he loves you." Grady walked in circles, but stopped and turned to her. "Love is sometimes not enough. Sometimes, lass, it can put you in more peril than you'd like. Your relations with Keith will cause him and his clan trouble. Are ye willing to be foolish and uncaring for his people's welfare?"

She scowled at the harshness of his words and thought he meant to threaten her. "If you mean to frighten me—"

"Nay, not at all, *Lady Macleod*. Someone needs to speak the truth here… I don't mean to intimidate you and should explain… Come and sit with me. I promise to keep my hands to myself." He motioned her to a nearby rock and she sat upon it. Grady sat on the grass next to her. "I should tell you what I know about our betrothal."

Marren placed her hands in her lap and intended to listen. She daren't interrupt him.

"When I was a lad, Laird Mackenzie showed up at our keep with a wee lass in tow…you. He told my da that he took you as his ward in a treaty with the Macleods. Only Sidheag never intended to honor the alliance he made with Laird Macleod and he did not need a wife. He said he wouldn't allow his precious son to marry you either. So he got my father to agree to keep you even though my da had banned all women from entering our keep."

"Why would your da ban women?" Marren closed her mouth. She hadn't wanted to interrupt him and she was finally gaining an understanding of what happened to her when she was a child.

Grady leaned back against the rock, raised his knee, and rested his forearm on it. "My da disliked women and forbade them from entering our keep. It was my ma who turned him against all women. I was young then and mayhap a handful of years older than you when you arrived. I often hid behind the buttery in the great hall when my da had guests. It was the only way I ever found out anything... Mackenzie was a mean son of a bitch. He was as fiendish as my da, but I ramble..."

"Go on." She folded her hands and waited silently for him to continue.

"Mackenzie told my da that if he kept you, he wouldn't raid his lands or bother any of our clansmen, but he refused to be in an alliance with us. As long as you married a Mackay, he'd honor his word and leave us be."

Marren tensed. She knew what was coming. "So if I refuse to marry a Mackay, your clan will be troubled by the Mackenzies?"

"Aye, lass, and they'd make war against us as they have done with most of the clans here in the north. The Mackenzies thrive on war and often start one over minor squabbles."

"Is your clan capable of fending off the Mackenzies?"

Grady raised his handsome face which didn't show his concern. He neither smiled nor scowled. "I haven't been to my father's lands in years and know not the happenings there or how large my da's army has grown, but when I absconded they numbered in the late hundreds. I left a year after you arrived. Not that I care about what happens to my father, but the clansmen and women don't deserve to be desecrated because of a depraved alliance my father made with the Mackenzie."

Memories flashed in her mind: that of a lad who cried in the night. She'd always wondered who the lad was but never had seen him. "It was you…wasn't it? I heard your cries when I was there at your father's keep."

Grady flinched and a few seconds later, he gave a slight nod. "Aye, it probably was me. I have only spoken of this with Keith and I only speak of it with you now to make you understand. My da beat me often for naught. I never gave him cause, but I'd had enough of his cruelty and so I…left. I fled to the Sinclairs. My comrade's da, Edmund, took me in and allowed me to foster at arms with his soldiers. That's how I met Keith. He also fostered with the Sinclairs."

"I see."

Grady set a hand on her leg, near her knee, and gently squeezed her. "Lass, I understand you and Keith care for each other and you don't want to marry me. But if you marry him, you'll put both your clans in peril. Will you be selfish and put others at risk for the sake of your heart?"

Marren dipped her chin at his words. What he spoke dejected her. She wasn't uncaring and would never risk anyone's safety. She shook her head and averted his gaze.

"My father is not one to accept such a slight. He will probably get Sidheag Mackenzie to side with him against the Sutherlands. Their armies are great, fearsome, especially the Mackenzie's. It's said their soldiers number near a thousand. Many in the Sutherland clan will die."

"Surely neither the Mackays nor the Mackenzies will care about an insignificant woman such as me." Marren frowned and as much as she wanted to instigate Grady to beg off the betrothal, she realized he sacrificed his future to possibly keep people from being killed. She couldn't go through with the plan to be difficult, not when he was so noble.

Grady groused. "You are not insignificant. I tell you the

Mackenzies made a pact with my da. If either learns they were thwarted by the Sutherlands a war would be inevitable. Right now the Mackenzies have taken arms against the Roses over the paltry issue of a mile of land, a border dispute. They would enact their full wrath if they felt the Sutherlands purposely instigated them."

"Then I cannot marry Keith."

"Nay, you cannot. If you will have me, I would marry you and uphold the betrothal. I won't force you though, lass."

"I shall think about it."

"Don't think too long or hard about it." Grady stood. "If Keith insists on marrying you and you agree, I will do what I can to support you. Och lives are at stake and you must consider that."

She nodded. "I won't have anyone killed because of me. Keith will not marry me."

Grady whistled and his horse trotted forward. He mounted the steed in a swift motion and cantered off.

Marren walked toward the cliffs and stood a few feet from the edge. She gazed at the great waters beyond and at the sky. A beautiful sunset lit the horizon in a vast aura of colors. The view was spectacular and almost ethereal. She took it as a sign that she'd made the right decision. As she watched the sky pitch, she sat and folded her legs beneath her. She wished she could escape and sail away to a land where there were no wars or alliances or mean men who only cared about killing or hurting those who mattered not to them. Now she was sounding as wistful as Trulee.

"Marren?"

She startled at Keith's voice and hadn't heard his approach. He strolled toward her and sat beside her. She returned her gaze to the sea.

Keith took her hand and rubbed his thumb over the flesh of her knuckles. He kissed the side of her face and leaned his head against hers. "I haven't been here in a long time and had forgotten...how beautiful it is. Do you remember when we were young and we used to play on the rocks below?"

She smiled at the memory and nodded. "I do and of that time when we saw the ships coming ashore…"

Keith grinned. "Aye and we high-tailed it back to the keep and told everyone we were being invaded."

"Oh and your da yelled at us for scaring everyone when it was only traders coming from Tintagel. You always had me believing we were being invaded. We were overzealous in our imagination."

He nudged her shoulder with his. "We certainly were. It was easy to tease you. You made my childhood joyful and I never thanked you."

Marren sighed. "Grady just spoke to me about our betrothal."

"What did he say? If he insisted you accept him, you should know that I won't let you. I cannot lose you, Marren. There is nothing more important than us. Tell me."

"I won't accept him. There is much to consider though. Lives are in peril and I don't want to be the cause of people's deaths. It saddens me to say this, but there can be no us." She touched his face and caressed the hardness of his jaw. The look in his eyes tensed her heart, but she had to tell him the truth. "Keith, I cannot marry you regardless of how much I love you."

Chapter Twenty-Six

Keith stayed by the cliffs until it was too dark to see the water. Marren blurted out her decision and left him. He remained and tried to reason why she'd rejected him. He swore he would force Grady to repeal his betrothal to Marren. Keith wouldn't allow a simple pact made years before to come between him and the woman he loved. He left the cliffs and walked back in the silence of the night. But the voices made much noise upon reflection of all that happened since his return. Marren, Grady, Philly, and Samuel's words rebounded as he tried to make sense of the turmoil.

Throughout the night, he paced the small confines of the office, and a handful of times he'd clutched the knob. He wanted to seek Marren, to hold her, to assure himself she would be his. Before he sought her, he needed to speak to Grady and find out what in God's name he'd told her. Obviously whatever he'd spoken forced Marren to reject him.

Keith passed the great hall which was oddly silent. No one was up and about yet. He traipsed through the courtyard in search of Grady and made his way toward the gate. Marc stood before a group of watchmen who he directed in their morning tasks and the sentry who was sent to relieve the night watch. When he noticed him, Marc marched forward.

"Laird, you're up early this morn. I wanted to tell ye that in a week I'll be marrying the fair lass Cassie. She's agreed to be my wife. Will you attend?"

He nodded but barely listened as his guardsman chattered on about how pleased he was with his woman. Keith was happy for his friend, but his sorrowful mood at his own relationship woes rendered him incapable of offering him compliments.

"Have you seen Grady?"

Marc turned away and said over his shoulder, "He was headed toward the fields a few minutes ago." With quick steps, he returned to his duty.

Keith sauntered off and reached the incline within seconds. He shielded his eyes against the rising sun and tried to spot Grady amongst the soldiers who practiced arms on the vast field.

Aulay approached. "Laird, I'm gladdened you're here. The young soldiers will compete this day. They'll be happy you will watch. Many are a wee bit boastful, but—"

"I'm not here to watch the competition. There's Grady." He didn't give a word of parting but marched to the center of the field where Grady went at a seasoned soldier with his sword. He ambled toward him and called out, "I need to speak to you."

His comrade didn't glance at him but focused on his task. "Can you not see I'm a wee bit busy at the moment?" His sword deflected a strike from his opponent and he stepped back.

"It's important. I need to know what you said to Marren."

"I can tell you're bothered, but I can't right now." Grady turned and deflected another strike. "I'll come to you when I'm finished."

A whistle alerted him and Keith signaled to Marc that

he'd be along in a moment. To Grady, he said, "I'll be in the hall. Don't make me wait long." He hailed off to find out what Marc wanted.

"Laird, you have a visitor at the gate. Jumpin' Joe awaits ye."

He frowned and shook his head. "Why didn't he come inside?"

Marc shrugged his shoulders. "I raised the gate for him, but he said he wanted to meet you there and didn't plan to stay that long."

"Aye? I wonder what he wants. He rarely comes to Sutherland land. It must be important."

"He didn't say, Laird, but I'm off duty and if ye want I'll come along—"

"Joe's a friend. I'll find out what he wants. Go on and take your rest." Keith walked with spry steps toward the gate. When he got there, he noticed Joe's agitated state. "Jumpin' Joe, what brings you here?"

"My good comrade, Keith, I come with news. Aye, ill-tidings if I'm to be truthful."

"Why don't you come to the keep and we'll have some ale and you can tell me your news there." He was about to turn and head off toward the keep, but Joe shook his head.

"I cannot stay long. Let us move by the trees where we cannot be overheard."

Keith's curiosity was stoked to a great flame. He followed his comrade to a nearby copse of densely shaded trees and leaned against the bark of the thickest trunk. "Why the secrecy?"

"What I have to say might be upsetting, but I'd rather ye hear it from me."

He grimaced and was about to yank Joe's tunic to get him to spill what he'd come to say. "What in God's name are you talking about? What's your news? It doesn't sound good…"

"My brother told me that Lady Ophelia stopped by to visit him weeks ago. She told John that you were recently made chieftain."

"Aye, but you knew that."

"She also told him that you were to marry and she would send for him when the wedding would take place."

Keith nodded. "That's right. I was given an edict to marry to become laird. What's the problem, Joe?" He scratched his back against the bark of the tree and realized he had to be patient. Joe was taking his sweet time in telling his news.

Joe paced before him in an agitated state. "My brother… John took it upon himself to look into your matters and discovered that your da never married your ma. There is no record of their marriage. John keeps great detail of all the weddings and births."

Keith laughed. "Is that what concerns you? I'm certain my parents married here on Sutherland land. Perhaps they had a different priest perform the sacrament. It matters not."

"But it does matter, Keith. It's unlikely that they were married by another. Before John took the post here in the north, only Father Stephen served the area. He left all his books with John. There is no record that your parents ever married. But there's more…"

Keith scowled and paced before his comrade. His shoulders tensed as his friend continued.

"Not only is your parent's marriage in question, but so is your birth. There is no record of your baptism. Father Stephen would've noted it and you definitely would've been christened by him."

"I see." But Keith muttered and didn't understand the meaning of what Joe was trying to tell him. What did it matter if his parents hadn't wed in the area and there was no question Hendrie Sutherland was his father.

Joe rubbed his face in frustration. "My brother took the liberty of his account and reached out to the bishop. He serves the land near the Mackenzies."

"Aye, so? Why does that matter? I am confused as to why John would question these affairs."

"Your ma was married to Sidheag Mackenzie." Joe had exclaimed his news and stared at him as if he waited for him to refute his revelation.

The words *married to Sidheag* reverberated in his mind. Keith shook his head at what his comrade was telling him. He felt as though he was run over by his horse. He couldn't voice a denial because Joe wouldn't speak falsely about a matter of importance such as his mother's marriage.

Joe looked around as if he wanted to assure himself no others could hear what he spoke of. "That's not even the worst of it, Keith. There were two bairns blessed from their union...you and Kieran Mackenzie."

A fierce grimace came to him. "Do you know what you're suggesting?"

"Aye, Keith, och I am not suggesting at all. You and Sidheag's son, Kieran, are brothers."

He fisted his hands and he considered what Chester Mackay had told him when he'd found him in the woods: *I vow I was looking at you when I glimpsed him. He has the same shade of hair and eyes. His body build is the same as yours and his face; it was like seeing you, only it wasn't you. I almost made the mistake of calling him by your name when I first spotted him.* Keith flinched when he remembered Chester's words: *If you had a twin, it'd be the knavish Kieran Mackenzie.*

Joe set his hands on his hips and scowled at the ground. "If you disbelieve me, you can read it for yourself. John has the books in his possession. He says ye have no claim as laird of the Sutherlands. I forced him to keep quiet about his finding, but he won't remain silent for long. I thought I should tell ye before word got out. I'll try to keep John from spewing his rubbish."

"My thanks, Joe, for telling me about it and coming..." Keith's entire body tensed. He couldn't fathom the news or what it meant.

"I should go. If you need me, you only have to send a message—"

"You should go." Keith stood by the trees and the news

sat like a rock in his stomach. He wasn't a Sutherland but born of their enemy Sidheag Mackenzie. Why had his da lied to him all these years? Is that why he wasn't put off by him leaving the keep and fostering with the Sinclairs? Keith shook his head. Nay, Hendrie cared about him and his father loved him. But Keith was deceived by everyone. There was only one thing he needed to do—he had to denounce himself as laird.

By the time he reached the cottage he sought, the vigor of the news had lessened his steps. He was still resolved to amend the situation and rapt at the door.

"Ah, lad… Laird, what brings you to my door this early in the day?"

"Samuel, I came to give you this." Keith removed the ring given to him and placed it in the elder's hand.

"Why do you give me the ring? Are you abdicating your role as the laird?"

He nodded firmly. "I am."

"But why, lad? I thought you accepted the position and the covenant? If you are still irate because we insisted you marry, I will speak to the elders. I'm certain we can come to some accord. Your da would—"

"He's not my da." With renewed vigor, Keith walked away with solemnness in his heart. When he reached the keep, his shoulders slumped and he was defeated. He'd lost everything—lost all that he held dear: Marren, the lairdship, his clan, and his family. Betrayal overtook every sense of him and he was in the foulest mood he'd ever been in.

Grady called to him from the great hall. "There you are. I've been waiting for you. You wanted to talk about Marren?"

Keith poured himself a large tankard of ale and drank it down. He set the cup down with an angry bang and eyed his friend. "I only wanted to tell you that… Marren is yours. Treat her well and take care of her. She deserves a good husband, Grady."

Grady chortled. "Well, that was easier than I thought it would be. I'm glad you came to your senses because a war with the Mackenzies would've wreaked havoc on your clan. What changed your mind?"

He fisted his hands but wouldn't acknowledge the news he'd just learned. "I wish you well, Grady, but I must go." Without another word, Keith turned and made his way to the solarium. Grady called out to him, but he ignored his comrade and hurried onward. There was only one more thing he had to do before he left.

He found Philly at her tables. She didn't hear him enter or approach.

Philly startled and gasped. "Oh, dear lord, it's only you. You frightened me, Keith. What brings you here so early in the day?"

"I returned the laird's ring to Samuel."

She dropped the small wooden box she held and tilted her head to the side. Her gaze questioned him. "You did what? Why would you return the ring? Is it because of Marren and her supposed betrothal to the Mackay? If that is so…"

"It has nothing to do with Marren. Philly, I know the truth." Keith hadn't meant to be blunt, but the entire situation distressed him and his voice pitched with his confession.

"Keith, you're worrying me. What do ye speak of? What truth?" Philly tried to reach out to him, but he stepped back.

"That I'm not your nephew and that I'm not a Sutherland. All these years, my entire life, I have lived a lie."

Chapter Twenty-Seven

Cassie and Marc's wedding went off without a hitch except for Keith's absence and Marren's dismay. She was pleased for her friend because she received the joy all women wanted. How she envied Cassie's happiness. She'd never appeared more beautiful than on her wedding day with her long curling locks fastened with sprigs of flowers and a becoming gown that matched the colors of the Sutherland's tartan. The celebration was lively and all rejoiced at the happy couple's devotion. Marc had even worn a tunic for the ceremony which the men had teased him about. Their banter made Marren miss Keith more because he would've been merry to make fun of his longtime friend.

Over two weeks had passed since Keith's absence. He hadn't even bid her a farewell. His aunt appeared troubled and sad but wouldn't divulge why he'd left. Something happened to make Keith leave without a word to her. Marren felt remorse over her rejection of him and thought her betrothal to Grady was the root of Keith's departure. That was the only plausible explanation she could think of. But now she wasn't so sure that's why he'd gone.

She was lost without him and as each day passed to another, she realized she couldn't live without Keith. Regardless of the peril, she wanted to be with him. There had to be a way to keep her marriage to Keith a secret. Somehow she had to make Grady understand. He would accept her decision and she recalled his words: *If Keith insists on marrying you and you agree, I will do what I can to support you.*

Now she had to talk to Lady Ophelia and force her to speak of her discussion with Keith before he left. She waited until she was certain Lady Ophelia attended her plants in the solarium to confront her. At the entrance, Marren hesitated. But she had to do something to remedy the situation she had created.

"Milady," she called and curtseyed before she approached.

"It is good to see you here, Marren. I didn't think you would ever join me here again."

"I came not to enjoy the fauna, but to speak to you about Keith."

"Is that so? I wondered how long it would take ye to come. Sit and we shall have our discussion." She motioned to a stool.

Marren's knees shook because the discussion would be difficult.

Lady Ophelia turned her full attention to her. "Before we speak of Keith, I would tell you… I once had a great love. I should have fought to keep him but I was a coward. I hoped that you had more mettle than I did. If you love my nephew as you say you do, you won't let fear keep you apart."

"He left without a word to me. What am I to think but that he no longer loves me?" Marren tried not to let the woe of her words affect her, but tears shimmered and threatened to fall.

"His leaving wasn't caused by you or his aversion to you. Oh, here's Grady, Aulay, and Emmett. I sent for them." Lady Ophelia waved them forward. "They have perfect timing."

"Why did you send for them? I don't want them to hear

what I have to say." Marren turned a glance at the men who bounded into the solarium with grim faces.

"Milady, we're here as you bid us," Aulay said and bowed his head.

"What did you need of us, Milady?" Emmett asked.

"I have called each of you here because there are grave matters at hand."

"I shouldn't be here," Grady said. "If this concerns the clan, I should go."

"Wait, Grady, this does concern you," Lady Ophelia called in a soft voice. "You are Keith's closest comrade and he needs you. Aye, he needs all of you. To help my nephew, I need your aid if I'm to convince Keith to return."

"He'll come back when he's ready," Grady said. "He is angry about my betrothal to Marren."

Emmett snorted. "You're betrothed to her? What's this now?"

Aulay said nothing but stared at her as if she had done something dreadful.

Grady leaned against the table and nodded. "Keith wasn't pleased when he told me that Marren was mine. I should've gone after him, but I thought he needed time to come to reason. He probably went to Wick to see Joe."

Emmett fingered his beard and frowned. "But Joe was recently here. I saw him and Keith in a heated conversation near the gatehouse. Perhaps you're right and Joe needed his favor. It's possible he went to Wick."

Lady Ophelia adamantly shook her head. "Nay, Keith hasn't gone to Wick. Before I tell you what has happened... What I say here must be kept in the strictest of confidence. I want each of you to vow not to speak a word of what I say to anyone."

The men vigorously nodded and voiced their agreement.

Marren stood next to her lady and thought to offer her support. She grew concerned because Lady Ophelia seemed to become distressed. Her dismay was caused by more than Keith's departure or her rejection of him.

"Marren, your vow?"

"Of course, Milady, I vow to you I shall keep your confidence."

"Now then, that's settled. I shall get on with the telling. Almost a score and ten years ago, a woman arrived here at the Sutherland keep seeking sanctuary. With her, she had a wee bairn, a lad. My dear brother, Hendrie, took pity on the woman and allowed her to stay. He fell in love with her and her son. Her name was Vera and she was lovely, the kindest woman I'd ever met, and her babe was just as winsome. The poor woman was married to the meanest man alive...the Mackenzie laird...Sidheag. To escape him, she fled in the darkest of night."

No one spoke a word as the lady told her tale.

Lady Ophelia continued, "Hendrie didn't care that Vera was married or that Keith wasn't his blood son. He loved them dearly. It was his fondest wish that Keith become laird when the time came when Hendrie could no longer see to the clan or if he perished to the hereafter. Hendrie never told a soul who Vera or Keith was except for me and I have kept his secrets. Only I was privy to the truth. Sidheag Mackenzie never found out that Vera came here. At least, he never tried to contact her here. Somehow Keith found out the truth about his birth which is why he returned the laird's ring and banished himself from the clan."

Looks of abashment came to the faces of the men. Marren was astounded by what her lady told them. What Keith must've thought when he'd learned that unfortunate news?

Aulay was the first to speak, "If what you say is true then that means..."

Emmett scowled. "...he's the son of the Mackenzie, our damned enemy."

Grady pressed his hands over his face and groaned. "Damnation, that's the last thing I expected to hear. I imagine Keith is vexed beyond sense."

Lady Ophelia's mouth turned down in a pout, but she

continued, "Aye, he's Mackenzie's son, but Hendrie loved him. Keith feels deceived and that his life has been a lie. Perhaps he should have been told the truth. I am certain he is wrath with everyone for the despair those secrets cost him."

Marren's heart hurt at how Keith must be suffering. She needed and wanted to be with him, to hold and comfort him. No wonder he'd left without a word after learning such truth. To find out he was another man's son, let alone his enemy's, must've been more than he could bear. She knew how much the Sutherland clan meant to Keith, and for him to exile himself meant that he no longer felt privileged to call himself a Sutherland.

Aulay braced his legs and folded his arms over his chest. He appeared irate, but kept his tone civil when he asked, "What aid do you need from us, Milady?"

Lady Ophelia stepped closer to Emmett and Aulay and said woefully, "I know you were not pleased when Keith returned home and was proclaimed the laird—"

Aulay cut her off, "Lady Ophelia, I might not have welcomed him with open arms, but I was gladdened Keith came home. He belongs to the Sutherlands and shouldn't have stayed away. There's no other man I respect more except for Laird Hendrie."

Emmett spoke up, "Our father spoke of his desire to see Keith become laird. He was Hendrie's devoted soldier and we promised our da we would support his son."

"Then I will not have difficulty in what I ask of you?"

The men shook their heads and seemed to support Lady Ophelia.

"I want Keith returned even if you must force him to come. A missive from me is on its way to my brother. Hendrie shall come at once to remedy this situation. Keith must be here when he arrives."

"We will handle the matter, Milady," Emmett said.

"I know where he might have gone," Grady said.

"You must leave this day then. And Grady, I am privy to the situation and discord of your relations with your father.

Chester spoke of it often and has told me about Marren. If you love the lass then, by all means, marry her."

Grady's cheek twitched as he focused on Lady Ophelia. "And what if I don't?"

Lady Ophelia smiled. "Then don't let the possibility of a daft war come between two people who belong together. If the Mackenzies want to take arms over Keith and Marren's marriage then the Sutherlands will meet them on the field. All shall support their laird. Do I make myself understood?"

Marren was shocked that her lady would stand up to the men in such a way, but she was a force to be reckoned with. It was at that moment that she knew what she had to do. "I want to go with you."

All shot their gazes to her.

Grady scoffed. "Nay, you cannot. We might need to use force, Marren. Keith is an obstinate man and it will take great will to get him to return."

"Aye," Emmet said with a grin, "We will probably have to use our fists on him."

"Don't you dare lay a hand on him," she warned. "If you do so, you'll answer to me."

The men chortled and seemed not to take her threat to heart.

Emmett flashed a grin. "Och he might be a wee bit bruised, Milady, but he'll be in one piece."

"I mean it, Emmett, if you lay a hand on him, you shall never hear the end of it." Marren glared at the men but they weren't affected by her boast.

Lady Ophelia clicked her tongue and drew their attention. "Perhaps it would be best if Marren stays here. Just bring my nephew back posthaste."

The men absconded from the solarium before Marren could convince them to take her along. She rushed to her bedchamber and pulled a satchel from the wardrobe and rummaged through it until she found the glass bottle she'd gotten from Trulee. It was the one the healer left when she recovered from her ordeal of being trampled by Keith's horse. The potion was the perfect solution. Marren rushed down the stairs and hastened to the stable.

"Emmett, wait."

He dismounted his horse and approached. "What is it, Milady? You cannot convince me to take you with us if that's what ye mean to do."

She pulled him aside so none overheard their conversation. "Nay, but... Take this." Marren placed the bottle in his hand. "Keith has suffered enough pain. Don't lay fists on him. If he is troublesome, put a few drops of this in his drink. It's a sleeping potion."

Emmet chortled a laugh and nodded. "Very well, Milady. If we can't get him to come, we'll try this. But I won't promise that we won't give him a good wallop for being an arse."

"Be sure not to use too much because it is a potent mixture. He'll sleep for days if you give him too much."

Emmett bellowed and drew the gazes of the men who awaited him. "Well now, this might come in more handy than I deemed. Worry not, we'll bring your man back to ye."

She threw herself against him in a tight hug. "Hurry back." Marren left him and stood in the courtyard, not far from the busy stables. The men rode hastily through the gate. She walked with quick steps and her arms swung by her side until she reached Lady Ophelia.

Lady Ophelia's face reflected her sadness at the situation and she hugged her. "I'm sorry, Milady, that you've been so distressed. We shall make him understand why Laird Hendrie kept the truth from him. Keith will accept his place here."

"Once he does then we can work on his honor and get him to marry you."

Marren smiled for the first time that day. "I'm dismayed by the trouble I've caused Keith. But I'm gladdened you support our marriage. I didn't think you would approve."

"Oh, dearest, it's been my hope since you both were wee that you would marry. I secretly hoped he would return and find you here. All went according to plan."

She was astounded by Lady Ophelia's admission. "But why did you have the lasses come if you wanted him to marry me?"

"I couldn't make it easy for him, now could I? Besides, he had to see what was available to him to realize what was before him…you. Aye, the lasses were part of my plan to get him to admit his feelings for you. Whenever he came home for visits, he always asked after you. I suspected his regard long before he came home for good."

Marren chuckled. "You knew when I didn't."

"He always looked at you fondly, more than what a lad should when he peered at his friend. Keith has always loved ye. Everyone knew it but the two of you. It's time you married and made more Sutherlands." Lady Ophelia pulled her into her embrace.

"But I shouldn't marry him. If I do many will be in danger. The Mackenzies will war with us. How can I accept that? I appreciate your kind words, but regardless of your support—"

"Leave that to the men. Men like to war and besides Keith will find a way to thwart them. No one will be in danger. I vow that to be true. Lass, trust me in this matter."

"I pray you are right."

Thoughts rebounded and the most outrageous of them came to her. Keith was Laird Mackenzie's son. He wasn't a Sutherland, but the son of the one man she feared the most. God help them if Sidheag Mackenzie found out about Keith. And yet, if she married Keith as she was wont, it might possibly solve the issue regarding the alliance her uncle wanted.

CHAPTER TWENTY-EIGHT

Sinclair Holding
Sky, Northern Highlands Scotland

In the past fortnight, the Sinclair clan approached him numerous times to offer their objection to Keith's visit. Callum didn't want to send his longtime comrade away, but his clansmen were about to declare Keith their enemy. He needed to find out what was going on and what caused his comrade's surly mood. It was unlike his friend to be careless on the training field or sotted most of the day.

As long as he'd known him, Keith was a good-natured sort and friendly, except of course if they needed to raise arms. Hadn't he professed to want to marry a lass at his holding? Callum scowled in thought that a woman was surely causing his comrade difficulties. Try as he might, he couldn't get his friend to tell him what the problem was.

"There have been complaints, Keith." Callum stood in the dark confines of the barracks and disbelieved what he was seeing.

"Come, Callum, and join me in a drink."

"Haven't you had enough?"

"I'm celebrating my victory on the field this day."

Callum peered at his longtime friend and leaned against the wooden beam in the barracks. He'd invited Keith to stay in the castle, but his comrade insisted he stay with the soldiers. "You injured at least three of my fiercest soldiers. Their wounds will take long to heal. Are you intent to decrease my army's numbers?"

Keith scoffed derisively. "Ah, they weren't much of a challenge and they certainly are not fierce. I barely struck them. Your soldiers are a bunch of bairns. They'll heal." Keith lifted his cup with a shine to his eyes. "I find I'm enjoying sparring with the Sinclairs. It's been too long since I raised my sword arm."

"You mean to slay someone, do you not? You're besotted again and have been every day since you've arrived. What's up your arse, Keith?" His comrade shot to his feet but he staggered a few steps and fell against him. "You look like hell." He gripped his tunic to keep him standing. "Tell me why you're here and how long you plan to stay."

"There's nothing to tell and I have nowhere else to go. Can a man not enjoy a drink without everyone badgering him?"

Callum scoffed. "I will desist in badgering you if you cease sparring with my soldiers. Neil won't stop groaning about your intrusion on his training sessions."

Keith laughed. "Your commander is a wee bit sensitive. It is not my fault he cannot handle the soldiers."

He took hold of Keith's tunic in a tighter grip and forced him back until he fell upon his bed. "I won't have you fighting my men. Keith?" Callum called his name twice more before he realized his comrade gave in to his stupor. "Let's hope you sleep it off," he said to himself. "What in God's name happened to you?" But Callum didn't get an answer to the question he'd asked more times than he could count since Keith's arrival. His friend was broken of spirit. What had

Keith meant when he said he had nowhere to go? He was the Sutherland laird and had a home.

Since he'd come, his comrade remained closed-mouthed about why he'd come and why he took to drinking most of the day. It wasn't like Keith to imbibe to such an extreme. His friend usually handled his drink, but it was excessive which worried Callum. Keith divulged nothing even with the haze of drink muddling his mind.

He welcomed his friend and permitted him to stay as long as he needed to, but something troubled him about Keith's manner. His comrade was usually agreeable. It was a trait that often flocked women to him. Hell, Keith had even won over Violet when she'd first met him. Keith's demeanor changed to that of wrath. It was evident in his tone and his actions.

His commander had to force his soldiers to practice arms with Keith. None wanted to go against a man whose daemons rode him. His friend was plagued that was certain. The only way to find out what troubled him was to visit the Sutherland keep. Yet Callum didn't want to leave his friend even for a few days. He'd do what he could to help. Eventually, the matter would erupt and his friend would have to face whatever it was. Callum only hoped none were wounded in the eruption.

He left his slumbering friend and walked back to the castle. Inside the great hall, he ignored the liveliness of the servants and his children. Callum stood by the hearth in ponder of what to do.

Violet pressed her hand on his shoulder. She quietly watched him. "Something troubles you. I shall send the lasses to the gardens."

Dela yanked his tunic sleeve. "Da, will Uncle Keith come for supper?"

His daughter enjoyed Keith's company and his comrade often told her comical stories of his childhood. "I'm afraid not, lass. Take your sister and enjoy the sunshine." He kissed Cora's head and took his wee bairn from Violet. Holding his son allayed him and the tension of his friend's plight eased. The children left and quietness settled in the hall. Callum sat in the chair with his bairn lying against his chest.

Violet returned and knelt on the floor beside him and placed a gentle hand on the babe's back. "He hasn't told you what vexes him?"

"Nay and I am concerned because... He's like a brother to me, Vi. I've known Keith since we were lads and he's never been like this. Something dreadful happened to force him from his home and for him to take to drink. I'm certain of it."

"Why don't you send a missive to Lady Ophelia? Perhaps she can tell you what's going on?"

"I better do it before Keith ends up killing one of my soldiers."

"Do you think this has to do with a lady? Wasn't he supposed to marry? You said he was to choose between the lasses Lady Ophelia invited to his keep. Maybe he's been refused."

Callum grinned at the thought but shook his head. "I doubt it, lass, because he knows how to charm the ladies. If he offered for one of them, he'd be at his wedding. Besides, Keith wouldn't let a woman bring him so low. This matter is graver than a marriage rejection."

Violet pressed a kiss on his face. "Worry not, love. He'll come around."

"I hope so, sweetness. I'll give him a few days and then will confront him."

His wife sighed. "Are you certain you want to do that? You'll kill each other if you take to fists again. I won't have your handsome face battered."

Callum chuckled. Their brawls were fierce, but if he wanted answers, he'd have to force his friend to give them.

Keith groaned and opened his bleary eyes. The barracks were dark and as he adjusted to the dimness of the light, he spotted the jug he'd set on the floor. He reached for the cup next to his bed and poured more brew gotten from Eric, Sinclair's smith. He chugged it and remarkably sobered slightly enough to recall his discussion with Callum. Had his comrade forbade him from joining the soldiers in their practice at arms? He chuckled to himself because it was laughable. If the Sinclairs soldiers couldn't handle one Sutherland…

He blanched at his thought. He was a Sutherland no more. The matter of his birth was an ever-tightening noose around his neck. The noose almost choked him with the reminder that he was the blood kin of his enemy. Keith moaned at the inebriation of the drink and took smaller sips. He needed to keep his mind numb so he wouldn't think of the atrocious truth. He needed to leave the north altogether or be constantly reminded of the stigma of being a Mackenzie. Keith wanted to escape the memories of Marren, Philly, his clansmen, and his comrades, and the truth of his birth.

Being at the Sinclair holding only reminded him of what he couldn't have, that he was no longer connected to a clan he was devoted to for life. Keith's head swam with thoughts of where to go. He could cross the channel again and offer his sword arm in protecting the clergy and peerage. But he'd done that stint before and couldn't stay away from his beloved homeland for long.

Perhaps he should hire himself as a mercenary, but then he reconsidered. There weren't many who needed an army of late except for the Roses who were at war with the Mackenzies. Wouldn't it be befitting if he lent his sword arm to their cause? Aye, he'd happily fight against the Mackenzies for the Roses. They'd taken everything from him. Even though he was apparently blood-related, he felt more removed from them than he had when he only considered them a rival.

Hell, maybe he should go to the border region and support the English in their petty wars, but the thought of doing so put a sour taste in his mouth. Wretchedness overtook him and he rose and sauntered to the water barrel just inside the barracks. Keith dunked his head and hoped the cool water would refresh him. Drops of water spotted his tunic but didn't give the effect he'd hoped for.

No answer came to him of where to go. Callum's patience wore thin with him and he wouldn't blame his comrade if he insisted he leave. Keith staggered to the barracks entry and peered outside. He stepped out and stood in the rain. The heavy drops did little to sober him.

Callum walked toward him and held a bowl in his hand. "Here," he said and thrust the bowl at him. "You need to eat something. When you're done, take a damned bath in the loch. You stink. Aye, you're covered with my soldier's blood and I won't have you frightening my wee lasses. Come to the hall when you remove that grime and that pike from your arse. I need to speak to you." Without another word, he marched off.

Callum didn't await his retort or agreement. Keith tossed the bowl of stew on a table inside the barracks and grabbed the jug of brew and ambled with unsteady steps to the loch. He disrobed and dove headfirst into the chilly water. Within seconds, he was clear-headed. It didn't sit well, but the jug sat next to his belongings on the bank. He'd muddle himself again once he was clean.

Keith swam for a bit and floated in the depths of the water. Would it matter if he never resurfaced? Not bloody likely. He tried but failed miserably not to think of Marren, her bonny face, her winsome smile, and her becoming nature. He missed her, her touch, and her kisses. But she'd never be his. Keith had unequivocally no resolve left. Short of breath, he reached the surface and took a deep gulp of air. Not only did he fail in his quest to cease his mind from his misgivings, but he couldn't even end his existence.

Keith swam to the bank and crawled ashore until he reached his garments. He didn't want to face his comrade's questions yet again, not when he had no answers. Callum persisted to want to know what troubled him, but the matters were too extensive to give simple reasons. Keith wasn't ready to confess the horrible circumstances that led him to the bottom of many jugs of brew.

Thinking of such, he snatched the jug he'd brought and tipped it to his mouth. There wasn't enough to give him a respite from his maddening thoughts. He hastily dressed and forwent his upper tartan. It was too hot, but he wouldn't leave it behind. The night air would be cold enough outdoors and with nothing to offer warmth, he'd freeze his arse off. If he left the Sinclair holding as he intended to, he would need it. Keith clutched the cloth and headed toward the gate.

Oddly, the lane that led to the gate was vacant. None were about but that didn't deter him. He kept a fast pace and called out to Peter, the gate watch, to open it.

"I'm sorry, Laird Sutherland, but I've been given orders not to open the gate for you."

"Don't call me that and who the hell gave that order?" Keith shook the iron bars and growled.

"My laird told me to keep ye from leaving and if you gave me any trouble to have ye taken bodily to the keep." Peter whistled and two burly guardsmen came from the gatehouse.

"Open the damned gate, Peter," he shouted.

The two men grabbed his arms and forced him to walk toward the keep. As he fought ferociously, his strength depleted and he gave up the fight. Keith tried to free himself but their hold was too tight. Once at the castle, they shoved him through the entrance of the great hall. He turned on them. Keith punched the soldier to his left in his eye and grabbed the head of the soldier to his right. Before he could get in further strikes, Callum put his hand on his shoulder.

"That's enough, Keith. Be gone, men." Callum pushed him toward the table.

Keith leaned against the end of the table and rasped from his exerted efforts. When he raised his face, he noticed Grady, Aulay, and Emmett. They sat as pretty as they pleased with a trencher full of food before them. He remained silent since no one greeted him. After an unnerving minute or two, he cleared his throat and eyed the jug on the table.

"It appears I've disturbed your supper. I'll be gone." He slunk next to the middle of the table and was about to snatch the jug when Callum blocked him with his arm.

"Sit down and shut your trap, Keith. You are going to listen and listen well."

He grimaced and viewed the looks of pity on his comrades' faces. "Bloody hell, what do you want?"

Callum remained standing and took a breath. "I know why you fled the Sutherland holding."

"Aye, well, bollocks and good for you. So you're privy to my downfall too? All of you are? Do you want to gloat and tell me how daft I was to believe I was…?" his words fell away.

Callum pressed him into a chair at the trestle table. "We don't intend to tell you what an arse you're being. Aye, 'tis the truth you're doing a fine job of that by yourself."

Silence weighted the room in a heavy quiet and he closed his eyes. When he opened them, his comrades stared as if he was a ghost or something as ghoulish. He stood in an offensive stance. "I want to leave. Tell Peter to open the damned gate."

"Nay."

"Then let me return to the barracks."

"Nay."

"Bollocks then, Callum. Speak your peace and then I shall go." He retook his seat and poured himself a drink from the pitcher. A taste of refreshing ale would allay him while he waited for Callum to bring him lower. Keith choked on the liquid as he swallowed. Damnation. Water. "Well, get on with it. Say what you want." He glared at the men and decided to keep quiet.

"You're certain you're through?" this came from Grady.

"Aye, obviously you all wish to rebuke me, so go on."

Callum leaned forward. "You came here to hide, did you

not?"

"Your days of running are ended, Laird," Emmett said.

"Lady Ophelia wants you returned even if we must turn your bonny face blue to do so," Aulay said and grinned.

"Why in heaven's name does she want my return? I'm no longer a Sutherland and certainly not your laird," he gritted out to Aulay and Emmett. His throat had gone dry and he poured more water into his goblet and gulped it down.

"If you put your efforts into accepting your plight instead of thrashing my soldiers—"

"Your soldiers needed a good thrashing. I accepted what's been told to me. And I will not return to Sutherland land. There's no reason to." His eyes blurred and his head felt strangely light. The faces of his so-called comrades waved before his eyes. "Damn you. You poisoned me." His head thumped on the table and he groaned before darkness took him.

Emmett grinned. "I told you it'd be easier than brawling with him."

"Aye, but I still say we should tie him to his horse," Grady said with a chortle. "It's what he deserves."

"You mean my horse. Keith took my horse again when he left," Aulay explained.

Grady scowled. "Why did he take your horse? Where's his?"

Emmett snickered. "Keith's horse sort of went maddened and ran off into the woods. Winddodger hasn't returned, but we have the sentry on the lookout for him."

"God Almighty, no wonder he's so irate, and his horse abandoned him too. Poor Keith," Callum said with a grin. "He's been through hell, hasn't he?"

"We should get him back to the Sutherland keep before he awakens," Grady said.

"Worry not for I gave him enough of the dram to make him sleep for days," Emmett said with a shine to his eyes and his grin wide.

"Hell, I hope you didn't kill him," Callum said.

Aulay grinned. "He still breathes. God help us though when he does awaken."

The men laughed as they hoisted him for his trip to the stables and his journey home.

Chapter Twenty-Nine

Someone dropped a boulder on him. That was the first coherent thought that came to him. Keith groaned and opened his eyes. The familiarity of his bedchamber met his gaze. He didn't comprehend how he'd arrived back at the Sutherland keep. His recall was nil and he barely remembered being at the Sinclair's.

"Keith."

He shot a glance at the sweet voice that caressed his ears. "Am I dreaming, love? It's you."

"It's me. Don't move. The effect of the potion hasn't quite worn off yet. You've come to twice since you were brought home, but succumbed again."

"Someone poisoned me?"

Marren gently pressed her fingers on his face. She smiled and gave a slight nod. "I'm afraid it was the only way to get you back. Otherwise, your comrades would've used their fists on you, and I couldn't have that. I like your face the way it is."

"You did this to me?" he was astounded she'd be so underhanded.

"I had a hand in it, but the men gave the potion to you. They only sought to help you. You shouldn't hold it against them. Promise you'll remain calm?"

Keith took a deep breath. "There is no fight left in me, lass. And who are the 'they' that you speak of?"

"Your comrade Callum, and the Sutherlands... Aulay and Emmett. Oh, and of course Grady. They were sent to fetch you. Lady Ophelia ordered them to bring you home."

"They ambushed me."

She patted his chest. "For your own good. Try to rest. Your da will come soon."

"My da?" Keith tried to shake the haze away, but his mind wouldn't focus on his thoughts. He closed his eyes and when he opened them again, he was alone. Had he dreamed of Marren? Was she really there beside him? He was in his bedchamber and in his comfortable bed. Still, he groaned at being back at the Sutherland keep.

The door creaked open. His father stepped through the threshold. Keith's breath halted at the sight of him. He'd never put the name of da to any man except for Hendrie. The fact that he wasn't his father gave him pause and a mournful mood overtook him. He couldn't think of Hendrie as anything but his father, but the man lied to him. Emotions he'd drowned came upon him, but he suppressed them as best he could.

"Son, rest easy. Are you alert enough to speak with me?" His father handed him a cup.

Keith drank down the water, grateful to wet his throat which had gone dry. "I'm alert. Say what you've come to say. It doesn't matter because, in the end, I am not your son. I don't belong here."

Hendrie yanked the chair by the wall and set it next to the bed. "You'll always be my son."

"You lied to me," he said with more than accusation in his tone. Keith wanted to lash out with his anger and to speak of the treachery that rendered him completely dumbfounded.

"Aye, I did. I had no choice but to. I promised your ma."

"She lied to me too."

"Sometimes, lad, a mother must tell falsehoods to protect her bairn."

"Why? I didn't need protection. I needed the truth. Why keep it a secret?" Keith wasn't sure he wanted to know, but he asked anyway. He shifted his position and sat up so he could look Hendrie in the eye.

"We decided when we took our vows that I would claim ye as my flesh and blood."

"You mean the false vows since she was already married to another? She's deceiving and—"

Hendrie smirked. "I know you're angry, Keith, but don't speak ill of your mother. She was the best thing that ever graced this keep. I loved her and still do. We spoke our vows privately to each other. It didn't matter that our pledges weren't blessed by the priest or before God. As far as we were concerned, God understood."

"Why would you accept another man's child as your own?"

Hendrie smiled lightly. "I was married, lad, twice before I met your ma. I couldn't get either woman with a child. I accepted the fault and discerned I'd never father a child. It was a blessing because both women turned out to be vexing and difficult. One died when she fell off her horse and the other ran off, never to be seen again. I was grateful to meet Vera."

Keith scrunched his eyes as Hendrie continued, "Your ma was caring but as bonny on the outside as within. She never asked for anything except that I promise to claim you as mine. Of course I did, and wouldn't deny her anything. You were the joy of my life. When you were a lad, seeing you reminded me of her. I was saddened when God took her from us, much too soon for my liking."

He refused to allow emotions to overtake him, but Hendrie's words affected him. Keith took slow even breaths and tried to remain calm and unmoved.

"Our clan never knew the truth of your birth. Even if

they did, they would never deny my claim that you were mine. I promised your mother on her deathbed that I'd keep her secrets and I had until Philly told me you found out. How?"

"Father John stuck his nose in my affairs."

"Ah, Father John is a stickler for the church's rules. There are ways to keep him quiet."

"I cannot be laird." He blurted out his declaration and hoped his father would accept it.

"Why the hell not? It doesn't matter that you're not born of my blood. You are my son in every sense except by blood and have been since ye were the wee age of three, the day your mother walked through the door of my keep. No other will be laird here but you."

"Samuel will not agree. I returned your ring to him. When he finds out we lied to him—"

"I told him the truth before you returned home. He's privy to all my secrets. Samuel agreed that you are the best man to lead our clan. I won't hear your denial."

"But da… I don't feel worthy, not now." There it was, the confession he'd long since buried within himself. Denial of his worthiness and acceptance sat like a rock in his stomach.

His father pressed his arm. "You, dear lad, were birthed by a woman who had more courage than the entire Sutherland army. She wouldn't give me an unworthy son. I see her strength in you."

"What about the Mackenzies? If they find out about me—"

"Sidheag is aged. He cares more about defeating the Roses than about matters that happened years ago. Besides, he thinks you and your ma died."

"How is that possible? Why would he think us dead?"

"Because I took matters into my hands and had Callum's father send him a missive which gave the grave details of a woman and bairn found drowned in his loch."

"And Sidheag never questioned it or asked for the bodies returned?"

"Nay, he was a knave and cared not that Vera left him. He was a brutal warlord and she was too delicate a woman for such a life."

Keith sighed discontentedly at the discussion of his mother, a woman he knew little about. Hendrie always spoke kindly of her, but he loved her. "Did Sidheag mistreat her? Is that why she left him?"

"He didn't bodily harm her, but he was cross and unkind with his words. He thought of her as his property and she was forbidden to leave his keep. She was forced into captivity from the day she married him."

"He might as well have beaten her then if he kept her imprisoned. My brother…Kieran… Is he aware of my mother and that she left him?"

"Not to my knowledge. I have never laid eyes on Kieran, but word has reached me that he thrived. Reports tell that he goes into battle with his father. Sidheag is close to Kieran and they are from accounts, brutal adversaries."

Keith lamented at the contention of their conversation. "Why did she leave Kieran behind?"

Hendrie sat back and seemed surprised by his question. "I asked her that once when she lay dying. It broke my heart to hear her speak of it. She wept and grieved for the loss of her son."

"Her reason?"

"If she'd taken both of you lads, Sidheag would've gone after her. She knew he'd stop at nothing to get his sons back. Vera couldn't leave without one of ye. Sidheag cared not that she left so she hoped by leaving one of you behind would appease him. Her safety counted on her abandoning her son and she regretted it until her last breath. She left the elder."

"I kind of feel empathy for him."

"Chester Mackay kept abreast of him, your brother, throughout the years. Chester wasn't told about you or your connection to him, but Philly asked him to keep informed, and he appeased her. I deem Chester was pleased to have a reason to visit Philly. She'd told him she was curious about the warlord and his son. Chester never questioned why she wanted to know about Kieran. Kieran Mackenzie is much like his father, a warlord who takes little compassion on his enemies."

"Does he know about me?"

Hendrie fingered his beard before he answered, "I doubt he does unless his father confessed to him about you and your mother. I wouldn't worry about Kieran. His lands lay far from here and I doubt ye shall cross paths. The only people who know about your...situation is Samuel, Grady, Aulay, and Emmett. They have taken a sworn oath to keep our secrets. Now, are ye ready to leave that bed and get back to your life, lad?"

"I am."

"Don't let your wounded pride force you to lose all I wish to give you, son. You won't deny me again? I am your father and I wish you to acknowledge me."

"Nay, Da, I won't deny you." Keith's chest eased and he had a better understanding of why he'd been deceived. If only his mother hadn't died, she might have told him the truth long ago.

"Good. You haven't forgotten the edict of being proclaimed the laird, have you?"

Keith shook his head but raised his brows in awe that his father still insisted he take a wife. He wasn't about to follow through with the edict especially since he couldn't marry Marren. "I told Samuel I wouldn't marry the lasses Philly brought."

"So I've been told. You must fulfill your pledge and take a wife. Your wedding will take place as soon as Father John arrives. I will have a word with him about what he's learned. Have no worry that he'll spew damning words about you."

Keith tensed. "The woman I want to marry is pledged to another. There will be no wedding."

Hendrie grinned and guffawed. "She's been released from her betrothal."

"Won't this cause the Mackenzies to take arms against

us?"

His father cut him to the quick with his viewpoint. "They won't find out and if they do, what can they do about it? War with us? She'll be wedded to you and they'll have to accept it."

"I don't like the thought that the Mackenzies might come to declare war because of me."

Hendrie patted his shoulder. "Lad, if it comes to that, we'll answer their call. Betwixt our soldiers, the Mackays, and the Sinclairs, we outnumber them by a great number. The solution to the problem shall remedy itself. Grady's father is gravely ill and soon, the lad will be called to lead his clan. He will support us as the Mackay laird."

Keith nodded and was in awe of all that his father had told him. How long had he been under the effect of the potion? Perhaps long enough for everything to sort itself.

"Now, you must claim that sweet lass before she changes her mind." Hendrie laughed as he exited the chamber.

Keith lay back and pressed his hands over his face. He couldn't and wouldn't ever deny the man. And he certainly had enough doubts of late, but no more. As far as he was concerned, he belonged to the Sutherlands, and Marren belonged to him.

He reached the basin and splashed water on his face and shook off the remnants of his sleepiness. Keith left the bedchamber and was eager to rejoin his clansmen and to see Marren. At first, his movements were unsteady, but he made it to the great hall. He sat at the table and ate until his hunger abated and he felt stronger.

Grady entered and joined him.

Keith raised a brow at the sight of his friend's face. "Whose fist did your eye meet with?"

"Laird Hendrie's."

He bellowed with laughter. "My da punched you?"

"Aye, he surely did. He meant to convince me to break my pledge to Marren."

"And did you?"

"What do you think? None can refuse your father. I did even though I warned him against allowing you two to wed. I only wanted to protect you."

"My thanks, Grady, but I don't need your protection."

"Nay? Well, I told Marren she was free of me and she disbelieved me. You might need to convince her she can wed you. Are you certain you wish to marry her? She's a wee bit haughty."

Keith's brows drew together at his friend's choice of words. "What do you mean haughty? Marren is the sweetest, most gentle-natured woman."

"She has a hard slap, aye, and almost made me infertile when she damned well kneed me between the legs." Grady chuckled low. "Ah, but she's sweet to you, is she not?"

"She is. Where is she?"

Grady shrugged his shoulders. "Last I saw her, she was picking heather blooms in the field adjacent to the keep wall. Aye, she's a sweet lass to all but me. You're a fortunate man, Keith. She gave her blooms to a wee one who was crying. Marren brushed off the lass and sent her happily skipping away."

"She has a way, doesn't she?" Keith rose. "I should find her and get to my convincing."

"Is that what you're calling it now?" Grady chortled when Keith threw a hunk of bread at him.

Keith grinned to himself and went in search of Marren.

Chapter Thirty

Marren stayed away from the keep most of the day. She couldn't bring herself to see Keith. Even though she was pleased he'd returned, she was uncertain if he still cared for her. Seeing him hurt and lying in bed nearly broke her heart. She didn't want him to put himself in danger because of her and if they ignored the threats her uncle had made, they'd surely invite more troubles.

Grady Mackay insisted she release him from the pact his father made with her uncle and the Mackenzies. He forced her to admit there was no connection between them. She realized that when he'd kissed her. Marren supposed most women would be pleased to be kissed by him. His lips were soft and yielding and his hold was formidable. She felt absolutely no attraction to him, and likewise, him to her. Still, he cajoled her to refute their betrothal and she hoped she wouldn't regret it. Perhaps it was best for all if she didn't marry at all.

She spent the morning by the keep's walls plucking heather and decided she might get back to making scents. There had to be a hawker in a nearby town that would sell them for her. When she spotted the wee Ellen weeping because the lads wouldn't play with her, she gave her the heather she collected and soothed her wounded pride. The lass scampered off and Marren smiled after her.

She entered the solarium and hugged herself to ward off the chill. A breeze picked up and whipped at the fauna along the lane. Marren glanced at the table where she created scents. It had been a long while since she eased herself with her passion, but she couldn't bring herself to try until now. Later, she would collect more flowers and herbs and would perhaps make a scent for Cassie. She hadn't given her a wedding gift.

But now she wanted to be alone. She bent her knee and ducked under the table and crawled beneath. She lay on her back and closed her eyes. The events of Keith's return, Grady's harassment, and her uncle's threats exhausted her. She was tired of thinking about the situation she'd put everyone in. She about pummeled Emmett for giving Keith too much of the sleeping potion. Keith was fortunate he hadn't died from the excess of the medicinal.

Marren lay on her side and pulled her legs close and grew drowsy. Being in her secret spot comforted her and she was glad to be alone. Someone touched her leg and she startled. She found Keith staring at her. He knelt by the table and had lifted the cover.

"It's you. You scared me."

"Aye, it's me. I'm sorry, lass, I didn't mean to. You looked peaceful."

"What are you doing here?"

Keith pressed his hand over her hair and smiled. "We need to talk."

"We do. Your aunt told me what happened, about what you learned. I'm sorry if you were upset. I wish I could have soothed you or offered some form of comfort. If you'd rather not discuss it, I understand." Marren hoped he would speak of his birth and about his parents, but she wouldn't press him.

He crawled to sit beside her and his face was staid with seriousness. "I was taken aback and I intend to tell you what my father told me. But before we get to that, there's something I need to do."

"What is it?"

"Kiss you." Keith pressed his lips to hers.

Marren moaned when he added his tongue to the mix. The kiss turned passionate and excited her. She rejoiced that he held her and she perused her hands over his hard chest. He cuddled her cheek with his palm and continued the desirous kiss. His tongue gently stroked hers and his groan rumbled his chest. Her fingers caressed the strands of his hair by his nape and she pulled him closer.

Keith pressed his hands over her breasts and caused her to moan with desire. A sensual essence overtook her and she needed to get closer to him. A desire for him brought forth dizziness to her body and she trembled with longing. Marren moaned again and Keith pulled away.

His voice sounded hoarse, "Lord, I missed you. Missed this…" He placed kisses on the side of her face and trailed his lips to her neck. He was about to kiss her lips again when they heard voices.

Marren placed her head on Keith's chest and spied their unwanted company through a slit of the cloth. Lady Ophelia seemed upset. Marren glanced at Keith, but he signaled her to be quiet with a touch to her lips. She didn't recognize the man who accompanied Lady Ophelia into the solarium.

"I didn't mean to upset you, dearest," the man said earnestly.

"You tell this to me now? It is bad enough that you come and visit occasionally and remind me of our past. I have tried to forget you," Lady Ophelia said.

"It is our future I'm concerned about, Phee."

"Don't call me that, Chester. Please, you're making it difficult to send you away."

"I love you, Phee, and always have. Och, I was a coward to let my brother interfere."

"I love you too but as long as your brother lives there is nothing we can do."

Chester pulled Lady Ophelia into his embrace. "There's plenty. I'm my own man, Phee, and I say what decisions I make for myself, not Simon."

Lady Ophelia caressed Chester's bearded face. "It's too late, my love. Besides, your brother will banish you if you disobey his order."

"I care not about Simon. Marry me. I should've forced my brother to accept my decision years ago. All I need is you. You're the only woman I have ever loved. Marry me."

Lady Ophelia pressed her eyes and wept.

Keith tensed and she felt his body turn rigid as he watched in awe the romantic discussion going on in the solarium. Keith looked at her and tried to move from their position, but she held him tightly. She thought they should stay where there were and not interfere. Marren shook her head at Keith and caressed his face to get him to stay put.

Lady Ophelia dabbed her eyes with a cloth. "I want to say aye, but too much time has passed. I'm an old woman now."

Chester kissed Lady Ophelia's cheek. "Ye still look like the bonny lass who captured my heart."

"And you still resemble that arrogant Highlander who thought I was drowning in the loch when I only screamed because a fish touched my leg."

Chester laughed. "It was the happiest day of my life, the day I gave ye my heart. I shouldn't have listened to my brother and should have married you then, but he was my laird and I was...too daft and loyal."

"And now? What has changed?"

"Simon never deserved my loyalty. I know that now. I made the biggest mistake by letting you go, Phee. Please, don't deny me now."

"Oh, Chester," Lady Ophelia said and leaned against him.

"I promise to make our remaining days joyful."

"I have only ever wanted you. You're so handsome." Lady Ophelia caressed his stark white tunic with her dainty hands. "Of course I shall marry ye."

"We should go somewhere where we won't be disturbed." Chester kissed her longingly. "Then I will prove to ye that I thought of you every day."

Lady Ophelia clasped Chester's hand and they absconded from the solarium.

Keith peered beyond the table cloth until she drew him with a touch to his face.

"That's your aunt's long-lost love?"

Keith scowled with a nod. "Aye and I don't know if I'm pleased or not by what I just heard."

"It's romantic. She deserves to be happy."

"Aye she does, and so do you." Keith pulled her until she lay on top of him. "And so do I. Kiss me hard, lass, and I will prove to you how much I love you."

Marren set her mouth on his and rejoiced as his tongue rekindled her desire. She kept her mouth on his as she fumbled with her skirts and his lower tartan. His body tensed beneath her palms on his chest as she joined their bodies. She couldn't stop herself from thrusting against him and her longing spurred her to take him with maddening pleasure.

Keith set his hands around her back and forced her to stop. "Lass, take it slow. I want to enjoy this." He pressed her lips with gentle kisses and moved lethargically until she squealed from the intensity of his teasing.

"It's been too long. We'll take it slow later," she rasped. Marren thrust against him and moaned as pleasurable twinges shook her legs. She kept her gaze on his face and her heart swelled as she watched him. His handsome face tensed when she culminated and landed hard against his chest.

Keith helped her move and he groaned as he met an intense end. Marren lay against him and listened to the maddening rush of his heart clashing his chest.

"Do you really love me?" She lifted her head and stared into the blue hue of his eyes.

"Aye, I have since the day I saw you in the great hall. How can you ask that after what we just shared—?"

She kissed him hard with as much passion as she could dole.

Keith flipped her body and leaned over her. "Now is there something you want to tell me?"

"Aye, I love you too."

He chuckled. "I know you love me, lass. Not that, love, about our wedding... My da told me I'll need to do some convincing."

"I want to say aye, but I fear—"

He set a gentle kiss on her lips. "My aunt pined for her love for years because of fear. I won't let us have such regrets. Regardless, Marren, of what happens, we will confront it together."

"Even war? I want no one hurt because of me...us."

He gentled his hand over her cheek. "You're a sweet woman to be concerned for others, but there's no need to worry over that. I give you my pledge this day that our union won't cause the Mackenzies to war with us."

"Then aye."

He scowled hard. "Aye, you'll marry me?"

"I will."

Chapter Thirty-One

The day of their wedding arrived. His aunt insisted on inviting many which included the clan of Sinclair, Gunn, Grant, Gordon, and Robertson. Keith wasn't sure he wanted to see the lasses he'd courted, but as a means of amenity, Philly wanted to extend her appreciation for allowing the lasses to come. He forbade Philly from inviting the Frasers because if there was one woman he hoped to never see again, it was Lady Eedy.

Keith smiled to himself that of the seven lasses he'd courted, Marren was the only lass he could ever love. As he waited for his bride to join them, he stood next to Father John who wore a disapproving scowl. But the priest often wore such a look and it had nothing to do with his knowledge of Keith's parentage. Apparently whatever words his father had with Father John persuaded him to accept Keith as Hendrie's son.

Marren walked toward him with his da escorting her and his entire clan smiled as she passed them. When she reached him, Keith took her hand and grinned. He couldn't help but be elated to make her his.

"You look beautiful," he whispered by her ear. She wore the becoming gown she'd worn on the night of his welcome home feast and looked as lovely this day as she had then.

She squeezed his hand and smiled back. "And you look handsome."

Father John's voice boomed forth as he spoke a litany about the duty of husband and wife. He spoke of God's expectations and the love between a man and a woman. Keith doubted the priest understood what that meant. He glanced at his da and realized his father must have loved his mother as much as he loved Marren. To accept him and respect his mother's wishes could only be kept by such a man as Hendrie.

Father John bid them to make their pledges.

"Marren, I vow to love you until I take my last breath." He needn't say more because all he felt at that moment was spoken with those little words.

Father John rolled his eyes and Keith almost laughed.

"Keith, I will love you all the days of my life." Marren's gaze was full of affection for him.

He didn't wait for the priest to permit him to kiss his wife. As he did so, Father John proclaimed them married. He grinned as he heard the calls and whoops of his clansmen. Keith took her hand and guided her to the feast. It was too cold to remain outside and Philly had the keep readied for the great number of guests that attended.

Inside the hall, he left Marren to get her a drink. He returned to her with a goblet of wine and chuckled when he handed it to her. "I hope you'll limit your cups of wine. Otherwise, you might make unbecoming comments about me when I try to put you to bed."

Marren laughed and pinched his arm. "I intend to only have one cup. And you? Callum told me how besotted you were at his keep. You won't take more than a few cups of ale?"

Keith groaned. "Don't remind me. I'm not taking a sip. I want to be clear-headed this night."

Jumpin' Joe approached and set a jug in front of him. "To help ye recover from your night of pleasure." Joe guffawed and gained a reproached look from his brother.

He blanched at it and would save it for another time, and perhaps would drink it when he had his first bairn. "My thanks, Joe. Join us."

Joe sat next to him until Aulay forced him to shift on the bench. His comrades joined them and Marren conversed with Cassie, Marc's wife.

"Laird, you made a good choice. Milady Marren was the bonniest lass amongst the hens," Emmett said.

Aulay shoved his brother's shoulder. "Don't speak of our laird's wife with disrespect, brother. But aye, of all the hens ye courted, she was the most winsome."

Grady shoved Aulay aside and took his place on the bench. "Keith, I have a surprise for you. Aulay and Emmett helped me set up a jousting field beyond the keep. We'll have a tournament to celebrate your nuptials."

Keith grimaced. "I'm not going to joust with you, Grady. I recall the danger involved." He remembered seeing the injuries of a jouster on many occasions when they'd traveled across the channel. The sport drew much fanfare, but he thought the participants were daft for risking their lives.

"Oh, are you afraid of a wee challenge?"

"Hell aye, I am. I'd rather toss cabers than joust. If you recall the last joust we witnessed..." The man who made the challenge was struck in his gullet and slain before he hit the field. "Why do you want to joust?"

Grady grinned. "Because I mean to take to the sport. I want to race horses, too. Sir James by the border has a good stock of horses for sale. I mean to breed them, race them, and make a good profit."

He scoffed at the absurdity. "You don't need the coin unless you spent your fortune?"

"Nay, I have a good amount of coin left. Come, Keith, don't be a coward."

As much as he detested being called a coward, he

wouldn't accept Grady's bait. "I don't like to wear armor, especially not atop a horse with a pointy lance coming at me. It's a mad endeavor, Grady, but I wish you well with your pursuit."

"Come outside and at least watch the spectacle. Laird Gordon got one of his men to go against a Gunn. They'll joust and you'll see, it will be fine entertainment."

The men vacated the hall. Keith wasn't sure he wanted to see the joust, but he'd humor Grady for a few minutes. Behind the keep, a long plot of grass was set up with a wooden divider. Each man would ride on his side of the barrier. With a six-foot lance, he'd ride at his opponent and try to gain points striking various places on the rider's target. Whoever was the first to knock the other from his horse would claim victory. It was barbaric to Keith's way of thinking. The riders took their position and waited for the call to ride forth.

Something caught his eye and he spotted his horse, Winddodger, near the curtain wall. Had his horse been inside the wall all this time? "My horse!" He was pleased his steed returned.

Grady set off to get him. Winddodger meekly lowered his head and allowed his comrade to take his reins. "Damn, he's a fine horse. He'd make a good addition to breed with my mares. How much do you want for him?"

Keith adamantly shook his head. "I'm not selling you my horse."

"I'll give you double what you paid for him. He's a good sturdy steed and would make good racers if mated with the right mare."

At that point, Dain wedged himself between him and Grady. "M'laird, you have racers? I always wanted to race horses. Before I came to Laird Hendrie, my da raced horses for Laird Monroe."

"Is that so?" Grady lifted the lad from under his arms. "You're light enough. Throw in your squire, Keith, and I'll pay you triple."

Keith waved him off and walked away. He shouldn't entertain Grady's offer, but Winddodger was useless to him now. Grady gave him the greatest gift by calling off his betrothal to Marren. It was the least he could do to give him his horse and squire, although, Keith wasn't about to make it easy on him.

Back inside the keep, he found Marren sitting with Cassie. Their laughter lightened him. Just looking at her softened his demeanor and his comrade's banter was forgotten. He waited eagerly for the celebration to end.

Throughout the night, the lasses who had come to be courted by him approached. Caroline Gunn and Lindsey Gordon were betrothed to men from each other's clans which forced an alliance between them. Their row in the mud hadn't caused a rivalry between them. Iona's father, Laird Grant, attended, but he told him his daughter was on a trek to the Far East with her brother on a quest to find birds of a certain variety. Keith gave thanks to God above that he hadn't offered for that lass's hand. He would've been pecked at all his years about the feathered creatures.

Robina Robertson gave him hostile looks from across the great hall. She hadn't received an offer of marriage yet and Keith suspected she probably wouldn't. But she'd likely lead her father's army one day. In an attempt to avoid her, Keith took Marren's hand and tried to lead her from the hall.

Cassie laughed and rubbed the swell of bairn bump at her middle when Marren chastised him.

"It's too early to leave. Our guests are still here." She gave him a sympathetic pout and finished the remainder of the wine in her cup.

He cared not that they'd leave their guests unattended and forced her to follow him. Before they reached the stairs, he spotted his Aunt Philly and Chester. For two old people, they sure liked to kiss, but they had much time to make up for. Their wedding had taken place the day before in a quiet ceremony with only a few in attendance. Chester was a good sort and he didn't worry about his aunt's happiness.

Keith reached his chamber and shut the door forcibly and slid the latch to lock it. "Finally, alone. Come here, lass, and kiss me hard."

"Before I do, did you remember to tell Marc to have the sentry keep watch for Trulee?"

"I promised I would. If she comes on Sutherland land, they'll find her."

"I worry about her."

Keith pressed his hand on her shoulder. "I know you do. You know what I'm thinking about?"

She untied the strings of her bliaut and teased him with a little show of her skin. "I could guess." Marren giggled but ceased when she noticed his serious gaze.

"When I held Callum's son... I kept thinking of how I longed to hold our son."

She smiled sweetly at him. "Well, we should get started on that, shouldn't we?" She let the fabric of her overdress fall and he took her in his arms.

Keith pressed her back on the bed and grinned. He'd wooed the right lass and his life would be filled with happiness. "Aye, we definitely should get started on that."

Author's Note

Dear Readers,

In the 1390s there was much turmoil regarding King Robert II and his son and their inept rule. They were notably two of Scotland's worst kings having no interest in protecting their lands from the ever-invading English. Neither had like-mindedness attention for soldiering and left such details to lower countrymen which caused a divide in the nation's allegiance. As such, the clans in the north likely stayed to their lands, protected their interest, and kept out of politics as much as they could. (At least, that is this author's opinion.)

Be sure to look for book three in the Lairds of the North series, *Making Her A Mackay*, Grady Mackay's story, coming in 2021. Grady's story tells the tale of two people whose hearts are connected by their circumstances. Their experiences lead them to love and understanding, and to have the compassion to always be accepting of each other.

Lastly, don't miss book four, which features Kieran Mackenzie and Trulee Macleod in *The Warlord and the Waif*. I hope you're finding this series as enjoyable as I found writing it. If you do, please be sure to leave a review or send me a message.

Happy historical reading,

Fondly,
Kara Griffin

OTHER HISTORICAL TITLES
By Kara Griffin

MYSTIC MAIDENS OF BRITAIN SERIES
PENDRAGON'S PRINCESS – Book One
* THE GOOD WITCH & THE WARRIOR – Book Two
* A KNIGHT ENTWINED – Book Three

LAIRDS OF THE NORTH SERIES
* THE SEDUCTION OF LAIRD SINCLAIR
* SEVEN LASSES & A LAIRD
* MAKING HER A MACKAY
* THE WARLORD & THE WAIF

LEGEND OF THE KING'S GUARD SERIES
CONQUERED HEART – Book One
UNBREAKABLE HEART – Book Two
FEARLESS HEART – Book Three
UNDENIABLE HEART – Book Four

GUNN GUARDSMAN SERIES
ONE & ONLY – Book One
ON A HIGHLAND HILL – Book Two
A HIGHLANDER IN PERIL – Book Three
IN LOVE WITH A WARRIOR – Book Four

THE PITH TRILOGY
WARRIOR'S PLEDGE – Book One
CLAIMED BY A CHARMER – Book Two
LASS' VALOR – Book Three

* *KEEPERS OF THE KINGDOM* (series)
* *THE MARVELOUS MACLEERS* (series)
* *DAUGHTERS OF DUNFELD* (Halloween anthology)
* Denotes COMING SOON

Praise for Kara Griffin's Books

The Legend of the King's Guard Series

CONQUERED HEART "WOW! What a great start to a series, this book is fast-paced action, but then what did I expect, Kara Griffin writes strong-minded and compassionate characters and embroiled them into adventure and romance." Amazon reviewer – 5 Stars

UNBREAKABLE HEART "A sensational story of love and forgiveness. A roller coaster of emotions, a swoon-worthy hero, and a heroine who gives our hero a run for his money. The author did an awesome job in transferring the anger and devastation Makenna was feeling as well as the love that eventually conquered their hearts!" Maira/Books & Benches – 5 Stars

FEARLESS HEART "Heath and Lillia are perfect together. Friar Hemm is amazing. Its a sad, tearful, astounding, amazing book. Can't wait to read the next." Debbie Hoover, reviewer – 5 Stars

UNDENIABLE HEART "A good historical set in the time of Robert the Bruce. Kara Griffin's writing draws you in like you are right there with the characters. I enjoyed it so much that I have gone on to read the first three in the series as well. A must for anyone who likes Scottish historical." China36, reviewer – 5 Stars

The Gunn Guardsman Series

ONE AND ONLY "I just finished this book ten minutes ago and I'm still smiling. Wonderful. Absolutely wonderful… This story has so many truly fantastic scenes. Oh, the days of men of honor, governed by loyalty, duty, and chivalry. And to top it off, they are all strapping warriors wrapped in the Gunn plaid. Need I say more? This author writes truly wonderful historical romances." Past Romance, Amazon (reader) – 5 Stars

ON A HIGHLAND HILL "WOW! Holy Highlander! Those Highland Hills will capture your heart and soul not to mention the men. Fast-paced and passion-filled." My Book Addiction and More (blogger) – 5 stars

A HIGHLANDER IN PERIL "This book has intrigue, mystery, murder and incredibly romantic scenes that you will have a problem putting it down until the very end and then you will wish it had another chapter so you could keep reading the story. I did not put it down until the last word was read. I recommend this book to any who enjoy historical romance with intense intrigue and suspense." Jusnana, Amazon – 5 Stars

IN LOVE WITH A WARRIOR "Oh what a great romance lover's dream book. In Love with a Warrior was such an enjoyable historical romance, I read it all in one night. Talk about realism, romance, passion, the heat of battle, and remarkably accurate history. This fast-paced and adventurous plot moved quickly and kept me interested all the way through." Renay Arthur - 5 stars

THE PITH TRILOGY

WARRIOR'S PLEDGE "Kara always writes intense but sweet romances, always great character and plots. I'm already almost done with book 2 to the series. This is one author you don't want miss out on reading." Heather SS, Amazon (reader) – 5 Stars

CLAIMED BY A CHARMER "Enjoyed!....every bit, moves along no wasting time in the story. Kept me wanting to know what or who is the other enemy besides one of her relative." Kgose5, Amazon (reader) – 5 Stars

LASS' VALOR "Lass' Valor was a thoroughly enjoyable read. Kara Griffin did a wonderful job with the character development and storyline, spinning a tale full of adventure, love and a little mystic." KVD, Amazon (reader) – 4 Stars

About The Author

Read a Scottish or Medieval Historical Romance book by Kara Griffin and transport yourself to the mystical, enchanting realms of the Scottish Highlands and Medieval Britain. Stories of noble warriors and strong, but sweet, heroines will have you rooting for them as they encounter dastardly villains. Be romanced with unconditional love in sweeping tales of romance. There's always a Happily-Ever-After in her stories.

Kara Griffin is the author of Scottish/Highlander and Medieval Historical romances. She always had a vivid imagination and has been an avid reader since her early years. Inspired by her grandfather's heritage, she loves all things Scottish. From the captivating land to the ancient mysticism, all inspire her to write tales that make you sigh.

Kara enjoys family life with her husband. They spend a lot of time with their daughters, who live close by. Their grandbabies are the joy of their lives. When Kara is on hiatus from writing, she usually spends that time with family. In the Pinelands of New Jersey, she enjoys the outdoors, especially the beach and wooded areas near her home.

She enjoys hearing from readers. If you have enjoyed her books, let her know by reaching out. Follow her on Facebook, Pinterest, Instagram, and favorite her on book sites. Be sure to visit her blog where she posts insight into her writing. Kara's books can be purchased at all retailers. She appreciates any reviews that are left at retailers and book sites, so please be sure to let her know what you think of her stories.

Visit Kara on Facebook at:
www.facebook.com/AuthorKaraGriffin

Or visit her website at:
http://karagrif66.wix.com/authorkaragriffin

She always enjoys hearing from readers, so be sure to say hello. For questions or inquiries, please email: karagrifin@gmail.com

If you enjoyed this book, please take a moment to post a review on your favorite book site. Reader feedback is so important and much appreciated. Thank you.

Made in the USA
Coppell, TX
12 June 2024